The ~~Wedding~~ Fund

Gill Scott

Copyright © 2017 Gill Scott

All rights reserved.

ISBN-13: 9781973389934

DEDICATION

For Dad

ACKNOWLEDGMENTS

This book would not have been possible without the help and support of Edward, whose encouragement, patience and critical guidance has kept me going throughout this time.

I'd like to thank my mother for her amazing help and guidance, her love of the English language has kept me on track.

I'd also like to thank Spiffing Covers for providing me with a jolly spiffing cover.

And finally, to all the wonderful people I met in Thailand who helped paint the background for this novel.

PROLOGUE

I dig out my most flattering outfit, straighten my hair and attack the street stalls of Thailand for some shopping and a kick up the arse.

The stalls are awash with colours and flimsy clothing essential to keep you cool in this unbelievable heat. With everything so cheap, I think I might just go a bit mad. I try on a few cute dresses and realise 1) I am not 19 and look ridiculous in 'cute dresses' - when did everything get so short? and 2) People in Thailand are small and buying things in a size L (if I'm lucky) doesn't quite have the feel good factor I'm after. Why is it when you want to shop and spend money you can't find anything, and when you don't have a pot to piss in you see something you want every time you blink?

I watch groups of people wander up and down

the rickety streets and pavements, how have they managed to work out summer chic and festival cool? Well, they've probably been on holiday in the last three years unlike me so perhaps they've had time to work on it. Not me, and what better time for a fashion reinvention. There's lots of tiny daisy duke denim shorts - nope, too fat for that shit; mini dresses - too old for that shit; tie dye trousers that make you look like you're wearing a nappy– not 'traveller' enough for that.

I suddenly feel about as trendy as a geography teacher, so I have a pit stop and order a glass of wine. I dig out my phone and look through all my photos, trashing everything I'm wearing in all of them, whilst doing my best to ignore the six-foot tall bugger beside me in almost every photo.

The pictures span around a three-year period. There's pictures of the weddings that we have attended, all fresh faced in floaty knee length dresses; pictures of weekends up North in hiking boots walking the hills; and then the main ones that I am looking for - pictures of picnics and gatherings in Hyde Park during the beautiful days of summer in the city. I cast my eye across the different styles of the girls which includes cut off denim shorts and halter neck tops, long t-shirt dresses and oh my god, someone here is wearing a crop top, at least it's not me.

Jesus, why don't we get a card through the post

from the fashion police to say 'Eh, just a note to let you know it's time you moved up an age category in your attire; I'm not quite saying mutton and lamb just yet, but you know, have a think about it. Kind Regards, The Fashion Police.'

Then there's a photo of someone in a floaty skirt and a vest top looking relaxed, pretty smart casual, and no bulging bumps sticking out of inappropriate places. In another, an outfit of knee length dark denim shorts with a white linen shirt. These individuals obviously got the letter from the Fashion Police. As for the rest of us, the less said the better. Note to self, I'm not sure double denim was ever OK.

Hitting the shops in the heat again, I try on a long floaty dress, one size fits all it says, now that's more like it - no big L screaming out at me from the label. Well, this is remarkably age appropriate and sophisticated summer cool. Sure enough, the floodgates open - I have become a boho fashion victim, with a whole new wardrobe for £75. I just know this will change my life - a new independent, travelling spiritual me is born - Ta da.

CHAPTER 1

I study my face in the mirror as I put the finishing touches to my makeup on and rehearse for the hundredth time how I will tell Pete the big news. I imagine his expression of awe that I've done this for us, saved over £7000 to pay for the wedding we've always wanted but couldn't afford.

Today, I finally get to share my secret. We're off to John and Suze's wedding and I can hardly contain myself. Not because they are Pete's closest friends or because we get to go to The Savoy (OK, well I'm a bit excited about that), but because I can talk about what I've been holding in for years now.

Pete and I have been together for seven years and have been talking about marriage for the last three - predominantly at the twenty-four weddings we have been to between then and now. 'Do you think it will ever be us' I would muse after I had taken the brave tablets of a few glasses of wine at the first few weddings. Pete always said that it was a nice idea but we don't really have the money for it just now, that it's something we will talk about again once we've worked our way up the career ladder at work, once we are able to spend some money on it. Not that he wanted anything big mind, something low key, none of this showing off to the world lark. I've heard a lot of this chat, and yes, I guess he's been right - but now I have just the right amount for our perfect little wedding.

Over the last three years I have relinquished my cocktails, eBay addiction, new shoes, bags, winter coats, eaten leftovers for lunch and even put up with bobbly tights in the name of creating 'The Wedding Fund'. It's going to blow his mind when I tell him, and what better place to do it than at another wedding, at The Savoy even. I can picture it now, us glowing in the quiet knowledge that we're getting married too but not wanting to share the news right there and then and take any attention away from John and Suze on their own big day.

'Taxi's here Al.' Pete shouts down the hallway. OK, ready, one last deep breath to calm myself.

As we pull into The Savoy, the doorman complete with top hat guides us through the reception area in all its marbled glory. Everyone is gathered on the terrace overlooking the River Thames in preparation for our move into the ballroom which is a sea of white and gold. Huge white candles grace the end of each row of seats. The white seat covers each have a large silk gold bow tied around them. Orchids look like they are exploding out of gigantic gold vases and the sparkling lights hang from the ceiling in front of ruched chiffon. The sun is shining and the reflection on the water echoes the inside golden colours of the ballroom.

The bride walks down the aisle glowing, the train of her Vera Wang dress sashaying behind her. She looks amazing, a bit more glitz and glamour than I will go for - a subtle off white fluted dress, and maybe a fur bolero in keeping with a winter wedding at the end of the year. I know people say you need at least twelve to eighteen months to plan for your big day, but I already have three years on that, so seven months is more than enough for our intimate little do. Pete doesn't really do flowers, romance and organizing things, but I've arranged enough valentine's days, birthdays and parties in my time (not to mention this wedding in my head) to know that I can do it with my eyes closed.

A very many glasses of champagne later our dresses are stretched to the limit from the delicious smoked salmon, beef wellington and raspberry dacquoise dessert. We are drifting into the party part of the evening, the delicate sounds of the string quartet finishing to allow for the speeches, while the wedding band set up behind the scenes to kick off the dancing.

I've already decided on my moment to surprise him. Once everyone starts to get up on the dance floor we will have the chance to slip away briefly. Pete doesn't dance, I've tried many times in the past to get him bopping about with no success, so I've no reason to expect that today would be any different.

We had a big party for my 30th birthday four years ago that Gail and Lisa, my best friends, arranged. James Bond themed with everyone whooping around the dance floor in slinky ball gowns and all my favourite music playing one after the other - a real 'disco' feel. Everyone, and I mean everyone, was up dancing when Jackson 5s I want you back came on except for him. He was propping up the bar. I can still recall my heart plummeting when he refused to join in, but that's Pete, he watched from the sidelines and smiled at me with his Jack Daniels in hand, laughing at the bouncing mayhem.

Just as the first wedding dance finishes and everyone starts to get their dancing feet on, I get a glass of the free-flowing champagne and a double Jack Daniels from the bar for Pete and suggest we take a wander out to the terrace.

'It's been a beautiful day, hasn't it?' I say.

'Yeah, sure. Shame it had to take place on the

same day as Arsenal in the FA Cup. I suppose this helps to ease the pain.' he jokes, raising his fifth JD for the day.

He kisses me gently on the forehead and tells me I look beautiful, a rare but not unique sentiment expressed.

'Sooo, I have a surprise for you.' I say, as I link my arm in his and gaze out to the river, the lights shimmering across the surface.

'You're going commando?' he raises one eyebrow.

'Awight Pete, did you see Giroud's goal today?' Dave shouts as he wanders out to join us on the terrace with a cigar and the football highlights on his phone. Bloody great.

'Awight Dave.' says Pete as he shakes his hand.

Ten long minutes and a discussion involving 'the referee's a wanker' later, the guys start to wander back into the ballroom but I hold Pete back.

'Hon, come here a minute.' I pull at his elbow.

Leaning with our backs against the balcony looking in at the dance floor, I start our usual wedding conversation.

holiday or can't buy a car, you've been hoarding seven grand?'

'Well, I've not been hoarding it, I've only just got £7000 now. It's been gradual over the last couple of years.' I stumble, thinking this isn't how I planned this discussion going in my head, not once during the hundred rehearsals I had with the mirror.

'Three years. Three years and you didn't tell me you were doing this?' he spits out.

The tears start rolling down my cheeks, I can't quite believe this is happening. The last three years of saving, denying myself everything, dying my hair at home (believe me, this is a risky sacrifice for a blonde), using my will power to stash away every last penny I could and he's angry with me? Well, I'll show him anger, how dare he behave like this.

'Pete, I've done this for us! Isn't being together, happily married more important than two random weeks in Spain? This is what we want, isn't it?' I'm shaking and crying and gritting my teeth to stop the words escaping from my mouth in a volume that draws the attention of the masses swirling round the dance floor and cavorting at the bar.

'You're having a bubble aren't you? Please tell me you're joking. I just can't fucking believe you've hidden this from me. Secretly plotting how to get me down the aisle…' Pete replies.

'What? Secretly plotting? We've talked about this. You said that it was money that was stopping us, saving is hardly secretly plotting. If you have a problem, if this isn't what you want then…' I interject, absolutely fuming.

'Oh Al, calm down. Sure, yeah, this is what we want.' he brings me into his arms.

'Relax, will you. Now go and sort your face out, you've got black streaks running down your cheeks. I'll see you back at the bar.' he sighs.

'OK…but we are getting married?' I whimper.
'Yes Al, it looks like we are.' he sighs affectionately.

So I, Alice Appleby, am finally getting married. Let's just say the proposal didn't quite live up to my childhood fairytale expectations, but I suppose Pete was just taken aback by it all. Yes, that must be it. Once we start planning everything I'm sure it will be completely different.

Not that I live in the land of make believe, I am a thirty-four year old woman after all and more than aware that the shit that happens in movies, is just that -

Hollywood bullshit. Romantic comedies portrayal of wedding proposals is akin to hardcore porns portrayal of sex. Thankfully, with a bit more experience of the latter we are fully aware that what you see on a porn movie (so I'm told obviously) is complete science fiction compared with real life.

Proposals in movies on the other hand - well we don't have too many experiences to compare that to, so when it comes to our expectations there, we are a bit more away with the fairies. Well not completely, I suppose I could compare it to how Rob proposed to my best friend Lisa - which was with a diamond and sapphire ring on top of the Eiffel Tour during a weekend getaway in Paris. On second thoughts what is it we apparently learn once we've entered our thirties, don't judge yourself against others, everyone walks their own path in life. And so it is, slightly bypassing the proposal I've now realised never actually happened, my path is leading its way down the aisle, and my mother can finally buy herself a new hat.

***

I met Pete whilst standing in some posh cocktail bar in Soho seven years ago. I'd been at the bar for an eternity, well twenty minutes, still it was too long to wait for a drink and having been passed over for Angelina Jolie, Cameron Diaz and Brad Pitt's lookalikes I was getting increasingly impatient.

Pete turned to me and laughed, 'look at you up on your toes - if looks could kill. Not getting attention at the bar eh?'

I started laughing, 'They're bloody ignoring me.'

He told me he would see what he could do to shunt the waitress in my direction. We spent the next five minutes discussing the pros and cons of cocktail bars against local English boozers and as the bar girl approaches Pete, not me, he ordered drinks for me and my friends along with his own. He helped me over to the girls with the glasses and we shared the next few drinks together, oblivious to everyone else around us. I hadn't really met a proper cockney cheeky chappy before. You'd think that living in London they would be everywhere, but they certainly hadn't been where I was looking, every Londoner I met was like me, from a different part of the world drawn to the bright lights of the City. He was tall with the most gorgeous green eyes, dark blonde hair, a cheek to him that you couldn't help but be taken in by, and an accent that I almost understood. He made fun of my northern accent and country roots and most importantly, he just made me laugh.

I wanted to spend the whole evening with him, but after a while my friend Lisa collared me to say we were moving on elsewhere. I gave her the 'Can't we stay, I think I like him' eyes, and got the 'If you think you like him, then we really need to go' eyes. Lisa was a big fan of the leave them wanting more mantra. We all know the act cool drill, but Lisa is great for making sure we follow through. I'd quite happily have spent the whole night talking to Pete, and who knows what else, but Lisa does get this stuff right (she was the first one of us married after all). As I was leaving the bar Pete asked for my number and after an excruciating four days staring at my phone willing it to ring and kicking myself that I didn't take his number, he got in touch to invite me out to a picnic that weekend in Regent's Park, pretty smooth I thought.

We met at the underground station and Pete led the way, guiding us through the park where we settled underneath a tree not too close to anyone else. He opened his rucksack and pulled out eight cans of Stella and a family size bag of Walkers crisps. Hmm. Not quite what I had in mind for a romantic picnic, but other than the pitiful spread we had a really special day, laughed continuously, made up lives for the people around us, shared stories of our own lives and he took it well when I suggested perhaps we have cava and Kettles crisps next time. Point taken cheeky, so there will be a next time he said, moving towards me for what was our first kiss.

The first year of our relationship was filled with adventures, nights out with friends, and nights in exploring each other. Pete was from London and took me to parts of the city I had never been to. He took me on the Jack the Ripper walking tour where the guide kept telling him off for offering his own thoughts on who was responsible for the infamous unsolved murders; he chaperoned me through the not so scary streets of Brixton; and he introduced me to the world of "The Arsenal". I was always keen to take part in whatever this city threw at me - live music, new restaurants, quirky pop-ups, the constant tickets I seemed to obtain to be in the audience of game shows; you name it - if it seemed like fun and something different I wanted to be a part of it and Pete was dragged along for the ride. Such is the energy and enthusiasm you have both at the start of a relationship and in your mid - twenties as I was then.

Pete had been accepted by my parents as the new beau in my life after a slight grilling from Dad. They jovially forgave him for being from 'dawn sawf'. Pete was a charmer who always asked for seconds of Mum's food (smart man) and generally my parents were delighted that this boyfriend had both a job and a 'nice' haircut; and no blue hair, facial piercings, motorbike or the need to call my Dad 'my man' at the end of every sentence (just a whistle-stop tour of the delights of my youth).

After two years we decided to move in together and found a great flat in Finsbury Park which we stretched ourselves to afford at the time, it was a couple of minutes walk from the tube and on the Victoria line (do you know, this was almost called the Viking Line), so it was less than an hour to get anywhere in London. In the throes of passion we relished having our own space and christened every room in the flat. We had what I expect are the usual teething issues related to moving in together too - he couldn't understand why I had so many cushions, I couldn't understand why he had so many gadgets with cables; I washed and emptied the washing machine, Pete filled it up; neither of us could comprehend how long the other spent in the bathroom (really, how long does it take a guy to have a shit I ask you?).

My mum had always been the 'house manager' keeping us all in check, ensuring the milk wasn't eight days old and still sitting in the fridge looking pretty, making sure that the sock drawer was fuller than the washing basket. I was happy to take on that role, and Pete was happy to be looked after. I love cooking and spent my evenings coming up with new creations in the kitchen while Pete rocked his ridiculously massive headphones collecting keys or guns from a phantom video game world during the week and at the weekends we would party and hang out with our friends.

Eventually we were at that age -the big 3-0s, marriages, promotions, the occasional friend's child being born, and life was starting to change for us and the rest of our friendship group. Our friends were either saving to buy a home or were starting families and weekends out were becoming less spontaneous and needed slotted into the diary a month or so in advance. People were dropping off the radar and Pete would say 'Another one bites the dust".' as they walked down the aisle or as we heard the news of another baby on the way.

It was that time in your life when you know that the lack of responsibility and pressure won't last forever because senior jobs, marriage and babies may be around the corner, as they had become already for some of our friends. Except it didn't seem to be round the corner for us, Pete and I had talked about marriage at the point when everyone around us seemed to have been struck down by weddingitus. It was like an epidemic at one point and Pete seemed to be the sole proprietor of the magic immunity potion. That was three years ago, and he said that it was time to concentrate on our jobs and that we really couldn't afford it. We hadn't really spoken too much about it since, but that was the point I decided if money was the problem for us to get married, then money would be the solution, and therein began the Wedding Fund.

For the last few years we have been concentrating on work, Pete is close to his second promotion in the insurance company and I've been steadily building up my salary as a Careers Advisor in a college. I don't like to say that we've been boring, but, well yes, work and box sets on TV had taken over our life (school nights and weekends). I still looked up all the exciting things that were going on in London, new bands, new restaurants and festivals but Pete was normally too tired to get involved. I went along to some of these things with my girls, Gail and Lisa, but an after work drink with colleagues or going to the pub with mates to watch football seemed to be all that Pete could muster the energy for these days. I suppose I could have done more myself, but you know, I just didn't.

While he was at his after work drinks I was stashing away the cash, only spending money on my catch ups with the girls and the latest fitness crazes, well - I had to look good in my wedding dress when I finally got there didn't I? Unfortunately a crash diet didn't quite cut it these days to prevent gravity dragging your tits to the floor unwillingly (I curse the seventeen year old me who loved having big boobs), and what happens to your arms? It's as if you wake up one day and all of a sudden realise that the top of your arms have doubled in size when flat against your ribs and when you lift your arm up to check what's going on the skin doesn't come with you. It's just hanging there in all its saggy glory - the underarm dingle dangle has arrived, and with each body revelation a new exercise regime is commenced for a month or so until something else takes over.

We did have a wobble last winter and I wondered if everything was going to collapse around me. Gail, Lisa, me and our significant others went to a country manor in the Cotswolds. It was beautiful with roaring fires, gardens as far as the eye could see and sumptuous furnishings everywhere. Lisa and Rob had arranged it as a thank you to Gail and me for helping out so much with their wedding that had taken place in the Summer.

Gail's boyfriend Tarquin used the setting to propose to her on the first night, and while we rejoiced in her happiness and toasted them with champagne I noticed that Pete had become quiet and closed off, drinking at double the pace of everyone else in silence.

I took him for a walk around the grounds and asked what the problem was, why he was being so rude to everyone when they had treated us to this weekend away. He didn't ask to be there he said - who wants a boring weekend in a country retreat with all these married people. As opposed to a boring weekend at home I asked, why don't you want to do anything anymore? It was like the life had been sucked out of him, he was shrinking like a prune not remotely interested in anything that wasn't a night out with the boys or work.

Now, I may have been slightly influenced by the fact that one of my best friends had just been proposed to and they'd only been together eighteen months no less, but I confessed to Pete that I cried my eyes out watching cheesy proposals on YouTube and was starting to question if he ever had any intention of marrying me. Why was I hanging around? He assured me again that we just needed to concentrate on work for a while and once we have more money we would revisit this. Thank god I thought, otherwise my wedding fund would have been a complete waste of time, and I was already over halfway there.

CHAPTER 2

Dinner with the girls is a regular occurrence in our favourite Soho spot. As the wine arrives, brought over by the spritzing Davidos (David, from Essex really), I almost wet myself waiting for my turn to update on the last few weeks.

Gail, Lisa and I have been friends for over fourteen years and still meet every couple of weeks to chew the fat. We met at University when the three of us were immersed for the first time into London life. Each of us having left our much smaller towns and villages for our studies in the big smoke. We met in halls of residence and in our second year we found a flat together, cementing our little London family forever more. We shared our twenties, discovering and enjoying the shops, parties, music and all that this crazy metropolis has to offer.

Having come from a small village, London was a far cry from my home town up North, where there is a choice of two pubs to frequent, and recently a fancy 'gastropub' has arrived in town. Shopping relied on a lift from Mum or a thirty minute bus ride to the closest biggish town where the main street had a small shopping centre and you could treat yourself to a new outfit from Topshop, Warehouse or Oasis.

The girls were equally enamored by London's big city lights and over the years we have secured our places in each other's hearts. Though we don't live together anymore, our catch ups in our favourite Soho restaurant have remained a constant, only the topics of conversation changing over the years.

During our university years we confided in each other, celebrated the highs, had our coming of age girlie holidays in Spain, as well as sharing our shameful embarrassing moments on men, boozy nights and bad decisions. I don't think anyone will ever forget the time I turned up at the house with my shoes in my hand unable to wear them home due to the fact that while I was upstairs having a rough and tumble with a nice young boy from the student union, one of his housemates it seems was downstairs taking a ginormous shit in my shoe. Not that I realised it at the time, I was halfway through the walk of shame home in the morning when I realised in my hungover state that my right shoe was painfully tighter than the left. I removed it to see what was going on only to discover that my toes had been squelching in poo, and it was caked between my toes. Looking inside the shoe I realised that there was still a huge lump in there and so me and my manky feet made a run for home where Gail and Lisa, in hysterical laughter attached a hose to the outside tap and scooshed me and my shoes to within an inch of our lives. It takes a good friend to help scoop a shite out of a shoe.

Any road, I digress, nowadays we are much more sophisticated ladies (well, most of the time) who enjoy dinner, a drink and a chinwag after work in our little spot where we keep up to date on the latest trials and tribulations of each other's lives.

Gail is from Somerset and is most definitely the hippie amongst us, making sure we are all up to date on the latest climate changey things we should be doing (to be fair, I do most of them for a couple of weeks until I forget to continue, but using eggs to wash your hair instead of shampoo was taking it a bit far). She has endless enthusiasm and has probably been the best at continuing to take advantage of London and all its opportunities with her boundless energy. Gail lives on a houseboat with her fiancé Tarquin, who she met at Blissfields, a festival in Hampshire concentrating on 'green issues' and new bands. Tarquin, as you may have guessed, is a public school educated chap from a fairly well-to-do family. Unlike the rest of his clan however, he doesn't work in the family company and instead drives a souped up campervan to festivals and events where he sells all things falafel. Gail makes jewellery which she sells alongside him at the various London markets, local shops and festivals. She is the most thoughtful person I know, and is endlessly giving us little gifts that she has found that are just perfect for us.

Her dinner updates at the moment are normally on the latest spirituality classes she's been to, the self-help books she's just finished or updates on the wedding plans, but she tends to keep those brief which I'm pretty sure has something to do with me and my lack of wedding plans.

As flighty as Gail can be, Lisa is the sensible one, all strong and practical. If you have a problem Gail is all ears and sympathy and Lisa sets about finding a way to fix it.

Lisa is also from up North, with solid northern roots. She is fairly blunt and straight talking; and she doesn't suffer fools gladly. She's passionate about everything and could start an argument with the Dalai lama. Lisa and her husband are taking the music marketing industry by storm with their own consultancy, and are currently working their socks off. When we catch up Lisa is generally putting the world to rights or discussing the wonderful world of politics and I have no doubt that she could give any local councillor a run for their money. And when she's not fixing the world or her work, she's generally sorting out the pair of us.

My updates tend to cover the latest fitness fad I've taken up and dropped, the stories of the crazy college kids I work with who make us feel old, and the growing status of the wedding fund.

'So ladies, do you fancy traditional pastels or something a bit more quirky?' I ask.

'Al, what are you on about?' says Gail.

'£7263, I've done it...so are we going full length or...' I start.

Lisa splutters her wine across the table as she pieces it together, 'Are you serious? Oh congratulations, to be honest we never thought he'd say yes, even with your bloody fund that's left us drinking shitty wine from the top of the menu for YEARS.'

Gail jumps in, 'Eh, it's not that we thought he'd say no, it's just, he'd put it off for so long, even after he got that promotion...Davidos, champagne please, our Alice is getting married.'

'Sure thing, that's fabulous dahling.' replies Davidos.

I'm so caught up in everything I wait until the

champagne toast before filling in the rest of the story, that being...well Pete didn't really take the news too well if I'm brutally honest.

'Euch, that's not good.' Lisa looks worried.

'I know,' I reply, 'but I think he was just shocked, everything is great now and the plans are all under way'.

'How was the 'we're getting married' sex?' Gail asks, 'Tarquin and I went wild when we got engaged, it was like anything we wanted to do before but had been too shy to mention came out.' she giggled.

Gail doesn't hold back on these things, as she continues, 'We were all in the country manor remember, and he stole one of the cleaning ladies' outfits from the maintenance cupboard that had been left open and had me dress up and clean the room while he slapped me on the ass for not doing it properly and every time I missed a spot he had a different punishment for me.'

'What about you Lisa?' Gail nods towards her, 'You were in Paris, any French maid scenarios for you?'

'Oh puleease,' Lisa says, 'but he did get what I reckon is the best night of his life for investing in this' she flaunts her rock in our face and giggles.

'Do you know that the top of the Eiffel Tour

moves as much as 18 cm, swaying around in the heat and the wind?' I add, anything to move the conversation on.

'Good God, I'm glad I didn't know that at the time.' Lisa replies.

'Oooh, when are you getting your engagement ring?' Gail asks, 'And can we arrange engagement drinks?'

I'm delighted that the conversation has moved on as I didn't realise "getting married sex" was a thing. Actually, that's a lie, before the big day I'd been to the beauty salon to get a bikini wax and I'd ended up telling the beauty therapist all about my plans to surprise Pete with the wedding fund (how do these people manage to extract the most intimate details of your life from you, perhaps it's something to do with your vulnerable nakedness). Anyway, she was full of suggestions on how to make it even more special - and so half an hour later I left the salon with a Hollywood wax and a bright red heart shaped vajazzle to boot.

Not that Pete actually saw my jazzy lady garden. After the proposal he consumed a lot more drinks and by the time we got home his flaccid parts were as sleepy as he was, nothing was getting that bad boy up. A few days later we still hadn't consummated the news and my heart was starting to lose its shape one fallen diamante at a time until I painfully removed the rest and put the whole ridiculous experience in my box of never to be told memories.

'Yes, tell me if Pete needs help choosing the ring - you did such a good job with mine.' Lisa says.

'OK I will, but as it's not a surprise I expect that we'll choose something together.' I say.

I hadn't even thought about this, will this come out of the fund or will Pete spring for this separately. Traditionally he should be spending two months salary on my ring I guess, but that's a bit OTT, one month should be more than sufficient, especially if I get to pick so I can choose something that looks a million bucks.

'Oh, OK,' Lisa nods, 'how about beginning of next month for the engagement drinks though, the first Saturday, can I arrange it?'

'Sure, but keep it low key.' I say, 'I don't want to freak Pete out.'

'What's up Al, since when do you want things to be low key? It's your celebration too.' Lisa demands.

'I know, I know. Sorry, and thank you for offering to arrange something. I'm sure it will be fab.' I smile weakly.

I notice the girls glance at each other. I'm not sure

why I'm so hesitant about this engagement party, normally I'm the first to whoop and holler about a party. I have a slight sense of trepidation about this, something just isn't sitting right, but I'm sure I'm just being silly.

***

It's a couple of days before the engagement party and we're tying up some of the details tonight to get them booked. I've done all the ground work, and put together a trusty file of everything, so tonight is decision time. Pete has done the square amount of bugger all so far, so I want to thrash it out and then we can update everyone at the engagement party.

I've rushed home from work to cook all the canapé options we could have at the wedding...nothing fancy - spring rolls, pigs in blankets, mini fish and chip cones and it's all set up at the dining table along with my wedding file and a chilled bottle of white wine.

I've put a list in the front of the file with the things we need to decide on - the bits that we really need to confirm to secure the dates we want. I've probably got around a 90- minute window of attention before Pete loses the will to live. Not to mention, Game of Thrones starts at 9pm, so I've got no hope after then.

7.45pm and no sign of him yet. I pop the canapes back in the oven to keep them warm, but where the hell is he, he knew we were going over the wedding stuff tonight. I'm on my second large glass of wine by the time the front door opens at 8.24 pm (yes, I have been watching the minutes tick over).

'All right?' Pete says.

'Hey, where have you been?' I ask, desperately trying to keep the frustration out of my voice.

'Drink with work, what's up?' he nonchalantly throws his suit jacket on the sofa.

'I told you this morning I was getting dinner and we'd go through the wedding stuff - we said 7.30.'

'Sorry, didn't know it was a set time - can't we go through it now?' Pete asks defensively.

I bring the now somewhat less appealing canapes out of the oven and put them on the table.

'Now, the main things we need to sort are venue which I have down to two places; Food - buffet or sit-down meal; and the guest list.'

'Sure. This food is a bit dry isn't it?' he says tucking into a fish and chip cone.

'Well, you will be 54 minutes late.' Moving on

quickly I continue, 'Any road I have it down to Public House restaurant or The Chapel music venue - both are easy to get to from the town hall.'

'The music venue.' Pete replies whilst casting his eyes over the shrivelled up food, looking for anything appealing to refill his plate.

'You haven't even heard the pros and cons of each?' I whinge, frustration setting in.

'OK, Public House then, you obviously didn't like that choice.'

'It's not that, I have a whole list here of what's what in each venue.' I sigh, handing him the typed up sheet entitled Public H v. Chapel MV.

'Shit, I don't care Al, honestly, really whatever makes you happy.'

'What would make me happy would be your input. I've done everything so far, a little contribution wouldn't go amiss.'

Avoiding his eyes, I refill my wine glass and concentrate intensely on my plate whilst he reads through the pros and cons sheet.

He grabs my hand, 'Sorry Al, it's just been a tough

day. Give me a butchers at that list. Hmm. Hmm. OK, Public House. Food there is great and...' he glances down again at the pro list, 'it's less than five minutes from the town hall.'

Great, decision made, and only like pulling a couple of teeth. 'Next, the food - buffet or sit-down meal?' I smile, knowing his answer to this one already.

'Piece of piss, sit down meal. Hate buffets - there's never enough and always a jostle to grab crap you wouldn't want to eat any other time.'

Finally, some enthusiasm, I knew he would have an opinion on the food.

'Ok, so just the guest list to sort and that's it for now.' I say, grabbing the provisional list I've put together and placing a copy in front of each of us.

I wander into the kitchen to get another bottle of wine from the fridge. As I'm searching for the bottle opener, I let Pete know that there are 80 on the list, but we need to get it down to 60 now we know it's a sit-down meal.

As I wander back with the newly opened bottle of wine, Pete is fiddling with the remote control. 'Did you hear me, we need to cut 20 out.' I say.

'Game of Thrones is about to start, just take out who you think. You know who I'd want there.' the back of his head tells me.

'No Pete, just NO. This is why I said 7.30. If you'd got home then instead of 54 minutes late we would have finished this, wouldn't have had a dried up dinner, wouldn't be…' my voice trails off.

I know I'm raising my voice and I know that with this tension a new bottle of wine is not a good idea but I've had enough.

'Record that and give our wedding day some bloody attention.' I shout.

He takes the list, and in the five minutes that covers last week's recap and the ridiculously long intro, he scores out 20 names from the list, returns it to me, kisses me on the forehead and dares to jest, 'See, just needed a bit of male efficiency.'

I am absolutely seething, how dare he underestimate the work I have put into this. I pack up the wedding file, fling it in my handbag and look over at Pete lounging in front of the TV, blissfully oblivious to the fury burning inside me. The silent assassin that is banging at my ribs to get out and beat the bejeezus out of him.

I clear the table, clattering as much as is physically

possible without actually shattering the table and start loading the bin with the leftovers, it's far too dry for second day lunch. Pete comes in oblivious to my pain and tops up his wine glass with one hand and catches a mid-bin spring roll in the other.

'You coming through? It's started.' he asks.

As I rinse the plates, my eyes well up and I swallow the lump in my throat. He couldn't have been less interested. Every hurtful, thoughtless thing he has done in the last few months flits through my mind. He forgot our anniversary, he seems to have forgotten that he is responsible for taking the bins out each week, he neglects to tell me when he's going out. In fact, everything he does is just selfish.

What am I doing here? *We didn't think he'd say yes*...Lisa's comment comes back to haunt me. Could they see something I couldn't, or didn't until now? I chuck the plates on the drying rack and head to bed, mentally exhausted and filled with a sense of unease that I haven't felt since those early days when you have no idea if the other person feels the same way you do.

***

The day of the Engagement Party has arrived. It's been arranged for early evening so that my parents can come down and return on the same day. Pete and I are still on sticky ground from the evening of wedding planning, not that he seems to be remotely aware of this. He has gone out to watch the football with a couple of guys from work so I will be meeting him at the party.

I insisted on something casual and Lisa has reserved an area in a local bar with a big beer garden. She and Gail have decorated the area and made sure that there are wine coolers and bottles of bubbly chilling for the big toast.

'This is wonderful sweetie pie.' says Mum, 'Aren't you lucky to have such wonderful friends to arrange this for you…it'll be the hen do next, and then the big day.' she elbows me.

I think my mother is even more excited than I am about this wedding. After ten years of waiting I expect she feels relieved I'm finally coming off that shelf.

'So where is 'ye olde cockney geezer' then?' asks Dad, looking mighty unimpressed that he is not here.

'He'll be here soon.' I look at my watch, 'He had a ticket to watch the Arsenal match with some work mates.' I force a smile.

There's roughly twenty of us gathered around a big garden table with an oversized umbrella. Bottles of wine are chilling in coolers, champagne is at the ready behind the bar for when everyone gets here, well for when Pete gets here. Everyone else has been here for over an hour politely ignoring the fact that only one of the 'engaged' individuals is here to celebrate at present.

'Tell us how the wedding plans are going Alice?' says Pete's auntie.

I was kind of hoping that Pete would be here for this but as he hasn't responded to my message asking where the fuck he is I guess I need to hold court for a while. Everyone is eager to hear too, so it feels like doing a bloody presentation at work.

'Well, we're not having anything religious,' I begin, 'so we will be having the ceremony in Islington Town Hall.'

'And then we are going to have a sit-down meal at Public House. Just something small, but of course all of you here will be invited.' I smile.

'And when do you get your ring?' Ailsa, my brother's wife asks.

'That's what we were asking.' Gail says, gesticulating towards herself and Lisa.

Cue. Everyone looks at my left hand and realises that I'm not wearing an engagement ring. Good question

Ailsa, good question. I feel like I'm under interrogation, and all I want to do is shout 'Who the fuck knows'. It's the only bit that I don't really feel I should be arranging, yet it doesn't seem to be coming up from Pete's side either.

'Would you excuse me a sec.' I say to the crowd, as I make my way to the loos for a breather and to call Pete to find out where the sodding hell he is.

I ring him three times whilst hiding in the stalls but there is no answer. The football match finished two hours ago and is no more than twenty minutes away from here. I'm starting to panic that something has happened to him, but truth be told, if asked at gunpoint where he is I think it's more likely that he's ditched the party than he's ended up in a ditch.

As I return to the party I am fending off enquiries as to Pete's whereabouts with the usual, 'oh he's running late, you know what men are like, he will be here soon' until he finally picks up my call.

'Hey bllabe.' he slurs.

'Where are you? We've been here for hours waiting for you?' I ask, trying to hide the frustration from my voice in case anyone overhears me.

'Out wish the lad.' he replies.

'You're meant to be here, at our engagement party, you don't even sound like you can stand up.' I say.

'Sorry bllabe, no can do, I'm too pished. Need bed.' he says and proceeds to hang up.

Holy fuck, how can he do this to me? I summon Lisa and Gail as I need a bit of help here on what to do next. I can't tell everyone that Pete just couldn't be arsed coming. Or maybe I can, what a prick. Who does that? Who misses their own engagement party to go out and get shit faced with their workmates?

'I'm fuming.' I tell the girls.

'What's happened? Where is he?' Lisa asks.

'He's trollied. Somewhere around the Arsenal stadium or on his way to bed. Absolutely rat-arsed.'

'Did he forget this was happening today?' Gail asks, giving him a chance.

'No, he didn't bloody forget. I spoke to him as he walked out the door. Gave him a shirt to take with him to put on after the match before arriving here.'

'Seriously, this is it. He is so dead. But what am I going to do now?' I ask, 'What about all these people here, this is so embarrassing.'

'Right,' says Lisa, ever the solution finder, 'you can kill him later, but for now where does everyone think that he is?' she asks.

'On his way from the football.' I reply, pacing from one foot to the other, biting at the skin around my nails.

'OK, so here's what we say....' Lisa starts.

And then I spin my yarn.
'Hi everyone, can I just have your attention a sec please? I've just spoken with Pete and he has really bad food poisoning, must have been from something he ate at the match, a dodgy pie or something.'

I will myself to stop, stop giving so many details everyone knows that's the first sign of a lie, 'Anyway, I'm really sorry but he's not going to be able to make it and I really need to get home and make sure that he's OK.' I finish.

'There's a couple of bottles of champagne and they've already been paid for so please help yourselves and enjoy the rest of your evening' Lisa adds with a sympathetic arm around my shoulder, which is invisibly holding me up straight.

I make my way over to my Mum and Dad to say goodbye before dashing off.

'Poor soul.' my mum says, 'Don't worry about us, you get home and look after him, that's my girl. Your brother will get us back to the station. Cheerio sweetie pie.' she kisses me gently on the cheek.

'Thanks Mum, speak soon.' I gulp back the lump in my throat as I just about hold it together for the final five minutes of farewells to everyone else.

As I leave the bar, uncertain of what state I might find Pete in, or indeed whether he will even be there. I am consumed with humiliation over what he has done. I'm sure everyone knew that there was something else going on, all those questions about the wedding and my lack of engagement ring. Oh dear god, how can I face these people again. I could kill him. I will kill him. How could he do this to me. Bastard.

I take my time wandering home, drifting in and out of conscious thought. Instead of being full of emotion, I feel almost the opposite. It's like there is a huge void where my heart should be, hollow and empty. My head is making up for it though, overflowing with furious ideas on what I should and could do to him, how I can punish him for doing this to me. Again, I think. He was shitty with me when I told him I'd saved the money to get married. He was late and completely disinterested when we were arranging the wedding details last week and now he's just not turned up to our engagement party with our family and friends. I just don't know what to do with this, what would I tell a friend in this situation? Well, that's a no brainer - I'd tell them that their fiancé is an asshole and that they should get out now before they walk down the aisle with this dickhead.

After a couple of hours of staring into oblivion in Finsbury Park I finally summon up the courage to drag myself back to the flat. As I walk in I can see a trail of discarded clothing displaying said assholes presence. Behind the bedroom door I smell a waft of sweat and beer and peeking in I realise that he is passed out on top of the bed in his boxers. I have no energy to wake him and argue, so I remove the pint of water and the paracetamol that he has next to him on the bedside table and place them next to me in the living room. You want them, you can come and get them.

It's almost 10pm, when he surfaces from the bedroom. He at least has the courtesy to look shame faced as I stare straight through him.

'All right? Do you know where the painkillers are?' he asks sheepishly.

I hurl the box of tablets at him.

'All right? ALL RIGHT? Do you think I'm all

right?' I scream.

He puts his hand to his head, 'Ouch. Keep it down will you.'

'You've got a fucking nerve.' I scream, 'How dare you do that to me. You listen and you listen good! I have just had to stand in front of our friends, my family, YOUR family, at OUR engagement party wondering where the hell you were. And then lie to them all that you have food poisoning to cover for the fact that you are a selfish, hopeless twat who couldn't be bothered showing up for his own celebration.'

I start throwing cushions at his head as nothing seems to be evoking a response. He's lucky I only had soft objects to hand.

'WELL,' I say, 'What the fuck happened?'

He flops onto the sofa, legs dangling over the edge, the back of his hand pathetically strewn over his eyes, 'I don't know. I had a drink after the match and one drink led to another and…'

'I had to sit and lie to your parents Pete, to your aunt.'

'I'm sorry. But what happened to low key - my fucking aunt.' he moans, 'I see her about once a year, what the hell are you doing inviting her to my "low key" engagement party. This is turning into a god damn circus.'

'Don't you dare.' I'm shuddering with rage, 'Don't you dare turn this on me, make me out to be the villain here.'

'You know what Pete, you want low key, you got it.' I glare at him.

Thankfully he is in too much of a state to argue further. And I quite frankly am done. He wants low key, he can have it. How about no wedding at all, is that low key enough for him?

***

It's been a few weeks since the engagement party and things have escalated to an unbearably bad state. I haven't mention the wedding at all, and neither has Pete. As far as he knows, the Town Hall and venue had been booked and paid for. He is out all the time, passing out in bed at the end of each day in a haze of beer and whisky fumes. I'm up and out each morning before he wakes and the evenings we do see each other, it's like living with a random roommate who annoys the hell out of you with everything they do.

How did all this happen? Ever since this bloody

wedding has come up things have changed, they've gone wrong. Google tells me that planning a wedding is stressful and many couples experience the same thing. But did these women spring the wedding on their man, I think. Is this stress or does he just not want this? Hmm. What's that saying, if it looks like a duck, swims like a duck and quacks like a duck....

Everyone at work is winding down, the students are gearing up for the summer break so our workload has depleted and I've become obsessed with online quizzes like 'how to know he loves you', 'is he the one', 'problems when planning a wedding'.

Pete and I haven't had a proper conversation in days, weeks even, he sees more of our remaining single friends and work mates than me and we haven't as much a touched each other longer than I can recall. I've tried to talk to him, but he seems to have 'retreated' as the magazines put it. Every attempt to talk about what is going on is met with grunts and sighs and 'I'm too knackered for this'.

I've held off on confirming any of the wedding stuff, it doesn't take a genius to see that Pete doesn't want this. He would probably go through with this wedding, drift into marriage, but I can't do that now, not now I know. Our relationship has become a blunt old razor. Like a razor, you can still use it long beyond when you should but you get the scars to go with it. You don't think too much about the scars and scratches it gives you until the old bugger cuts you pretty deep, then you realise its really got to go, a fresh new one is so much better.

I'm beyond believing in thunderbolt moments, but there's got to be more than this. Someone who really wants to spend their life with me can't be too much to ask?

Nothing is booked yet; do I just not bother? How long would it be before he realises that we are not actually getting married. Too long at a guess, too long for me to be hanging about wasting my time.

I still can't believe that at thirty-four I am contemplating starting over again, but that seems to be exactly what is happening. Christ, I could have enjoyed these last three years if I'd known, not wasted my time on him, on wearing old clothes and foregoing decent holidays to save money. I could have been chatting up gorgeous men, having my sex and the city moments and going to exotic places like Thailand and Marrakesh.

Well, I'll show him, I'll show him exactly what a bloody good holiday looks like, show him what it's like to be by himself. It's about time I got out of this goddamn mess and had some fun for a change.

***

The next few days pass in a blur. I've arranged a sabbatical from work for two and a half months and I've replaced the wedding folder and its To Do list with my new list. 'The Thailand Plan'.

The girls have come round for dinner after work and I'm going to cook and fill them in on the new plan. I didn't have to tell Pete to take a hike and give us the flat for the evening as these days he's never in before 10pm. Working late apparently, funny how his office has recently started smelling like beer and fags.

'Jesus Al, I knew things weren't good, but you're off to Thailand, and he doesn't know the wedding is off?' Lisa asks in a somewhat dazed manner.

'I've had enough Lisa, never more has the phrase *he's just not that into you* felt so true.'

I continue to fill them in on how I was having lunch with Jane from work a couple of days ago and listening to her talk about her travels around Europe last summer. It got me thinking about doing something similar. I spent the afternoon looking up flights to Thailand, looking at all the recommended things to do there, and before I knew what I was doing I had put some flights on hold.

My creepy boss in his shiny suit came into our little office not long after that and mid ball scratch (yes, he's that kind of disgusting boss) he began asking me to confirm the stats I'd been working on for him. Jonesy, as he liked to be called thinking that it made him one of the team was a classic prick. He wore too much gel in his hair, sported an open collar pink shirt to accompany the shiny waistcoat under his suit and constantly spoke with a patronising tone and his head tilted to the right. I wouldn't mind if he was sarcastic because he was always right, but instead he was the kind of dickhead who was always wrong and only managed to slime his way up the career ladder by kissing the arse of everyone above him. The fact that he was positively despised by everyone below him seemed to go completely unnoticed.

So this particular afternoon Jonesy asked me to clarify our weekly figures for him, which I duly did. No, that's not right he told me, look them up again. I had the bloody screen open in front of me. This is not my math going wrong here, we have a fucking database that calculates this figure for us - it's not rocket science. Except Jonesy didn't actually even know how this thing worked - you know the kind - I can do your job better than you although I don't actually even know what the fuck it is you do. Prick. As Jonesy proceeded to berate me on how important it is that I provide him with the correct figures for him to take to management I nodded along obligingly. All the while, I was clicking back onto the screen where my flights were sitting on hold. 'You understand how important this is Al.' he's saying to the crowded office - crowded with both staff and students no less. 'You can't just take a punt, this needs to be accurate. Now I'll give you an hour to get it right and then you can update me.' Anyway, that was the precise moment that I thought I will indeed take a punt and at the exact same time that I told Jonesy, 'Yes, leave it with me' - I clicked the button confirming the transfer of my flights from hold to booked. Thank you wedding fund - simultaneously allowing me to stick two fingers up to both tossers currently tormenting my life.

Thank Christ that afternoon HR agreed to my two month unpaid leave over the summer, they could hardly say no having let Jane do it last year.

'It all happened so quickly.' I added, with a nervous laugh.

Gail squeezes my arm and gives me a gentle smile, 'You're the queen of surprises aren't you?'

'Well the last one didn't work out so well...I don't know, I can't sit about doing nothing, waiting for things to change. It's only delaying the inevitable, that he doesn't want to marry me. So I'm out. I figure venue deposit equals flight, wedding breakfast equals travel money. Why shouldn't I have an adventure.' I nod my head defensively.

Lisa bursts out laughing, 'You never cease to

amaze me. Why the hell not, I have no idea what you are doing, but good for you.' she raises her glass to a cheers.

Gail joins in with a more reserved smile, 'Alice, don't you think you need to talk to Pete? You do have a tendency to you know, act first think later.... I do think that Pete is a git right now, but are you sure this is what you want? For it all to end?'

'He doesn't want to talk, he doesn't want to spend time with me, so that's exactly what he's getting. I'll tell him as I'm leaving.' I shrug.

Lisa jumps in, 'As long as you're not expecting him to jump on a plane and follow you, drop to his knees on the sand and tell you he couldn't live without you.' she lets that linger, 'Are you prepared to come back to a life without Pete?'

A moment of doubt passes through my mind. Maybe I am expecting Pete to come chasing after me? It would be the most amazing thing ever, maybe we could even get married out there on the beach. No, this is just a moment of weakness, this is my adventure and this is the right decision.

'The best break up for everyone is when you can't bump into them, can't be tempted into one more night together.' I say.

He may just realise what he's lost if I'm not around too, but that's not why I'm doing this, really it's not. And, I can't very well tell Pete that he's become a selfish boring git without doing something to prove that I'm not boring too. This break is exactly what we need, sorry break up, I mean break up.

'OK then,' Lisa says, 'well in that case Rob and I will come and help you move your stuff out on Sunday. You can store it at ours and then you will have a base with us when you come back to start afresh from.'

'Oh thank you, what would I do without you guys.' I grab their hands as my eyes fill with overwhelming appreciation.

'You're really sure hun?' Gail asks again.

'Yes. I'm sure. To the £7263 Thailand fund.' I raise my glass and we giggle with nerves, excitement and astonishment.

CHAPTER 3

"Welcome aboard flight BA10 from London Heathrow to Bangkok...'

As I sit on the plane I feel absolutely wiped out, I'm wedged between two large middle aged men and fighting for a bit of armrest - why doesn't everyone know the rule that if you're in the middle seat on a plane you are entitled to both middle armrests. I close my eyes and think about the weekend I've just had. It's been nonstop talking with those closest to me. Mum and Dad, Gail and Lisa, and of course, Pete. Everyone giving their two pennies worth on what I'm doing. Having been on full throttle to get everything done, I'm now like a duracell bunny on its last hops, limping along on empty. I drift off exhausted and replay the weekend in my mind.

***

The weekend begins as I finish my last Friday at work for the summer. I take the train up to spend the weekend with Mum and Dad. The train is packed with happy weekend people, another working week behind them, the days longer and an evening of BBQs, beer gardens or parks most likely ahead of them. I gaze around wondering where each person is going, who they're going home to. No doubt they have a better evening ahead of them than me - which involves shattering my parents illusion that their last child is finally joining the ranks of the normal by settling down to married life.

As the train pulls into the station, I can see Mum and Dad scanning the carriages to try and find us. They're expecting me and Pete to be stepping off the train. It never ceases to amaze me how excited they look to see me. As I climb down I see Mum's frantic wave. Honestly, there are about fourteen people getting off this train, but they wave like they could have lost me at Alton Towers.

'Kooee, Kooee, Alice.' Mum's sings. Why is it that just stepping back into your parents' company you have the ability to feel like an embarrassed teenager. Dad gives me a huge bear hug, folding me in while mum has a quizzical look on her face that I think can only be her wondering why I'm on my own.

'Where's Pete?' Mum asks.

'He's had to work. He says hi.' I lie reluctantly, it's only until we're home anyway.

'That's a shame sweetie.' she says while giving me a kiss and stroking my hair.

Mum always comments on how sleek and sophisticated I look nowadays. I'm far from it by London standards, but I guess my Mum now looks at me the way I look at those sloaney girls in Mayfair bars. I think Mum just sees the straight blonde hair (naturally frizzy and darker blonde, OK light brown), my fitted wardrobe of black and white, a distinct lack of canvas on the feet, and the fact that I'm never out of make-up. There's nothing sloaney or designer about me, in London I'd be deemed quite dull and plain, but in comparison to the jeans and trainers look that I sported when I left and many of my old school friends have retained, I think she likes to think of it as the sophistication of London.

I did try lots of different looks in my twenties, but none of them seemed to stick. My hair has been red, purple, black and silver. I've tried the grunge look, the indie look, and the vintage look, but each time I just seemed to look weird - like I'd got dressed in a charity shop by shaking around in the dark and wearing whatever fell off the hangers.

One New Year's Eve I decided to get hair extensions, right down to my bum, they became dreads

after a two-day bender and not looking after them. It was going to cost as much to get them taken out as it had to have them put in for the few days I managed, so instead I spent three hours in the shower with a tub of butter and a bottle of olive oil yanking and tugging the buggers out.
And I only had garlic olive oil, so I smelt a right treat by the end of it. Needless to say, I am best staying away from the magazine's latest trends, unable to carry most of them off and uninterested in dedicating the maintenance level required for the rest.

There's something so comforting about being back home. The smell of the house so familiar, Dad's papers lying all over the sofa and mum's knitting needles and sewing basket sprawled across the kitchen table. Sean our terrier panting with baited breath and the smell of mum's soup. Always a smell of mum's soup - even if it's not cooking and you can't see it, I swear the smell of our childhood soup and crusty bread Sunday lunches is always there.

Tonight however, there's a lasagne stacked high on the counter ready to go in the oven. It's Pete's favourite I can't help thinking. Mum is one of those Mum's who thinks you always need a good feed, and you probably haven't had a home cooked meal since you were last there. Never mind the fact you're in your thirties, love foodie programmes, cook almost every night, own over twenty cookbooks and have done so for the best part of a decade. Still, right now I'm more than happy to indulge in the pampering of my parents while it lasts, and nothing beats the taste of your childhood when you need a pick me up.

I will fill them in on what's going on, let me just enjoy the comfort of being back home for a while first. I told Pete that they were clearing out the garage and I had to go through my old stuff to see what I wanted to keep so if he didn't fancy it, he could just stay in London. As predicted and desired, Pete jumped at the chance not to join me for the weekend.

I sit down with Dad to watch a Question of Sport, a family Friday night tradition. I know nothing about sport and have no interest in it but it never really seems to matter with this programme. Besides, Dad and my brother Adam always watched it when we were growing up and as the option tended to be help mum with dinner (my interest in cooking hadn't quite appeared at that stage of teenage angst) or watch Q of S with Dad and Adam - I feigned interest for so long I began to enjoy it. Right now especially, a bit of Phil Tufnell, some time with Dad, the TV to prevent further wedding questions, and some cuddles with Sean were just the ticket. At 14, Sean (after Sean Connery, I have an insane crush on James Bond) is getting on a bit, so I lift him up onto my lap to indulge him for a while with some petting and mutual comfort.

I've dodged a few wedding questions already and

I can see Mum giving Dad the eye, that look that says there is something not quite right with our baby and it's your job to delve Dad. I continue to laugh at the programme, ask questions about the guests and stab random wrong answers at the TV...anything to keep the status quo and stop an inquisitive line of enquiry I'm not quite ready for. I'm pretty sure this keeps Dad happy too. He's a soppy old git, but hates these awkward chats and would much prefer Mum to do the digging and leave him to the jovial banter, practical solutions and bear hugs. I know I must tell them what's happening, in fact, I'm desperate for them to know as I hate keeping secrets from them, but they are just such worriers.

    Dad has worked for the same company for thirty odd years and will think taking a summer off to travel because you have broken up with someone is a big risk, not to mention a frivolous waste of money. Mum, she is going to panic about me. It's not that she doesn't want the best for me, but at 34, she already thinks I'm leaving things late on the wedding and babies front, let alone going back to square one, alone, single, with no baby-daddy in sight. My old school friends' children are embarking on secondary school she regularly reminds me. 'Don't leave it too late.' she often says.

    Mum met Dad when she was seventeen and they were married and with child by the time she was twenty-one. Most of my town have followed a similar path, the age may have crept up slightly to married and kids by twenty-five, but the overarching feeling is the same. Life in this town is about finding someone, settling down, getting on with life, and bringing a new family into the world. To mum, being single in your thirties is horrifying - you'll miss the boat, be left on the shelf and all those other delightful clichés people like to dish out to poor unsuspecting souls in their thirties who are otherwise very happy with their lives thank you very much. She means well, but I'm not looking forward to her reaction, comfort is what I need right now, not a reinforcement of the fear I'm already trying to suppress.

It seems different in London - single, married, with children, without - there aren't age brackets for this like there are elsewhere, or at least it doesn't seem that way as most of the people who have children move out of London, so you don't see them anymore, leaving the childless in your line of vision who are unlikely to be asking you why the hell you don't have a ring on your finger and a couple of nippers yet. My rational side belongs to London now - you'll be fine, you deserve a better, happier relationship, so you're moving on, having a break to re-align yourself. My emotional side on the other hand, that's closer to mum's view than I like to admit even to myself.

'Tea's ready guys.' Mum hollers from the kitchen diner as she plonks a humongous lasagne in the centre of the table, along with the salad that generally goes untouched (we all do that don't we, to pretend we are eating a slightly more balanced meal than just cheese, pasta, meat and garlic buttered bread). This lasagne taunts me, the sheer size of it screams out - Pete is meant to be here with you.

'So, sweetie pie, how are things?' Mum asks whilst dishing up and dad is filling the wine glasses.

'Yeah, all good ta, can you pass the garlic bread please?' I don't know how long I can keep this up, hell let's just get on with it.

'It's yes, not yeah Alice. You know, you haven't mentioned anything on the wedding plans in a while?' Mum says, sounding about as breezy as Monica leaving her message for Richard in Friends.

Taking a gulp of wine, I begin.
'So I have a bit of an update on that. The thing is, Pete and I aren't really getting on too well, so I haven't done much on the wedding front.'

I've never actually told Mum and Dad that it was me who proposed to Pete, me who saved the money for the wedding. I'm not sure why, I guess they might think it odd, untraditional, perhaps even dare I say it desperate. But once I start talking, it all comes tumbling out - my surprise wedding announcement, the money I'd saved, Pete's lack of interest in the wedding, the fact that Pete was pissed and didn't turn up to the engagement party and didn't have food poisoning, my reflection on whether for Pete it was ever meant to last this long, our fights, our growing apart, right up to

'So, I'm leaving him and I've decided to go to Thailand for a couple of months. Clear my head and move on.'

To be fair, this is a lot of information for a woman who until now thought her biggest worry was what hat the mother of the bride should wear to a London wedding. She no doubt had numerous conversations about it in the local village with all the nosey villagers who often ask when that daughter of hers who upped sticks to the big smoke was going to get herself hitched.

As I stop to breathe I see a look of exasperation and fear across my mum's face. She knew there was something wrong, but she was not expecting this. A few times she tries to speak, but nothing that quite resembles a full word leaves her mouth. 'John' is finally all she can manage, looking at my Dad. This is code for - I'm not coping here and don't know what to say, will you look up from your bloody plate and step in here - you've been tagged into this conversation. Mum wanders to the kitchen counter to get some unneeded napkins, or maybe they are needed, I think I've just seen her discreetly wipe her eye with the back of her hand.

It's not that mum wants me to stay with a guy who doesn't make me happy, it's just different in her world - you have a boyfriend for that long - he becomes your husband - it's filled with ups and downs, but you just make do and get on, and the ups of the relationship (which are the majority of the time) tide you through the downs.

Another bottle of wine later, I think they get it. This isn't me just throwing in the towel at the 'downs'. They are overcrowding the 'ups' and even my folks can see that Pete has been acting badly since I proposed and this is not a good sign.

The conversation continues throughout the weekend. With them realising I haven't mentioned anything to Pete about the impending break up, let alone the whimsical date of buggering off to Thailand yet, I think Mum now holds out some hope that this is me being my usual dramatic self and that it may be much ado about nothing, only the cost of an unused flight in our wake. This time next week, she will be back to hat shopping and searching for heels just the right height for both elegance and comfort.

Dad's more realistic however, his glasses not quite as rose-tinted as Mum's. He's seen this all before with me, these spur of the minute decisions that I do seem to follow through on, even if Mum never thought I would...coming home with a dog (Sean, who is now the family dog, after I realised that 15 year olds don't actually like getting up at 6.30am to walk the dog before school), quitting jobs on a whim, the butterfly tattoo, piercings in various parts of the body (all of which were the top half, and all of which are gone except the ears), moving to London, generally stomping my feet and reacting with a bang to most situations.

With a sunken feeling of dread knowing I am on my way back to London to talk to Pete, I am deposited back to the station. Mum asks me one final time to think hard about this before getting back to the flat to talk with Pete and irreversibly turning my life upside down. Dad squints his eyes at me and purses his lips, which from experience I take to mean, I know whatever I say you're going to do this anyway, let's just not reinforce it out loud in front of your mother just yet though eh?

He brings me in for a big hug and says, 'Do what you think best love, your mother wants you to be happy, she just worries about you.' I wave a teary goodbye and promise to call them in the evening to fill them in.

***

Then came the chat with Pete.

'Hey.' I mumble as I unlock the front door and wander solemnly through to the living room.

No response. He's engrossed in his PS4 world of war and is shouting at the TV with those bloody headphone things on again. As I wander past to reach the bedroom he looks across at me and gives me an upward head nod of 'hey'.

'Pete, we have to talk.' I say as soon as he turns to me. I have to get this conversation over with before I'm sick, or change my mind...or leave for Thailand tomorrow.

Removing one big round doughnut ear just an inch, he looks at me with that universal, chin out, head tilt that means 'what are you saying, say again'. I'm so used to that move I could honestly say fuck off the first time I say something to him when he's on that thing and never offend as it's always at least the second time before he listens. Really, the amount of times I have to repeat myself following that bloody head move.

'We need to talk Pete.' I say not looking at him.

I make a coffee while he continues with his game. I'm pretty sure he is actually closing it down, but why can't he just walk away from that thing as soon as something needs to be done. He wanders into the kitchen, leans against the counter opposite me and it all starts to unfold.

'So, what is it Al?' Pete almost sighs, I get the

feeling he wanted to put 'this time' at the end of that question but didn't.

'This isn't working is it?' I start, staring at the floor.

Silence.

'Pete, we're meant to be getting married, and we're hardly even speaking.' I look straight at him this time.

Silence.

'Do you want to break up?' I may as well get straight to the point with all the feedback I'm getting.

'No, it's just, I don't know what's happened' he manages.

'Do you love me Pete?'

'Yes.' he sighs.

'Do you want to marry me?' I force out.

He stares at the floor, shuffling uncomfortably before saying, 'Why do things need to change, they were fine before.'

'For you.' I reply.

I'm getting angry now. I knew it wasn't the money that held us back, I've felt it for the last months and now I really know I was right.

'You know your problem, you just don't want to grow up. And you know what? You are thirty - fucking - five. We've been together seven years. It's normal for things to change. Instead, you've led me on for the last four years with no intentions of getting married and you humiliated me in front of everyone at the engagement party. And by the way - has it even occurred to you to apologise to me properly for that? For the humiliation you caused me?'

'Fucking hell Al, when did you get so middle aged' Pete shouts back.

He never was good at taking an insult, so I fling another straight at him, 'Really, middle-aged? Cause you're so filled with a lust for life...you never want to do anything.'

'And you're so exciting are you Alice?'

'No I haven't been, but I'm starting now.' I calmly reply.

He smirks, 'off to climb Kilimanjaro are you?'

'No actually, I'm off to Thailand for two months. I leave tomorrow. We're over Pete.'

I wait for his reply but as nothing comes I storm into the bedroom to start packing up. I empty the drawers and wardrobe contents onto the bed. I have bin bags in my handbag that I picked up on the way home and a couple of suitcases on top of the wardrobe.

Pete appears in the doorway, staring at me like I'm a mad woman.

'What are you playing at, why are you packing?' he's asks, angry, scowling and actually quite terrifying. This is the biggest reaction I have had out of him in months, 'You're not off to Thailand...'

'See for yourself.' I interrupt him throwing the travel agent's envelope complete with itinerary to the edge of the bed for him to see.

'If you'd even entertained any conversation I've been trying to have over the last eight weeks you would have had more notice.' I purse my lips and stare straight into his eyes.

'Lisa's coming round tonight to pick up my stuff...and me, and here's the next two months rent. Consider it my notice, you can do what you want with the place.' I say, throwing the second envelope filled with cash to the end of the bed.

For the second time in three months, he's dumbfounded. Walking out of the bedroom in a daze he disappears to the living room where I can hear him pacing back and forward unsure what to do with himself. I continue to frantically stuff my clothes, make-up and toiletries into suitcases and bin bags.

I notice a picture on my bedside table, it's the two of us on a beach in Cornwall. I remember it well, we had been together about a year and had gone there for the weekend in July. It was absolutely chucking it down all weekend and we were almost blown off our feet trying to take this selfie on the beach wrapped in gloves and scarves and hooded jumpers. Yet, we were so much in love, laughing through the terrible weather, enjoying wet and windy walks, drinking in country pubs in front of fires to dry off, our whole lives ahead of us. I haven't really had too many pictures like that to update this one with recently. In fact, that's six years old that photo. We quickly passed that honeymoon period and became, well, boring. Never really doing anything new, going anywhere different, not really making an effort. I pick up the picture and stuff it in one of the bags, a reminder of what could have been.

Where is he? Does he not even have the oomph to argue with me, get angry with me, maybe even try and stop me leaving?

He comes back into the bedroom an hour later as I'm balancing on the edge of the bed leaning across to haul the last empty case down from the top of the wardrobe. Grabbing the case down for me, Pete says, 'Can't we just go on as we were?'

'You just don't get this do you? I'm not happy. We're not happy. Surely you can't be happy?'

'I haven't really thought about it.' he says.

'Well I have, and this is not what either of us deserves - a half arsed attempt at a relationship, or marriage. It's run its course Pete and you've made that clear by lying to me with delay tactics about marriage when you're not remotely interested.' I say.

'I guess I've known it too, maybe that's why I wanted to get married, to paper over the cracks with some excitement.' I add, sadly.

A couple of hours and many arguments, discussions, tears (mainly on my part) and door slams (mainly on Pete's part) later, Lisa and Rob arrive to pick me and my sad little bundle of bin bags up. Thankfully, they have a big house so will be lending me their spare room for my belongings, and a stop gap for me until I get myself sorted on my return. Poor sods, what a scene to walk into.

'Hey there.' Lisa says with as sing song a voice as she can muster. Rob, not quite sure what to say having no doubt been forced into coming here, gives a bit of a head nod to both of us.

'All right mate.' Pete manages, shaking Rob's hand. Pete turns to me, sighs and heads out the front door, clearly not wanting to watch this scene unfold any further.

'I'll call you in the next few days.' he says.

'My flight is tomorrow evening.' I reply with my head bowed.

He just shakes his head in disbelief and closes the door.

It was never going to be easy, but the lack of fight really says it all. He didn't even try to keep me here, to make it work. Can you believe he just walked out and left me, not saying anything to make me stay? Charming, shows just how much I meant to him.

I plough on with the removal, but Lisa and Rob do most of the carting of the bags. I'm not in a fit state to be productive and my whole body is shaking in a combination of shock and anger. What did I expect, him to fall into my arms and tell me of course he wants to get married and sorry for being such an asshole over the last months? Maybe. Well, that's not what happened. Good riddance to bad rubbish. Fuck. Him.

CHAPTER 4

'Ladies and Gentlemen, please fasten your seat belts as we prepare for landing. The time in Bangkok is 1.25pm. We hope you've had a nice flight and we look forward to seeing you again soon.'

As I climb out of the train in Central Bangkok at the stop my minimal research at Heathrow told me was the right one for the hotel, I cannot believe how many people there are everywhere. I must have picked a hotel in the Oxford Circus of the city. Navigating my way through the throng of people with my wheely backpack flying around behind me as it bumps along the potted pavement is quite terrifying. I feel part nervous, part excited, very overwhelmed and a deep sense of not belonging. People are banging into me, the street signs are all in Thai (go figure), the cars are honking, and there's no space to catch my breath, find my bearings or work out what the hell is going on. Eventually, I succumb to the twentieth taxi wanting to take me somewhere and jump in, showing him my reservation slip with the address.

'No, no.' he says, shaking his head vigorously at me.

'Sorry? I'm just trying to go here...' I say showing him the address. Jeez, this guy is angry. He keeps flapping his arms and pointing down an alleyway.

'Go.' he says. 'There!' he shouts in exasperation, before speeding off to find his next victim, ehm, I mean lucky customer.

Cautiously, and exceedingly glad it's not yet dark, I wander down the little street he was determined I was to take. I couldn't really portray 'jump me now - I have all my luggage, passport, far too much Thai baht to be carrying at once and I have no bloody idea where I'm going' any clearer if it was written across my t-shirt.

A minute or two later, I'm elated to see the sign for my hotel. I get myself checked in and escape into the cool air-conditioned silence of my room - collapsing, shoes and all on the bed. A mild panic sets in as I realise quite how difficult just getting to the hotel was - nothing is in English, I'm a complete foreigner, an alien in this land. Exhausted and beginning to lose faith in myself as the courageous adventurous traveller I have been painting to everyone over the last few days, I quietly sob into my pillow and start thinking about home, wondering what on earth I've got myself into this time.

Shit. Home. I better text mum and tell her I've arrived safely. I smile to myself, I wonder if there's any age in life you reach when you go away and your mother doesn't say make sure you let me know you get there safely. Never mind the fact that you make it home in London every day successfully without notifying her.

Turning on my phone, I'm curious to see if there is anything from Pete. 5.30pm here, so it's mid-morning back home and he'll be at work my mind calculates, as I wait for the phone to find it's Thai network, signal or whatever it's called when you're abroad.

Ding. Ding. Ding. Three messages. At a guess, Mum, Pete and Gail, or maybe even two from Pete.

Wrong.

EE - Welcome to Thailand

EE - We're going to charge you a fortune for everything you do on your phone out here.

Mum - You there OK? Let me know you're safe. Love you x

My heart sinks a little, I really thought Pete would have contacted me. I haven't heard anything from him since he walked out when I was packing up with Lisa. He said he'd be in touch in a couple of days and it's been, actually not even two days yet. Still, I thought there would have been something, anything. I did expect a little text from him by now, not necessarily a 'have a great trip', but something. Anger, rage, upset, pleading, any of these would make sense as they reflect the feelings racing through my head every minute.

I meticulously type out my text to Mum. She is a stickler for grammar on texts refusing to believe anyone should succumb to shortcuts in language. 'It is just laziness' I can hear her saying. 'No wonder the youth of today don't know their there from their they're'. Feeling the need to converse with an English speaking national, I abandon the text and dial the house phone instead. Not knowing the language somewhere is fun when you have someone to share it with, to muddle through together, but on your own it's bloody horrible.

'Hello.' ah, Dad's voice.

'Hi Dad, it's me.'

'Hi love, how are you? You got there safely then?'

'Yes, I'm here. Just checked in.'

'You OK, you sound a bit odd?'

'Yeah fine, just tired probably.'

'Probably?'

'Well,' my voice catches in my throat, 'oh Dad, what the hell am I doing?'

'Where are you just now, pet?'

'I'm in the hotel, just in my room.'

Dad's silent, and then I can hear him taking a big deep breath.

'I thought this might happen. Now look, you've gone out there to see the world, have an adventure. Sitting in your hotel room is doing nobody any good. So, pull yourself together, go and see the place and if you're not happy in a few days time come home, OK?' he tells me.

'I suppose you're right' I huff, feeling quite pathetic.

'No suppose about it love, what time is it there?'

'Just before six in the evening.'

'OK, so get yourself sorted and then go out. Go and eat some of that spicy food I've heard so much about and start enjoying yourself. Now don't let your mother know I've said this, but I'm very proud of what you are doing, I'd love to have done something like that. It takes guts love, so go on out and start seeing the place. For the both of us. Why not go to a touristy spot where people will probably speak English?'

'OK.' I reply feebly.

'Right, off you go then.' he replies, with a tone that suggests I've done my part now, but I'm not very good at small talk, can I please go?

'Thanks Dad, is Mum there?'

'She's out in the garden, should I go and get her?'

What an odd question I think. He rarely wants to chat on the phone, always keen to pass me on to Mum. Ahh, he's worried she will say just come straight home and resume the life you knew last week. Good point Dad. Dad's do come highly underestimated for their thought process in the family unit, I begin to think.

'No, leave her be, just let her know I got here safely, and maybe best not to tell her....'

Dad cuts me off, 'No problem, now away and galavant, but stay safe. And take lots of pictures, I've always wanted to visit Thailand.'

'Thanks Dad, bye.'

'Take care love.'

Following the gentle but needed kick up the arse I get myself in the shower ready to face this crazy city. I put on my shorts and t-shirt, dig out my converse and I'm set to go. Well, maybe just a bit of TV first. As I flick through the channels I realise I have the English options of BBC News or the Sci-Fi channel, someone's really trying to tell me to stop procrastinating and get out there. I take a few deep breaths, and as I'm wondering what on earth I am doing here I remember, you're here because you are sick of doing nothing back home, because you're now on your own so you better damn well get used to it and learn how to navigate this world solo. I look in the mirror, give myself a quick 'come on this will be exciting' pep talk, a lick of mascara, and I'm off.

As I venture out into the street, guidebook in hand, I take in everything around me. It's like an attack on the senses. The noise is all consuming - whistles, motorbikes, drilling, shouting, someone emptying a hundred glass bottles in a bin, car horns, the sing song voices of the locals, phones ringing, text message dings. I'm surrounded by a hundred noises. And the smells are both good and awful, changing with every step. The street food smells so good, so good you mistakenly take a great big sniff only to catch the whiff of the huge pile of rubbish next to you too or the exhausts, or the drains. It's like being at a strobe light disco, except instead of the lights going on and off, it's the switching of smells from good to bad. The place is hot and sticky and polluted, you can almost feel the heat and dirt clinging to you, grabbing hold of you and saying hey mate, wherever you're going, I'm coming with you. As for the sights, there is just so much going on. There are four lanes of cars and taxis at a standstill, tuk tuks with flashing Christmas tree lights, bikes weaving through the traffic like stunt drivers, stalls running down the side of all the roads selling DVDs, scarves, wooden Buddha heads and designer boxer shorts, street vendors selling all sorts of weird looking food, old men and women shuffling down the street in their slippers, cables and wires in the thousands hanging above the streets and bags of rubbish everywhere.

Without my heavy bag and too hot travel clothes on, I'm less intimidated this time out. God knows why it's easier as I'm seeing much more craziness as I look around this time, but it occurs to me as bizarre as this is, I'm not afraid. Everyone is smiling, going about their day, working, shuffling somewhere or other, and as alien as this is - it's absolutely captivating. I stop for a coffee and get out my trusty guidebook. I planned to read it on the plane, but somehow got frozen on the front page, my mind unable to get past the 'what the hell are you doing' phrase floating around in there.

As I sip my coffee and read my book, something jumps out at me - Khao San Road. Now I've heard of this, I'm pretty sure this is where Leonardo Di Caprio discovers the map to that island in The Beach. Ahh, the beach, now that sounds appealing right now, only a few days until I'll be lying on the golden sands I've seen in so many pictures. I was toying with getting a sandwich to take back to the hotel room when this page in the book caught my eye, and Dad's words come back to me - go somewhere touristy, enjoy yourself.

Before I can change my mind, I pay my bill and hop in a taxi to Khao San Road. An hour and only two miles later, yes, an hour to get two miles, I get out the car at the same starting point good old Leo had for his adventure.

Wow. It's like a New Year street party down here. Neon lights protruding out from buildings all the way down the small street; competing sound systems pumping out dance music, Justin Bieber and Bob Marley along the length of the road; and excited backpackers drifting along in little tribes. I read on the ride over that this is a common starting point for backpackers who use Bangkok as their base, and Khao San Road as their student union. The excitement on these young faces is infectious, and I am entranced by everything around me. I pick up a mojito from a street seller and head down the street. Everything is so cheap and as I twist in and out of the crowds, I peruse the stalls filled with beachwear, wooden carvings, and hippie jewellery.

I've left all my silver jewellery at home to be safe, and looking down at my bare arms decide to get one of those woven thread bracelets everyone seems to be wearing. Smiling away to myself I think this is a symbol that I too am travelling the world, flying by the seat of my pants. I'm not just here on a two week holiday, I'm an actual traveller, a world adventurer. I have a backpack and everything - well OK, it's on wheels and I've not even worked out how to fold away the wheels and strap it to my back, but I am an explorer, a globetrotter, so I must get one of these threaded tokens, the universal passport that says I'm part of this exciting gang.

'All 100 baht.' the street vendor says.

'Oh, thank you, I'm just choosing.' I reply.

'Discount for 2, 150 baht for 2.' she says, obviously keen for the sale.

Decisions, decisions. There are hundreds of these bracelets, brightly coloured threads, twisted leather ones, some with writing…'Khao San Road' - too tacky, 'Love' - I don't think so, 'Dickhead' - well that could be a present for someone…then I spot one that says 'Peace'. Yes, that's the one, a little peace in my head would be quite satisfactory for this trip, so I pick this up along with a dark leather pleated one. 150 baht later, I scrunch them over my hand and watch them jingle perfectly on my wrist.

As I'm leaving the stall, drink in my hand and my travelling symbols around my wrist, a tall dreadlocked man taps me on the shoulder.

'You could have got them both for half the price.' he says.

'Sorry?' I reply, unsure fully if he is talking to me, maybe he bumped me by mistake but he certainly seems to be looking at me and speaking in my direction.

'The stalls' he adds, pointing back at the bracelet stand, 'you're meant to barter with them over the price.'

'Oh, I didn't realise, em...thanks.' I smile back.

I'm not quite sure how to take this intrusion on my wandering, people don't just start speaking to you on the street in London. In fact, it's known that if someone you don't know talks to you they must be crackers (charity muggers and tourists looking for directions the only exceptions).

'No worries. I'm Theo by the way.' he charges his

beer to my mojito.

'Alice.' I smile back, raising my plastic cup and taking a sip of my cocktail.

Theo and I continue meandering down the street together, which isn't too forced or difficult as it's so busy it's like you're walking in a queue anyway, at least it is for now before the orderly walking turns into what I can imagine to be drunken stumbling chaos later.

Theo is from the Home Counties in England. He is tall with brown hair in dreads to his shoulders. He has big MC Hammer style pants on covered in a blue and white elephant pattern, a vest top advertising some kind of Asian beer and of course many, many bracelets. As we wander Theo tells me that he is part way through his round the world trip. So far, he has been to India, Myanmar, Cambodia, Vietnam and he has just come here now from Laos, where the highlight of his trip was doing an 'awesome' pub crawl on the river, in which you travel from bar to bar on a rubber ring catching ropes to pull you into the river banks as you get to the next bar along. I didn't realise anyone who wasn't American used the word awesome, but I have to admit that pub crawl does sound pretty 'awesome'.

'Fancy a beer?' Theo suggests, pointing towards a shack on the side of the road with some upturned crates as stools, Jamaican flags attached to corrugated iron as a backdrop and a bamboo shelf as the makeshift bar.

'Sure.' I reply, thinking how nice it is to have someone to talk to, someone to enjoy this with, even if it is just for an hour over a beer. We take a seat on a couple of crates and Theo orders us some beers.

He is a peculiar sort of traveller I realise. Everything about him to look at screams hippie, spiritual wandering soul, which completely clashes with his accent which can only have been honed in an Eton type school. No guy I know says 'Fancy a beer'. He talks about his travels and the 'awesome' places he has visited, things he has seen since being away. Theo graduated from Cambridge last year, with a degree in English and he's now taking a year out to travel the world. He did this before Uni too, so this is his second gap year. I get the impression that he is a bit of a know it all when it comes to the do's and don'ts of travelling the world in what he considers the right way. But know it all or not, I'm certainly enjoying sitting on a crate with him in the middle of Thailand drinking a beer and chatting away.

'How about you, two months out here you said? What's the plan? What brought you here?' Theo asks.

I'd almost forgotten that I had a story. It's been nice to just listen to someone else talking, be taken in with where I am and not think about the shit storm I've just created and run away from. I think for a minute.

Well, I proposed to my boyfriend, was engaged for three months then realised he didn't want to get married and in fact he's a bit of a dickhead, so in the space of a few days I broke it off, moved out, and now I'm here with no real plan, a broken heart and I'm trying not to think about any of it, or the fact that I have bugger all to go back to when I return, except a guest bedroom in my friend's house.

Realising that no one out here knows me, knows my story, and it's not exactly the best way to strike up a nice evening beer session by dumping my problems on this poor unsuspecting young guy, I opt for a different response.

'I work in education so I can take the summer off and have always wanted to visit Asia, to explore Thailand.' I reply.

It's not a lie, just a very abbreviated version of the truth.

'Awesome, what are your plans while you're here?' he asks.

No idea, drink mojitos, feel sorry for myself, hopefully fall in love with a tall dark and handsome stranger who does want to be with me. If he could also happen to be from London and want me to move in straight away that would be even better thanks.

'Few days here, then I'm booked to go to Koh Samui, and I'll take it from there.' I say, trying to sound laid back, casual, like this solo travelling thing comes so naturally to me. I mean look, I even have the bracelets to prove it.

'What about you Theo, what's next on your itinerary?' (Itinerary. Jesus Christ, what am I saying, I'm showing my age here, not cool. What happened to this relaxed hippy chick thing you got going on).

With a slight chuckle, but at least the grace not to mention my ridiculous phrasing, he tells me he is heading up north for a couple of days and then on to the islands. Koh Samui first, then Koh Phangan for the Full Moon Party and finishing off at Koh Tao for some diving. It's a pretty common trail so he says, like a rite of passage for round the world trippers. Party on these islands before feeling like a broken being and moving on to the mainland or new countries and actually seeing things other than the bottom of a bucket or beer bottle.

As the bar fills up Theo starts chatting with the guys next to us. He oozes the confidence of a lion as he waxed lyrical about the places he had travelled and made recommendations on the best places to visit. The little group consisted of Kristian, Gavin, Jamie, Khloe and Ashley and we share our stories of where we've been, where we're going and what we're all about. This, I later discover is par for the course for backpackers.

Gavin was a soldier who spent some time in Iraq. He has now left the army and is making his way round the world looking for somewhere he likes to move to, he never quite settled after returning from the Middle East. He is keen to explore the world and is delightfully entertaining with his distinctive geordie lilt. He is a great storyteller and could easily command an audience, which I think he does on a nightly basis - an audience of one that is (I'm glad I'm not sharing a dorm with him).

Kristian is from South Africa and is an amateur boxer. He has an injury so is making the most of having six months off from training and healthy living...not that the time off seems to have had an effect on his body ...phwoar, I can't take my eyes off his six pack bursting through his tight black v-neck t-shirt, which I think is possibly the point of the attire. He is a gregarious chap, who although starting his travels alone, has been pretty quick to pick up companions along the way.

Jamie looks every bit what I would imagine for a Hawaiian chick, blonde surfer girl hair, someone who was born to wear beachwear, a great figure and just really comfortable in her skin. She's twenty-five, and an artist. Her last art commission gave her the money for four months abroad - that being a ginormous sculpted penis she created for HUMPfest! A porn film festival in Seattle - how fun is that. She mixes up her travels with some volunteering and has just come from Cambodia where she was working on a community project to build a library in a small village.

Jamie met Gavin and Kristian in a hostel in Cambodia and as they were all heading on to Bangkok they joined forces to travel together. Jamie seems to be the rock between these two alpha males and as she is one year their senior they seem to accept it when she is sticking the boot in to put a temporary halt to their never ending game of one-upmanship.

Khloe and Ashley are from Essex. They just met the others in the hostel this evening; they are already tanned in a glowing orangey kind of way; are dressed like they are going to a nightclub and their desert island luxury item would definitely be hair straighteners that manage that curly wurly 'I've just come off the beach but not really as this actually took me three hours look'. They're very sweet, but I can't help feeling like they could be my students, they are quite a bit younger than the others and exactly like the kids in my college. Good fun yes, but travellers they are not.

Jamie tells me Kristian saw the girls checking into the hostel and waited in the common room area for their re-arrival. Kristian thought it would be 30 minutes later, Jamie knew better so went out and got them a six pack of beer, which was about spot on; the girls, all twirly haired, appeared around 90 minutes later....and now here we all are.

'Anyone know where I can get one of those cheap Fendi handbags?' Ashley asks.

'You mean the fakes? Patpong, but you have to nod at the right person to get a good one.' Theo continues building on his know it all persona.

'Are they fake? I thought they were just cheap here.' she replies as everyone cracks up.

Not even here a day and I'm part of a gang, heading off on a fake Fendi handbag mission. Theo says we need to head to the night market at Patpong, which is met by a few 'whey hey' cheers from the blokes. I quickly realise that this is the infamous street, where ladies blast ping pong balls from their bits.

A few shots and a very hairy tuk-tuk ride later and we are...well, nowhere near what looks like either ping pong street or handbag city. However, it is where this man seems to want to drop us off, insisting this is where we asked to go. Jamie sees this cute old man sitting on the corner (yep, just in his deckchair on the side of a busy road) and asks him for directions. Five minutes later Tong, our temporary tour guide, is shuffling along in his slippers with us trailing behind him leading the way to the handbags.

Jamie and I are chatting to Tong, he asks if we've been to the Grand Palace yet. It is a very special place to the Thai people he tells us, the King has been very good to us he says, a beautiful man and we need to worship him. Tong is 87 (he actually looks about 107) and he has a laundry service which his daughter now runs. He loves the buzz of Bangkok, hence sitting on the street corner, outside his launderette in his deckchair and slippers watching the world go by.

I can tell we are getting closer now as I can hear the embarrassing noise that can only be associated with a group of British guys with too much beer in them seeing some tits.

'I can see the street now Tong, thank you so much for your help.' Jamie bows to thank him.

'No, no, I take you. They like to, you know, change the price depending on who it is.' Tong says. How nice, he's going to make sure we don't pay over the odds for our handbags.

We turn into the pedestrian street where there are rows and rows of handbags, watches and sunglasses down the middle with a little walkway on either side, and as you look up you can see nothing but neon signs of naked girls and their bits all the way along the road, all the while running the gauntlet of people placing laminated menus under my nose with em, 'girlie shows' in black and white, on a friggin' menu.

Tong leads us up some stairs and has a long chat with a rather, short stumpy Thai lady who seems to be the big mamma of the place. Then leading us through the curtains, he turns to Jamie and says I've told her you friend of me, no more than 1000 baht each. Jamie gives Tong 50 baht, says thanks and then we're in.

What on earth? What happened to shopping for a fake Fendi? Now I know that there are such things going on in Bangkok, I do live on this planet, but at what point was I suddenly going to one? I'm not sure if it's the horror at where I may be about to end up, but for the first time in months I am laughing hysterically, bent double and shaking.

'What the hell Jamie? I thought we were going for handbags?' I ask with shock written all over my face.

She laughs in reply 'I don't know what to say - I told him to take us to the handbags, I didn't ask him to take us here, I swear!'

Somehow, I'm sitting in a row along the back wall of the club, I am frozen in shock at where I am and what I am seeing. It doesn't take too long to get the gist of how this works and us girls, who thought that we were here to handbag shop, are desperate to get back out amongst the Chanel and Gucci, or is that Chunnel and Gicci. As I get up to leave, Kristian and I are thrust ping pong bats in our hands and there are balls flying through the air at me. I can tell you, I batted them away like you would a grenade, a two handed bloody hard backhand in tennis, with everyone cheering us on. This has to be the most surreal thing that has ever happened to me. Ever.

Get me out of here.

Parting with a bit more cash for my unwanted game of ping pong, I politely decline the souvenir ball on offer. We are back out on the street, adrenaline pumping, hoarse from nervous laughter, propping each other up like we've known each other for ever. A shared bizarre experience amongst us shaping my new 'Bangkok gang'. The girls purchase their fake Fendi bags, Jamie gets herself a pair of ray-bans, I take Kristian to the shop to get some anti-bacterial hand gel to douse ourselves in, and we reconvene for a beer or four in a bar chosen by me that doesn't have any extra services on offer. I drift further into a drunken haze as we make our plans for tomorrow, and realising I haven't slept for a very long time and with jet lag setting in, I make my way back to my hotel. Just think, I almost bought a coffee shop sandwich and stayed in tonight.

***

As I wake I stumble around the room looking for the mini-bar. Water, I need water. Oh my god, what a night. Each funny moment popping into my head like a slide show. Well Dad, I certainly did something touristy last night, although I'm not sure it's what you had in mind. I pop a few paracetamols to stave off the dull beer head that's on its way and dig out my phone to see the time. Bloody hell, forty-seven notifications on Facebook scream out from my phone, what the hell has happened.

I open Facebook and see I've been tagged in a photo - me, Kristian, Theo and Jamie - all swaying and laughing under the big lady bits sign from the bar. My first thought - thank god I'm not one of those people who are friends with their parents on Facebook. Swiftly followed by the fact that I am friends with Pete - oh shit, what the hell is he going to say. Nothing it turns out. I have forty-six messages, likes and smiley faces gracing this picture which is slotted on the news feed between a picture of someone's dinner and a video of some child falling over a bit of Lego. The forty seventh is a message from Jamie, she says they are meeting by the river at midday to take the boat to the Grand Palace, and sends me a map to the pier.

Navigating my way through the chaos once again, I catch sight of Theo's dreadlocks and multi-coloured hair band providing a beacon to their location. Theo is negotiating a price with the boat guys and Gavin is nuzzling on Ashley's neck (I guess they hooked up last night then) as Jamie sees me and waves me over. Behind her I see a sign on the wall saying 'Beware snatch thief' -

and point at my amusing find for the others to see.

'Wey aye man, I feel a flashback to last night.' says Gavin.

'Oi, shut it you pig.' Jamie says and takes a picture of the funny sign to add to her "What the Fuck?" sign collection.

Over the next few days, I take a boat ride in an exceptionally low long tail boat down a river that made the Thames look clean. I see a bloated pig floating upside down on the water which Neo our driver says was, 'running away from chef' pointing to the shack on the river bank. I visit the Grand Palace which is very gold and bling and is dominated by a gigantic reclining buddha; take a tour to the floating market to taste a hundred different fruits I never knew existed and venture into the second biggest shopping centre in the world.

Most of this I would never have done if I hadn't had the good fortune of Theo saying 'Hi' on that first night. I think how lucky I am to meet these people. Bangkok is an amazing big, busy city, but a terrifyingly lonely one at the same time if you don't have anyone to share it with.

I have a gang. I can't even tell you the last time I met a new friend. I wonder if that's normal when you get older or another sign of mine and boring Pete's life?

Things seem so different when you go away to places where backpackers are, meeting people in this atmosphere seems exciting, easy even. Jamie, Kristian and Gavin have only known each other three weeks, yet they have all these little 'in' jokes, they seem to really know each other, and take the piss in ways I do with my best friends of fifteen years. There's something quite special about the friendships you see amongst people who travel together I think, I don't quite know how it happens, but you'd think these three went to school or college together seeing the closeness between them.

Having someone to share these amazing places, experiences and stories really is quite special. So with a heavy heart, I say goodbye on my last night in Bangkok to my little crew as I'm flying to the island of Koh Samui tomorrow.

Jamie, Gavin and Kristian are off up North to Chiang Mai on their next adventure with Theo joining the group. We all agree we will catch up in a couple of weeks for the Full Moon Party if not before, and with that, I stroll back to my hotel, grateful for the last few days. The laughter, the company and for making me forget about the reality of back home, making me realise that I can cope on my own.

I am ready to be heading away from the bustle of Bangkok to the islands, to the beach. In the taxi towards Bangkok airport I see a sign outside a cafe offering a special on 'Hand Burgers and See Foot', laughing to myself I grab my camera and snap, I must send that on to Jamie for her collection.

CHAPTER 5

As I climb off the plane onto the melting tarmac, I feel like I'm in a different country from this morning.

A little train, open at the sides and covered in pictures of suns and waves, like something you'd find at Disney World, takes us to the terminal. I use the word terminal loosely - it's all open, no windows, no doors, just a wooden roof around various big circular huts. It's the most amazing airport I've ever seen, and as I look around at everyone while I wait for my luggage, I realise I am not alone in these thoughts. This place just seems to put a smile on everyone's face. Welcome to island life.

I am met with the warmest greeting as I reach the resort. I've booked a hut on the beach for two weeks to start off with, and as Nok shows me to my hut she points out the snack bar, the beach and the towel stand. We wander down a sandy track till we reach a little spot only a stone's throw from the beach. She kicks off her flip flops and steps inside to show me how the air con works, where the safe is hiding and tells me to come and see her anytime if I need anything, want to book any tours or hire a scooter.

Desperate to get my feet in the sea, I close my door leaving the unpacking for later and wander down to the beach. The sea is the most glorious turquoise colour and the sand so soft underfoot, it's exactly how I had pictured it. I paddle my toes and squat down on the sand, gazing out at the horizon. My mind drifts back to home, and the disaster I just walked away from. The last few days have been busy, and I haven't had too much time to think about anything, but now it all comes back to me with a bang, sitting here on this beach, on my own. I feel like someone is slowly piling bricks onto me one at a time, each one dragging me further into the sand.

With the weight of the world on my shoulders, I cry. Not those great big shoulder shaking can't catch your breath sobs. It's gentler than that, a release of tension, a realisation that I haven't really thought about Pete much at all these last days, haven't actually missed him.

There was a time years ago when I would miss him if I was just going out for the evening with the girls, making excuses that I had to get up for work early so I could rush home and be with him. I would get home and we would snuggle on the sofa and watch a couple of hours of TV together, or a film, it didn't really matter what we were doing; if we were together, we were happily entertained.

Now though, there's just nothing. I think of all I've done over the last few days. Pete would never have gone to the Grand Palace or the floating market, fair enough, he may have visited the ping pong street I mistakenly ended up on but what guy wouldn't. As long as it involved work, beer, computers or sleeping he'd be onboard. What the hell I was thinking wanting to marry that kind of guy, I've no idea.

Then it hits me, I really do need to build a new life when I get back home, to find somewhere to live, but what can I afford on my own, good god I can't go back into a house share. What will I do with my evenings? I'm not getting any younger - will I ever meet anyone else, get married? Have babies? Give Mum grandchildren? What if Mum was right and I've just thrown away my last chance...

I don't think I realised until this moment that I was actually moving on from Pete, not really, and I'm ashamed to say I'm feeling terrified of being on my own, not terrified of being without Pete, but just being alone. And with that, the tears turn into huge shoulder shaking sobs. How can I have wasted so much time, drifted this far.

I thought you were meant to be wise in your thirties, have all the answers. The only answer I seem to have found is that I know bugger all about anything, least of all myself, and maybe Mum's desire for me to have a nice secure man in my life was perhaps a little more imprinted on me than I thought. No wonder she was panicking, now I know why and I am too.

***

Feeling the need to get intoxicated and forget everything about my new discovery, I drag myself back to my hut and do what every woman does when she needs a pick me up. I dig out my most flattering dress, straighten my hair and go out shopping (yes, I know I mocked the Essex girls for their straighteners and brought a set too, but this is the first time I've used mine and this is an emergency).

It's a pretty incredible place to shop and with everything so cheap I can really indulge. Having tried on a few cute dresses I realise that 1) I am not 19 and look ridiculous in 'cute dresses' - when did everything get so short and 2) people in Thailand are small and buying things in a size L (if I'm lucky) doesn't quite have the feel good factor I'm after. I take a break from shopping to have a glass of wine, an ice cold red wine to be exact which is surprisingly quite nice in this heat. As I watch groups of people wander up and down the rickety street and pavements, I decide it's time for a fashion reinvention. Looking at all the travellers and holidaymakers walking around, I try to find something that would suit me. There's lots of tiny daisy duke denim shorts - nope, too fat for that shit; mini dresses - too old for that shit. Jesus, why don't we get a card through the post from the fashion police to say, 'Eh, just a note to say it's time you move up an age category in your attire in case you didn't realise; I'm not quite saying mutton and lamb just yet, but you know, have a think about it, Kind Regards The Fashion Police.'

So, here in the middle of Thailand, in the middle of a fashion crisis, I order another glass of wine, dig out my phone and look through all my photos, slating everything I'm wearing in every one of them.

The photos on my phone span around a three-year period. There's pictures of the weddings that we have attended, all fresh faced and floaty knee length dresses; pictures of weekends up North in hiking boots in the hills; and then the main ones that I am looking for, there are pictures of picnics and gatherings in Hyde Park during the beautiful days of summer in the city. I cast my eye across the different styles of the girls in the pictures which includes cut off denim shorts and halter neck tops, long t-shirt dresses and oh my god, someone here is wearing a crop top, at least it's not me. Then there's someone in a floaty skirt and a vest top, looking fairly relaxed, pretty smart casual, and no bulging bumps sticking out of inappropriate places. There's an outfit of knee length dark denim shorts with a white linen shirt.

These individuals obviously got the letter from the Fashion Police. Looking through the pictures they are the ones who look youthful and fresh, the rest of us in our young high street retailers clothes look just like that - thirty somethings in twenty somethings clothes. Oh dear, it is most certainly time for a change.

With this realisation and the renewed shopping confidence only possible from too many glasses of wine, I hit the road again. I try on a long floaty dress, one size fits all it says, now that's more like it - no big L screaming out at me from the label. And then the floodgates open - I have become a boho fashion victim who now owns three pairs of fisherman pants (not the one's with elephants on them, classy ones), 2 floor length skirts, 2 slouchy tops, 2 fringed tops, beaded jewellery, head scarves, beaded flip flops, sandals and even a tie dye vest top. All this for £75, and I just know this £75 will change my life - a new travelling spiritual me is born - Ta da.

It's been so long since I have treated myself to any new clothes that I am overcome with joy. Everything has been save, save, save and I'm like a kid in a candy store now. So many choices of what to wear, and I want to wear them all. Now. Three years of budgeting has taken its toll. A bit like the minute you go on a diet, you can think of nothing else but binging on crisps and chocolate. Well, I think I have just carried out the shopping equivalent of yoyo dieting.

I teeter back to my hut laden with bags, narrowly escaping a nose dive off the payment numerous times. Note to self, high heels and island life in Thailand are not a match made in heaven, especially after a couple of glasses of wine. The pavements are something you'd expect to have seen in 1950s Spain, all pot holes, wobbly drains and missing steps.

Throwing the bags on my bed with smug satisfaction, a transformed woman with a transformed wardrobe, I dig out the long floaty dress and swiftly stuff the heels back in the suitcase, never to see the light of day again until I reach Heathrow. As I'm zipping up the suitcase, I see a book Gail gave me poking out. 'Just in case you need it' she said, giving me her well-thumbed book for my trip, 'it's done me the world of good'.
Digging it out, I see there's a post-it note on the front:

I can see you rolling your eyes now, but it may just keep you company on the beach, G x

In keeping with my new spiritual being, I flop on the bed and read the back of the book. It says it's ideal for anyone struggling in a dead-end job or relationship.
I chuckle to myself, seven years too late, where was this book over the years. Probably being offered at every chance, but Lisa and I were too busy rolling our eyes to take any notice, sorry Gail.

Maybe I'll just pop this in my bag to take out

tonight, I'm not actually going to read it but I don't want to look like a sad sack sitting on my own. Actually, maybe this new boho chic chick that I am will read books like this, perhaps I'll become full of wisdom. I can see myself having profound thoughts gazing out to the ocean, people coming to me for wise words, a fountain of knowledge.

    Slipping my toes into my new beaded beauties I realise that my hands and feet could do with being part of this transformation too, so I wander to one of the beachfront massage and beauty spots and indulge in a manicure and pedicure to complete the look. As the ruby red polish is beautifying my hands and feet I see that the sun is setting across the horizon. The sky is a hundred shades of pale blue and light greys caressed with swirls of pink cotton candy, some more intense candy floss colours than others. It is magical to watch, and certainly there is no better place to complete the transformation. The external transformation that is, I think there's still a bit of work to do on the rest yet.

CHAPTER 6

I make my way along the beach in search of a cocktail, some food and a little sampling of Samui's nightlife to complete my first day in paradise. It's so much prettier along the beach side, you can't see the neon signs, or hear the stream of trucks advertising boxing, go-karting, and kinky massages. I stumble upon a little shack called Coconut Joe's that has the most amazing spicy smells drifting out and realising that I have opted for wine over food so far today, I kick my shoes off on the beach and head in.

'Can I have a mojito please, and what is that amazing smell?' I ask.

'It's Coconut Joe's Pad Thai.' the waitress says, pointing towards a massive wok at the end of the bar, 'It's all we do, but very popular, you want some?'

'Yes please, that would be great. Thanks.' I reply.

It's pretty empty in here, but there are a couple of people sitting enjoying a cocktail on a table near the water's edge, German I think, still in beachwear enjoying the end of a day on the beach, so his bright pink shoulders would suggest. There's a few young guys sitting at the bar having a beer and ordering Pad Thai to take away, and an older guy sitting at a table next to the bar with a glass of whisky, or rum or something dark like that. He's chatting with the guys who seem to know him. Coconut Joe I presume? Coconut Joe looks to be in his early 70s, a man who has lived life. He's in pretty good shape, strong slim legs in tight denim knee length shorts, and a vest top that I would suggest was purchased a while ago, perhaps before he stopped working out so much and let nature, and rum, take its course on the old midriff.

The waitress boxes up two Pad Thai's for the guys and brings over a plate for me.

'Thanks Kek, see ya Joe.' one of the guys says as they wander off.

Least I now know it is Joe. Joe of the truly amazing Pad Thai, I devour the dish in a matter of minutes, the noodles are perfect, the peanuts the freshest I've ever tasted and just the right kick to it. This is so far away from Thai food back home I feel like I'm in food heaven, I'm spooning up every last bit of noodle, beansprout and licking my lips to savour the spices and I can see Joe smiling over at me.

'Hungry?' he says with a smile.

'It was delicious. Absolutely delicious.' I reply as Kek clears my plate.

'Holiday?' Joe asks.

'Yes holiday, well a long holiday - two months.'

'Wow, lucky you.' he smiles as he turns to see another crowd of young guys come in.

'Hey Joe.' they collectively say and begin to chat away about their days. They are bar promotion workers and this is obviously their local bar before they head to work on the neon light party street.

Feeling slightly awkward sitting there on my own with nothing to do now I've finished eating, I dig out Gail's book.

'Things don't always go as planned.' it begins. No shit Sherlock.

Distracted by the amusing chat between Joe and the boys, I am re-reading the first page over and over until I eventually give up, just holding the book up in place whilst I earwig on their chat. The guys are talking about the girls they met last night, not shying away from any details in front of dear old Joe who has the heartiest of laughs. One guy in particular is being wound up by the others for not 'getting any'. From what I can pick up he's the only one who has come out for the summer with a girlfriend at home, or at least the only one with a girlfriend who he is keeping his pants on for. I can see Joe chuckling away at the banter, but giving this particular guy a smile of admiration, a little wink, as if to say 'I'm laughing along here cause the chat is funny, but good on you mate, keep your pants up for her'. I get the feeling that Joe is a bit like a father, grandfather, brother figure to them, someone they chat to regularly.

Getting up to go to the loo, I struggle with a head rush and wobbly knees and realise just how many drinks I've had today; most of them of the alcoholic variety, so decide it's time to head for home.

***

I wake up slightly fuzzy, and all I can hear is rustling. Panicking, I imagine there are beasties everywhere, crawling all over me, until I pry my sticky eyelids open and realise it is all the plastic bags on the bed containing my new boho wardrobe. Thank god for that. I rejoice again when I see the new wardrobe in all its glory. Although what I was thinking about with that tie-dye effort I'll never know.

With a desperate need for water, I throw on my bikini and sarong and head out. Ooft, the heat. Drinking when you have to wake up to this sticky weather is not good. My skin is clammy, my thighs are rubbing together with sweat and my head is pounding. I think I'll lay off the booze today.

Suitably hydrated, I lay my sarong down on the beach and head towards that turquoise water. The sand is scorching so I pick up the pace, what a relief as the soles of my feet hit the water. It's like a warm bath but at least I'm no longer being scalded. Finally in, and floating merrily, it occurs I have a whole seven weeks of this beach. Sheer bliss.

My hangover is starting to subside with every wave that laps over me. The beach is fairly busy; families building sand castles, babies being bobbed up and down in their father's arms at the water's edge, older couples reading their books on loungers. It's the first day I have woken up with no plans. Between travelling days and the plans made with Jamie and the gang, I haven't really had to think too much about organising myself. Today's plan will be making plans. I head to the reception and pick up all the leaflets I can find, grab my notepad from the hut and resume my spot on the beach to get started on my list, god I love a list.

With all the flyers and leaflets spread out in front of me I start to build the list:
- Stand Up Paddle Boarding
- Jungle tour
- Elephant trekking
- Waterfalls
- Thai cooking class
- Quad biking
- Boat trips
- Snorkelling
- Diving
- Thai Massage

I can't help feeling a sense of loneliness at doing all these things alone. I know how ungrateful I sound, two months in Thailand and all I can a think is 'poor me, I have to do it alone'. I wonder what Pete is up to? Nothing probably, boring old Pete is up to exactly the same things he does day in and day out, so it's time to pull yourself together or you'll be just as boring I think to myself. Besides, the answer is work. It's still a weekday so he will be going to work like the majority of the people back home.

Looking around all I see are couples and families. I'm sure there are other solitude people here, but somehow they escape my gaze. Even after this trip I'll have no one to plan holidays with, the days of girly holidays long gone. So I better learn how to get used to this and enjoy it. How do people meet boyfriends nowadays anyway, I've been out of this game a long time. Online, yes I'm pretty sure people now meet online. Oh bloody hell, I've heard nightmares about online dating, and people sending you willy pictures, and all this writing a profile to sell yourself. Yuck, I shudder at the thought, what would I write?

Boho chic adventurous girl, enjoys travelling, scuba diving, elephant trekking and cooks a mean Pad Thai...

Better get on and actually do these things then. List complete, I head to Coconut Joe's for some lunch and a reprieve from the baking heat. Sitting in his same seat, Joe greets me with a smile that shines through his eyes.

'Hiya honey.' he says.

'Hi Joe.' I reply, shaking the sand from my toes as I enter.

After an afternoon of chatting, Joe it turns out has quite the story to tell. He is from a small village in Northern Thailand. He moved to Bangkok in his early 20s and worked as a waiter in a hotel. He took every chance possible to learn English - talking with customers, reading all the books he could get his hands on, picking up newspapers left by the guests. He worked his way up to Hotel Manager of a pretty swanky hotel on Bangkok's riverside and was fairly chuffed with his achievements.

In the early 90s the opportunity of a lifetime came up. Joe was walking around the breakfast area of the hotel checking that the guests were happy, when he approached a table of men discussing the location for a scene in the film they were making in Thailand. The agreed location had just fallen through and with only a week until filming they were in panic mode.

'How's everyone today? Anything I can do for you?' he asked, as he always did.

Well, he certainly did something for them. Joe suggested they could perhaps use his home village, he knew the village "Head Man" well, and also happened to know that the village temple was in desperate need of restoration, so a generous donation to assist with that could lead to a deal being done quickly to fit their filming needs.

The man, a huge film director in Hollywood, negotiated with the hotel owners a week off for Joe to accompany them and help get everything sorted, and so began his next career as a film consultant. Used to solving problems as the hotel manager of a five star hotel with a very demanding clientele, Joe was no stranger to making the impossible happen. Throughout that week he was more than the location finder, he became an indispensable member of the team - correcting unrealistic Thailand scenes, and finding everything from a chef for the crew to seven fire jugglers. The director asked him to stay on for the whole movie shoot, offering him more than his annual salary for the eight week period. It was a no brainier Joe said, he was in his late 40s, had no family and had a great Assistant Manager who he thought could step up if the hotel agreed. Joe was actually kept on for the next six months for post-production, living and workin in Los Angeles as a continuation and accuracy consultant and earning him another three years Thai equivalent salary.

Joe travelled around Asia as a film consultant throughout the Nineties and the Noughties spending his time off in Koh Samui. He still does some consulting, but they mainly come to him now, being a bit too old to be trailing around on location for days on end.

Joe prefers the simple life and never quite felt at home on the other side of the table in fancy hotels and restaurants and Coconut Joe's was born eight years ago.

What an amazing life.

'So that's my story.' says Joe, 'Now, your turn.'

I tell Joe everything; my relationship with Pete, the proposal, the break-up, the decision to come here, the fact that I'm terrified that I don't know what happens next in my life.

He listens attentively, nods along, not asking any

questions, just digesting it all. It's remarkably easy to talk to him, and feels cathartic to say it all out loud.

After a not uncomfortable silence, Joe replies, 'I never met the right person to settle down with. Maybe I could have made it work along the way, but I just think that marriage is so damn hard that if you're having doubts before you even get hitched you're never going to make it. And it sounds like you both were. I think you've made the right decision honey. It's difficult now but just look out for the signs, they'll make you smile.'

I can see Joe's gaze seems slightly distant and I get the feeling he might be thinking about the one who could have been his wife.

Snapping back into the present, Joe asks, 'Now, want to keep an old man happy and play me at chess?'

'Sure thing, but you'll need to teach me.' I smile back.

We whiled away the rest of the afternoon casually drinking a few beers while Joe taught me the difference between a pawn and a rook, how to get out of check and something called a lektine's gun whatever that is (I think he may have overestimated my ability to digest all this). We stop occasionally and Joe has a chat with the various locals who dropped in to see him, he seems to be quite the social butterfly on the island.

One of the local's mentions a beach party taking place tomorrow night and Joe encourages me to go.

'Are you going?' I ask him.

'Nooo.' he laughs, 'My beach party days are behind me, but you should go. What you doing tomorrow otherwise?'

'I'm doing that Stand-Up Paddle Boarding tomorrow.' I tell him.

'Well there you go, that's during the day and then you'll be ready to party in the evening.' he says with a twinkle in his eye.

CHAPTER 7

The beach is scattered with little bamboo shacks, jet skis lined up on the water's edge with paddle boards piled up behind them.

I've read that paddle boarding is the new fitness fad in the States. The sport had more first timers than any other in 2013. I've seen the Real Housewives of Beverly Hills cruising around on them with ease. It's meant to be a complete core and arms workout, but it looks pretty easy to me, and it's certainly going to help give me a fab all over tan.

I select my board from the collection, strap the velcro around my ankle and wade my way out until I'm deep enough to climb on.

Hmm, it's not quite as easy as I first thought. I

spend around half an hour climbing on, tentatively trying to stand up and falling off over and over, sometimes bopping my head with the paddle as I tumble into the water. Undeterred, as I seem to be getting closer each time I keep trying and eventually I wobble my way up to success. Finally standing tall I am met with a series of whoops and cheers. Unknowingly, I have provided the last half an hour's entertainment to my audience who were relaxing on sun loungers behind me. With a polite smile I take a cheeky bow and head out to deeper waters.

The sun is beating down and I feel a wave of euphoria as I pass the paddle from side to side and glide my way further out of the bay. My body must be swimming with endorphins from the exercise and I just want to keep going and going. Until that is, I sneak a peek behind me and realise just how far I've drifted out, I'm almost outside the bay, seeing the palm trees and sandy beach coming to an end as I look both left and right.

I paddle continuously on my right hand side in an effort to turn the board around and realise that I should have perhaps worked out how to turn a bit earlier than this. It's not quite as simple as those Beverly Hills chicks made it look.

With each attempt to turn I seem to be getting nowhere closer to facing the other direction. Exhaustion and sheer terror consume me. Perhaps I could just jump off, swim my way in? But no one else is out this far, maybe it's too far to swim? Maybe there's bloody sharks out here. Now I wouldn't mind a bit of weight loss, but not in the form of a missing leg. Fuck. What the hell am I going to do. I'm going to die alone out here and no one will ever know. No one will even look for me until I don't arrive home in two months time.

I keep pulling and grinding the paddle through the water to no avail. My breath is getting shorter and faster, my energy levels depleting and I'm dizzy with the heat. Hopefully my audience is still watching me and will alert someone that I'm heading towards my death.

I didn't think it could get any worse and then I see a speedboat shooting towards me. I summon the energy to wave my paddle above me, like a gladiator in a jousting match. Please for the love of god, don't run me over.

The boat continues towards me, but to my relief it is slowing down as it gets to me. Although not before the wake shakes my wobbly legs and catapults me off the board. I disappear beneath the waves, water up my nose and the board above my head stopping my resurface. I'm fighting under the water when I feel two arms under my armpits hauling me up out of the water and over the edge of the boat.

'You alright there me love?' someone says.

Coughing and spluttering I sense someone leaning

over me, sitting me up so I can cough out the remaining water swishing around my throat.

'Eh, yep. Yep I'm OK. Err, thanks.' I reply, saliva dribbling down my chin.

As I look up I see a vision of Patrick Swayze from Point Break standing over me (without the 90s hair.). A beautiful face it is, his eyes are piercing blue and glistening with the reflection of the sun and the water, his hair is all sun kissed blonde in a messy style and his tanned toned limbs popping out of his shorts and t-shirt don't leave me in any doubt of the quality of the body underneath, a slim build with the perfect amount of muscle.

Am I dead? Am I in heaven? Maybe this is a mirage and I'm actually drowning?

Then behind him I see six other faces staring at me, jaws dropped and eyes on stilts. OK, it's not that shocking is it? I just drifted out in the water a bit far…

'Hey,' Patrick Swayze says, 'You might want to…' he nods towards me, pointing at my chest.

Still coming to, I look down and realise that the two triangles covering what dignity and modesty I had left have found themselves sitting in my cleavage, my breasts hanging towards each armpit in all their glory.

'Oh fuck. Shit. Sorry.' I jerk my hands up to my chest and awkwardly return the bastards to their triangles.

With a cheeky smirk on his face, he rescues the paddle from the water and slowly takes the boat, the shocked tourists, me and my bloody paddle board back to the beach.

I sit on the floor of the boat with my head in my hands, humiliation washing over me as the boat grazes into the sand at the shore. I let the tourists disembark first, they are an older crowd who seem absolutely shell shocked by the whole experience.

I gather my stuff to get off as well and he asks me where I'm staying, at least I finally worked out that's what he meant. He actually asked me 'where you be?', in his funny West Country accent.

'Samui Beach Huts.' I reply.

'Stay on the boat, it's quite far down the beach from 'ere so I'll take you over. Just give me a sec to sort out these guys.' he says.

'Thank you.' I'm too exhausted to argue. Although the shame makes me want to jump off here and walk, the thought of any further exertion on a hike back home is unbearable.

'I'm Sam.' he says as he climbs back on the boat.

'Alice.' I reply, and then burst into hysterics.

'I'm so sorry your guests saw more than they bargained for there.' I say through tears of laughter and disgrace.

'Hey, they've seen all sorts diving with me today but I reckon you'll be what they're talking about this evening.' he says, focusing on where he is going but with an amused little smile on his face.

'Oh don't,' I cover my eyes and bite my lip, 'how embarrassing.'

'How did you end up out there anyway, it looked like you had a death wish. Especially at hoye toyed.'

'Hoye toyde?' I ask.

'Oh sorry, it's me West Country accent. High Tide.' he pronounces in the Queen's English.

'Ah, more like an overinflated idea of my capabilities. Thank you so much, I really don't think I'd have made it back on my own.'

'No worries, it's all good.' Sam replies.

I hear Sam singing a song to himself as he steers the boat towards my hotel. I know the song but can't quite place it. And then I do.

'Everybody needs a bosom for a pillow.' he's singing away to himself.

'What was that?' I ask.

'Oh shit. I didn't realise. The song must have popped into my head. I don't know why. Well, I do. But. Shit. Sorry.' he laughs.

'I'm just here.' I point towards my hotel.

'OK. Ere, have you been to Coconut Joe's next door?' he asks.

'Yeah. You know him?' I ask.

'Course, everyone who lives out here knows Joe.' Sam replies.

'Thank you so much again.' I say clambering off the boat with the bloody board and paddle banging against my legs.

'Can I buy you a drink to say thanks?' I ask, nodding towards Coconut Joe's.

Sam checks his watch, 'Sure, that would be lush, I can have a quick one.'

***

'Honestly Joe, you wouldn't believe it. They were completely out and I had no idea.' I tell him.

'And my guests,' laughs Sam, 'nice group, but an older bunch. Ere, I thought one of the wives was going to thump her husband. He couldn't tear his eyes away.'

Joe's eyes crinkle and he lets out a belly aching laugh as he takes in the details of the story.

'And were you scared?' he asks.

'I was terrified. I thought I was being cast out to the seas for good.' I reply, 'Then I thought I was going to drown.' I add, 'Then I thought I was going to die of humiliation when I saw these puppies were out.' I finish.

'Oh honey, you've made my day.' Joe says as we all crumble to pieces around the table.

'Well then it was worth it.' I reply and we clink glasses.

'Anyone for another?' Joe asks raising his tumbler

of rum.

'Sure. I've earnt it today I think. As have you Sam, it's on me.' I reply.

'No, really I must get back after this one.' Sam says.

'So how's the family?' Joe asks Sam, 'I haven't seen you in a while.'

Family. Oh well, of course he has a family. All the goodies are taken at our age. I think Sam's about the same age as me anyway; it's difficult to tell when people have a tan. Everyone looks so much younger and sexier when they're glowing with Vitamin D.

'Great yeah. I have to head back as it's just Sarah and the twins tonight.' he replies.

'How old are the twins?' I ask.

'They're two.' he replies, raising his eyebrows.

'Anyway, I've gotta go. Nice to meet you, hopefully see you again soon - although perhaps not as much of you next time.' Sam winks playfully.

I shake my head wondering if I will ever live this down.

'Oh Joe - I have one for you.' Sam says.

'Go on then.' replies Joe.

'Distorted Vision?' Sam asks.

I give a quizzical look and Joe tells me that Sam has a penchant for quizzes and cryptic clues, in particular for bands.

'Distorted vision.' Joe repeats to himself as he looks around gazing into nowhere.

'Got it,' Joe slams his hand on the table, 'Blur.'

'Well done mate' Sam shakes Joe's hand, 'See you soon.'

Sam and his family live a couple of islands over in Koh Tao where they run a scuba diving centre. So he's often back and forth dropping off guests doing day trips from Samui. Occasionally he stays over with Joe for the night if he has an evening drop off and morning pick up from here. Does Joe know everybody on all the islands? It's starting to seem so. Sam is every bit the island living dive instructor. He's relaxed, fun, scruffily sexy and I would imagine he could put any diving novice at ease. Both he and Joe have hearty, dirty laughs, combine that with Sam's slight West Country ooh err my lover accent and being around them is a complete tonic.

'So you going to go to that beach party tonight?' Joe asks.

It takes me a second to tune in, I've been watching Sam drive off on his boat heading over the horizon. It's like I've woken up inside all of a sudden, with a renewed faith there are decent men out there. Not Sam in particular, some lucky bugger has already snapped him up. Signed, sealed and delivered with a set of twins to boot and well done to her. But to have that sense of excitement when you look at someone, to know that is out there when I'm ready to start looking for it again fills me with hope.

I had been debating whether to go out to the party or not. I didn't want to be the older bird sitting there on her own, people around me asking each other who brought their mother with them. I mean realistically I could be one of their mothers, I'd have had to have got knocked up behind the school bike sheds when I was an early teen, but it is possible.

However, having a good time with Joe and Sam has made me want to go out and be part of the action.

'Yeah, why not, I'll go along and see what it's like.' I shrug my shoulders, whilst glancing out to the water again.

'He's a nice guy eh?' Joe tilts his head towards the water.

'Hmm?' I swivel my head back round, 'Yeah, nice guy. My hero today.' I laugh.

'Yes, he's a right knight in shining armour.' Joe teases.

'Give over.' I elbow him playfully.

CHAPTER 8

I think I've walked into Spring Break.

As I turn down the alley leading to the party beach bar I hear the pounding bass of house music thundering towards me. Happy house I think it's called, although that could be very 90s and it's something completely different. Turning left onto the beach, it's like a scene from an MTV pool party. All the sunbeds have been pulled together to make big beds and tables as chill out areas and dance spots; there are huge bean bags dotted around everywhere and people are dancing on each other's shoulders, girls in bikinis, topless men, all standing in front of a DJ tower facing the beach and the fire show on the water's edge.

The atmosphere is electric with people laughing and dancing. I'm mesmerised by the fire show, or more accurately the six packs on the men who are throwing the fire - let's just say the act of fire throwing must be very physical, these are some seriously tasty looking torsos. I don't believe that this kind of six pack exists back in the UK. The men look no more than nine stone each, are ripped as hell, yet as narrow as a flat screen TV. Talk about washboard stomachs, you really could wash your laundry on their stomachs - sorry, enough. But seriously, this is unbelievable. It's safe to say that I am well in the process of getting over my ex. Get a grip Alice.

I'm delighted to see that whilst the beach is full of backpackers, travellers and most likely some of my college students, the bar area has a bit more of an eclectic mix of ages allowing me to not feel like the teacher at the student party. I order a beer and take a seat at the bar, watching the shenanigans unfold. 'Shenanigans', really how old am I.

Looking at the waif like bodies on all the bikini and daisy duke clad girls, I am delighted that the stress of the last few months has resulted in a half stone weight loss. I'm not normally one to fuss too much about my muffin top, but it's difficult not to think about it here, between stunning stick thin Thai women, the itsy bitsy beach girls and the ridiculously sized clothing. Keeping this stress weight off could also help me snag a new man, you kind of need to be back in shape when you're single again, especially with all this online stuff and people looking at your profile pics. I'm far from ready to be looking for someone else, but if I were, it certainly wouldn't be on this beach with the Pool Party candidates as my competition.

Sipping my beer, I think I hear my name being called. I look around but can't see where it's come from. I hear it again, and then see Kristian bounding over to me, and giving me a massive hug.

'Kristian, what are you doing here? I thought you were in Chiang Mai.' I say.

'I was going there, but a couple of friends I met in Laos said they were heading to Samui so I thought I'd come here early.' he replies, pointing towards his friends.

'Aaahh, I bet you did.' I laugh, as I realise the two friends that Kristian has come to meet up with are two of the most gorgeous specimens I've ever seen, of the Swedish variety by the looks of it.

'What can you do.' Kristian shrugs with a snigger, 'I'm just off for a piss, I'll grab you on the way back.'

I wander down into the Spring Break area with Kristian. There's a crowd of people on one of the bed / table/ sunbed things with a few bean bags pulled around. Kristian introduces me to Heidi and Pippa from Sweden, two friends doing the South-East Asia trip during their summer university break. The girls are gorgeous, good fun and actually remind me of a long haired blonde version of the cheeky girls - all bum cheeks, boobs, giggles and smiles...I reckon they could get around the world without spending a penny if they wanted to. Then there's Duke, as you can probably guess, he is from America, Boston to be exact. Duke, I can tell straight away was a fraternity boy, probably into a game of beer pong or a wet T-shirt competition. He has that amazing Boston accent, where all the r's have turned to w's. All I can think of is Matt Damon and Good Will Hunting and if I close my eyes, I could be sitting with Matt right in front of me.

A few drinks in, I can't resist asking Duke to say 'How d'ya like them apples?', getting ready to close my eyes and visualise Good Will himself.

Duke isn't quite sure what to make of this. 'Why do you want me to say that?'

'It's from Good Will Hunting.' I reply, 'You know when he meets the girl in the bar and gets her number?'

'Yeah, I know that film, I know the line.' he replies.

'But he's from Boston...I, oh, forget it.' I say.

I have a feeling that this may be a British humour thing, who knows, however from then on Duke is known to everyone as Good Will Hunting. Not that I think he understands why, at all, or how on earth it is funny. I'm not sure the rest of them quite understood the logic of the appointed nickname either, but as soon as they could see the rise I seemed to be getting from it (lightheartedly of course) the name just stuck and everyone played along.

'Do you know that there's a dog named Duke who is the Mayor of a town in Minnesota?' I tell the group.

'Hey, that's BS.' replies Duke.

'It's not.' I laugh, 'I'm serious.'

'Why would you know that,' adds Good Will Hunting, 'That's complete bullshit.'

Kristian jumps up, 'Fucking Hell, it's true.' he says reading from his phone, 'You Americans are off the crazy scale. No shit, there is a dog that is the mayor of a town and he's been re-elected twice.'

'I always wondered when I was going to be able to use that random bit of knowledge.' I giggled.

As the night went on, buckets of cocktails with multiple straws appeared at the table, men walking around with monkeys approach to get us to pay for pictures, and young kids are running around selling us flowers and garlands. I even realise that down on the beach what at first glance seemed like a very young crowd was actually quite mixed in age - so I don't feel quite so much like the teacher anymore.

Throughout the night I discover that Good Will Hunting was indeed a frat boy and I am keen to know if the American movies I watched were true to life. It certainly seems so. Good Will told us about his hazing pledge days which involved things like eating a whole raw onion, being deposited with a bag over his head and stripped of his clothes in the town centre and having to run home, and the worst story I've ever heard; he described having to mud wrestle in a paddling pool at a party but instead of mud, there was a concoction of shit, vomit, piss and vinegar (and I thought my poo story was bad). I struggle to understand why anyone would put themselves through that, but he was determined for me to see the 'good' that the Frat mansions also displayed. He told me how throughout the year they would run events that would raise money to make sure every kid in the local orphanage and hospital would get a toy for Christmas, and how if you wanted to stay in the frat house you had to obtain a certain GPA (grade point average). I honestly thought that the films were a complete exaggeration of what happened in these places, now I realise I was watching a tamed down movie version. I'm not sure whether I admire him for going through all this shit or think he's a bloody eejit.

The cheeky girls are hilarious. Contrary to my theory that if you are as good looking as them you must have been in the back of the queue when they were handing out brains and funny bones, the girls seem to have it all. They have just finished their third year of studying to be doctors and have a few more to go, so are spending their summer letting loose. They're typical medical students, and by that I mean that they love drinking, smoke fags and like to be around until the end of a good party. Perhaps that's because these docs to be know the stressful job they have in the future. Who knows, but I'm yet to meet a medical student who doesn't love a good party. They have these two guys wound round their little fingers and, although they don't take advantage of it, the boys are like little lap dogs vying for their attention.

As the night continues and more shots and cocktails are consumed, Kristian and Duke strip off and run into the water skinny dipping.

'Come on,' they shout back to us, 'Come in.'

'...and bring beers.' adds Kristian.

The cheeky girls looked at each other for a brief moment debating whether to join before dropping their clothes on our seats and making a dash for the water. Holding their hands over their oh so pert boobs, their little peach bums are the focus of everyone still slumped in a stupor at the party as they watch the pair of peaches bounce towards the water.

'Come on Alice, the waters gorgeous.' they shout back.

Not a chance in hell I'm thinking. Not only is this a horrific idea in general, but who wants to see my boobs that are beginning to look like tennis balls in a pair of socks or my arse that is more like a semi deflated football than any form of ripe fruit.

'Naaah, but I'll get a round of beers.' I say, hoping that my proffering of further alcohol will prevent any further insistence on my joining them.

I wander down to the water's edge with the five beers in hand and wade out slightly so the water is just around my ankles to pass around the beers. As I'm heading back my own beer is grabbed from me by Duke and Kristian rugby tackles me under the water.

Coughing, spluttering and laughing I resurface, 'You bloody bastards.' I scream, splashing at them.

'Oh come on, you're in now.' one of the cheeky girl's shouts, 'Take your clothes off, join the fun.'

It does seem like they're having a lot of fun, and I

suppose now that I'm in I don't have to worry about the rest of the beach watching me wobble into the water.

What the hell, I said I wasn't going to be boring this trip and with sufficient alcohol in me to think it's a fun idea I whip off my shorts, top and bra, toss the clothes on the beach and sink myself under the water.

'Now can I have my beer back?' I jest.

'Only once the panties are off.' Duke holds my beer high above his head.

The word panties makes me cringe, it's knickers or pants I think. Not panties. And certainly not when they are M&S specials instead of some lilac lacey efforts. In a courageous brazen moment, I chuck my knickers towards the rest of the clothes and thankfully am rewarded by the return of my beer.

The water is blissfully cool on my body and we spend a good while enjoying the water and the naughtiness of floating around there in our naked glory until some guys starts shouting towards us.

I'm not surprised to hear men shouting for the cheeky girls, they are after all a vision of inexplicable beauty. We all turn around to see who is shouting and they slur a drunken babble out again.

'Oi, Miss! Miss?' they shout as their heads and

shoulders are wobbling around while their legs are working overtime to keep them up straight.

'They seem to be staring at you.' one of the cheeky's says.

'Give over, I think the whole beach is looking at you two.' I nod in their direction.

'No,' Kristian says, 'it does seem to be you they're trying to talk to.'

'Miss Appleby, is that you?' they shout.

Holy mother of Jesus. There's only one place that I'm called Miss Appleby and that's at my work, at the college. I look again, squinting my eyes to see better in the dark and realise that standing there right in front of me, with my knickers and bra bundled by their feet are Ed and Dan, two of my students.

'No, wrong person.' I shout back.

'Aaah, it is you. I knew it.' they shout back, and with that they pick up the clothes lingering around their feet. Ed puts my knickers on his head, Dan puts my bra over his, they grab the rest of the clothes and then do a runner.

The four naked bodies around me are falling

about with laughter while I remain stiff as a board, hiding right up to my chin under the water hoping for a wave to come and take me under and put me out of my misery.

My first thought, how the hell will I get home with no clothes, although this seems a small fry of a problem in comparison to what Jonesy is going to say to me once he hears about this. Can you get sacked from work for something that you have done outside of work? For skinny dipping on your holiday? Ed and Dan are now finished college, this was their last year and they won't be back so perhaps it will just be a funny story for them to tell their college friends in the pub, never to land on the ears of any of the staff. Besides, there is always denial. No Jonesy of course I wasn't skinny dipping in the middle of a remote tropical island in Thailand (remote my arse, that's two people who've called out my name tonight alone). I have no idea what you've heard but we're talking about a case of mistaken identity, not me. Deny, deny, deny. There you go, problem two solved now back to problem one.

'Right, seeing as they didn't nick any of your clothes who's going to help a girl out?' I hold my hands up in desperation.

Kristian, ever the hero, grabs Good Will Hunting's t-shirt and brings it to me in the water.

'Oi, why my T-shirt bro?' he shouts.

'Because you seem to have it off more than on anyway.' Kristian snorts.

'Thanks - I'll give it back to you tomorrow.' I turn to Good Will Hunting and bow to him in thanks.

I stretch the t-shirt down to cover my nether region and hunched over to maximise both bum and front bum coverage, I begin a quick wiggly jog home.

***

As I wake the horror of how the evening ended flashes back to me. Did I really get caught by my students skinny dipping? What the hell was I thinking. Although, other than 'the incident' it was a great night. A proper full on beach party, I think I'm starting to make up for my lost youth spent with dull old Pete. Can you believe that bastard still hasn't been in touch? It's been more than a week now and not one message, not one email. It's not even as if I can snoop on him as he doesn't put anything on Facebook, his last update was a 'cheers for all the birthday messages' note seven months ago.

After a few hours lounging on the beach with my trusty self-help book I realise that as much as I flick through the pages there is no chapter for what you should do if you're caught naked by your students.

I abandon the book and go visit Joe to take him up on lesson number two in chess. We have a couple of drinks as I regale him with stories of Kristian, the Cheeky Girls and Good Will Hunting. I had no intention of telling Joe how the evening ended but somehow it just spills out. Joe has a way of making you continue talking, confessing the embarrassing stories that you'd rather lock up in a cupboard forever more.

'I'm starting to see a trend here honey.' he laughs. 'This is your second incident involving a lack of clothing in as many days.'

'Anyway, sounds like a good night.' Joe laughs.

'It was fun, obvious incident excepted of course. Who knows how I'll cope again tonight.'

'Where to tonight?' Joe asks.

'We're meeting at the same bar then some ladyboy show I think…'

'Ha, be sure not to sit at the end of a row at the show unless you want to be up on stage.' Joe warns with a giggle.

'Really? Well now I know where Good Will Hunting is going to have to sit.' I laugh.

'And what you got planned for the rest of the week honey?' Joe asks.

'I want to do the elephant trekking and jungle tour in the next few days I think.' I reply.

We meet in the bar at nine (back home I'd be halfway through my evening by nine o'clock, now I'm not even meeting until then). Most of the guys have spent the day sleeping off the night before either in their room or on the beach, and they're now raring to go again.

'Tequila.' Kristian shouts as the waiter brings us over a round of shots someone has sneakily ordered.

We wander along the street and are playfully dragged by the ladyboys into the dark red cabaret show. The first act is 'It's raining men' and the stage is filled with beautiful specimens. Some of these lady boys look like super models in their diamante dresses and leotards.

I can't help looking for their bits and pieces, which I've read are sellotaped up their backside to remove the telltale bulge in the knicker area but you wouldn't have a clue. I've sat myself cleverly one seat from the end of a row, with Good Will Hunting in what Joe says is prime position.

As we get further into the show the music and dances are becoming more comical - we have Whitney Houston gesticulating blow job movements during I will always love you; a stunner singing and gyrating about to Britney Spears and then comes the audience participation part. It's Lady Marmalade from Moulin Rouge and there's a seat in the middle of the stage. They are asking for someone to join them and I can't help screaming and pointing to Will sitting next to me.

He turns in mock fear and anger, although I know he's secretly loving the attention. Sitting in the chair, the cast of moulin rouge start toying with him and caressing him with feather boas, the crowd is whooping and Good Will, I have to admit, is taking it in very good humour.

Half way through the song I realise that I have been snapping away with my camera and hadn't noticed that one of the ladyboys had drifted into the audience and was approaching me. Oh dear god, what is happening. The next thing I know I have been grabbed by the hand and I too am being dragged up onto the stage. I try to protest, but somehow it is drawing more attention to me so with my head hiding in my hand I allow myself to be dragged up. I'm then given instructions to copy Lady Marmalade in her twerking, slut drop and leg around the pole moves. I'm completely flushed, shaking in horror and hilarity, and after the most torturous and unglamorous shuffle around the stage both Will and I are released back into the crowds, and to our little group who

I have no doubt will never let me live this down.

Tequila - beers - cocktails - ladyboy show - just your regular Monday night.

***

The day's repeat themselves over the next week, well not that I went to the ladyboy show every night, but certainly the fashion with which I was consuming a variety of alcoholic beverages. A familiar rhythm was settling in, that being a hangover start to the day, drifting into the booze blues at lunchtime where I'm annoyed at myself for drinking so much the previous evening and having no energy or inclination to do anything with my day. This is followed by some further wallowing about my lack of life both here and back home, then as the afternoon comes round I kick myself up the arse to get out of my funk and go visit Coconut Joe's to cheer myself up. A couple of games of chess later and I'm on track to being jolly again, then I get ready, head out for an evening of partying and so the cycle continues.

Over the last eight days we have been to six beach parties, tried most of the bars in the area, and averaged a get to bed time of between four and five AM, most evenings ending on the beach with a motley crew of somewhere between 8 - 15 people, plastic bags of cheap beer and Kristian's iPod.

Kristian hooked up with Pippa earlier in the week and has been trying to make it happen again all week, unsuccessfully. Good Will Hunting has had us seeking out every beer pong and wet t-shirt competition going, the former to win and build up his travel funds and the latter, well that speaks for itself (see, my initial judgement there was correct).

Unlike the Bangkok gang, this seems to be more of an evening crowd, with little planned for the daytime except for sleeping off the night before and for me, chess with Joe. The nights are fun, but as the days go on I'm starting to feel worse and worse in the morning. It's been years since I've drunk like this, and a cloudy head each morning is taking its toll. I wake each morning gasping for water and wondering where Pete is, what he's doing. Is he missing me? Why hasn't he been in touch? Does he remember that today is bin day? Has he thrown away the out of date milk in the fridge? Why oh why hasn't he been in bloody touch?

OK, so I have a secret. I might have drunk dialled Pete last night. Maybe. My phone seems to think I did, but I'm not so sure. I don't remember so it didn't happen - that's how it works isn't it? My phone says that the call was only 4 seconds long so at least I know I didn't leave a message. But why didn't he answer my call. It could have been important. I could have been calling to say that I was in trouble and needed help.

Bloody buggery bollocks. The only thing I can think of worse than drunk dialling your ex is drunk dialling your ex and they ignore the bloody call. I don't really know why I called him anyway. It's not like I'm missing him or pining for him to take me back. I'm having way too much fun out here and he doesn't even know the meaning of the word fun anymore.

Perhaps the more important question here should be around the fact that I was in a state that I don't remember making the call...

CHAPTER 9

As I sit this afternoon with Joe, numbing out the thought of my drunken phone call and easing my hangover with a beer, I start to think about my holiday so far. Pretty boozy is what comes to mind, the reality is I've spent more than half my waking hours sedated by cocktails, and the other half recovering from them in a daze, barely able to hold a thought long enough to take any meaning from it.

The responsibilities of life back home are somewhat on hold, as if it's another Alice's problem, while this Alice is a twenty-one year old backpacker. Occasionally, it occurs to me that I should really be behaving more my age, but that thought is easily drowned out with a bucket of booze, or a basket load of denial telling myself this is the best way to move on.

'So, what's new honey?' Joe asks during game number two of chess for the day.

'Another day, another party.' I give an embarrassed giggle.

'You're certainly making the most of the parties.' he raises his eyebrows. After a pause, he continues, 'So, how many of those things on your list have you done yet?'

'Huh?' I say, looking up from the chess board.

'Elephant trekking? Cookery class?' he enquires.

'I haven't really had the chance.' I reply, trying to ignore the thought and concentrating very hard on my next move.

'...maybe getting to bed before the sun comes up might help.' says Joe.

He laughs, 'I'm not judging you honey, but you know, you told me Pete was boring, and, well, isn't getting pissed every night a bit dull too?'

'I'm just blowing off steam Joe.' I shrug defensively.

'What do you say in your country - the pot asking

the black kettle something?' he says.

Joe's English is fantastic and he loves all the funny phrases we use but never quite gets them right.

He pauses for a while, then continues, 'Not to mention, your looking pretty done in quite honestly.'

Oh he's a clever man this Joe. Wham. That was a blow straight to the solar plexus, knocked me right out. Everything he just said hits a nerve. I have the chance to do something really special out here, two months to travel, explore, rediscover my 'joie de vivre' and instead I'm behaving like a college kid and pissing it up the wall. What the hell is wrong with me? I've gone from a grown woman with a flat, a fiancé, a good job and responsibilities to this; a boring old woman who thinks she is in her teens getting trashed, not knowing how I got to bed each evening, waking up fully dressed gagging for water, a little bit more haggered looking each day, a little more lost each day.

'There's more to this island than bars and parties you know.' Joe continues, 'In fact, what are you doing tomorrow night? There's a market on in the next town - a bit of Thai culture, great food, not quite as good as mine,' he smiles, 'shopping, live music - what say I take you?'

'Sure, that sounds great.' I reply.

'And I want you to do something different during the day too, cross something off your list before you come and meet me here at 7. One of the many life changing adventures you have been talking about.' he smiles.

'OK, OK, point taken Joe. I'll get my arse in gear and do something.'

***

I wake up feeling refreshed from a night off from the boozy beach parties. After my chat with Joe I just didn't feel like going out with everyone. His words hit home about what I was doing, or not doing I guess, and I felt completely ashamed. I start the day in a quiet beach cafe, cappuccino in hand as I make my plans. I'm off to climb one of the waterfalls and ride on an elephant. Who's boring now, eh. Elephant trekking, climbing waterfalls, this is more like it, what a traveller I am.

Anxiously hopping on the back of a taxi scooter I finally leave this party town for the first time since arriving on the island. Bumping along the road I feel the breeze cooling my skin from the blazing sun and once I get over the fear of straddling a random stranger with my arms very tightly wrapped around his middle (really, shorts instead of a denim skirt would have been a better choice today), I take in the amazing surroundings.

The sea peeps up on my left in between the buildings as a beautiful reminder that I am currently living on a tropical island. Not on holiday, but living here. And at once I am ashamed again that this is the first time I have left the beach and neon strip. Having passed some of the most amazing secluded beach spots, I vow to make more of my time here. 'Stop wallowing and just start doing Alice.' I tell myself.

'What?' asks my taxi driver.

'Sorry…oh, nothing.' I reply realising that I've given myself a talking to out loud. I should probably get used to this trait if it's what spending a lot of time on your own does to you.

We turn up a final road and I see elephants on either side of the mountain road, free and wild, nothing to stop them from stampeding me, except they didn't pay me a blind bit of notice as they go about their business. I climb off the bike and Keng, my driver, says that he'll wait for me. He's going to wait for two hours, at no cost, unbelievable. I'm obviously not the first person to cling onto him for dear life then, as I thought he would whoosh off the minute he was released from my grasp.

Wandering into the park there's a few wooden platforms built into the trees on my left with saddled up elephants, awaiting the tourists to feed them bananas and clump around the jungle with them. There's a shop selling wooden elephants, key rings and all the usual paraphernalia and oh, another classic sign, which says:

Shoplifters will be prostituted

Erm, I hope that's a typo. Click. One more to send to Jamie.

I take a tour with Simon the elephant around the jungle accompanied by Rodney, my Thai tour guide. All the Thai people choose their own nickname he tells me, and he loves Only Fools and Horses, hence Rodney. Who would have thought it...Rodney is also a massive Manchester United fan and has been living in the onsite camp for ten years where he says he watches the Man U matches every week in his shack, leaving the door open so that Simon the elephant can watch too. What a hoot! There could have been something lost in translation there, but I swear he told me that the elephant watches the football with him. After giving Simon a couple of bananas and batting his trunk away from sneaking up my skirt (again, why on earth am I wearing a skirt), I make my way up the path to the waterfall.

Jesus Christ, I'm unfit. The tracks up the mountain are increasing in their gradient by the second, but oh it's so worth the sweaty effort. I reach the top of the trail and tilt my head to see the water cascading down the rocks into the pools at my feet. Nature at its finest, this is truly stunning and the pool so inviting that I strip down to my bikini and jump in, heading straight for the rock's edge with the falls refreshingly showering my face. Dare I say, moments like this could make me succumb to buying a selfie stick - but not quite - the waterfall will look exceedingly better without my bright red mug in it, and it does, even after the 28th photo I take.

**

I am gushing about my day and all I've seen and done to Joe later that evening as I meet him for our night out. We are just finishing a drink and getting ready to leave when one of Joe's friends comes in. I feel a flutter in my stomach as I realise that it is none other than my hero, Sam.

'Hi Joe.' he says.

'Hey there Sam, how's life?' Joe replies.

'All good. Just dropped a tour off and thought I'd say hi. What you up to?'

'I'm' just taking Alice here down to the walking market. Wanna join us?'

It's Sam, my paddleboard hero, maybe joining us. YES PLEASE, YES PLEASE, YES PLEASE.

'Sure, if you don't mind me gate crashing I could do with a night off from the kids, and I don't need to be back until tomorrow lunchtime. Can I have my usual spot for the night?' Sam asks.

'No problem, my sofa's all yours.'

'Great, I'll just set the boat up for the night and be right back.'

Now I don't mind telling you that the butterflies in my tummy started doing an involuntary dance. Sam was going to be joining us for the evening. What a fortuitous little happening that is. Not that I'm after him, but hey, there's nothing wrong with a bit of window shopping is there?

When Sam returns we grab one of the open pick up truck taxis and head off to Fisherman's Village, where contrary to my initial thoughts there are apparently no fisherman, it is in fact the posh part of the island. Two new towns in one day, and two strange forms of transport, I'm feeling proud. I finally have something to report back home that doesn't involve buckets of cocktails, stumbling into bed, or any other general antics associated with a girly holiday at the age of 19 in some part of Spain unfortunate enough to host us.

We wander the little beachfront street, looking at all the stalls and nick knacks, clothes, unnecessary items you feel compelled to spend your money on when you are on holiday that undoubtedly end up stuffed away in some drawer never to be seen again a month after you get home. I picked up a tall coconut vase. A fleeting thought tried to ruin my evening when it screamed out at me 'don't you need to have a sodding home before you start buying the fancy extras like vases??'.

We eat like Kings from the food stalls...prawns, noodles, spring rolls - and I even bought a bag of deep fried insects to try. Incidentally they taste like chewy twigs, pretty gross but at least they weren't gooey like those celebs on that programme back home have to eat which is what I expected. Once we'd eaten our fill and I'd spent enough money on tat, Joe led us to a bar at the crossroads of the market where we could people watch and he ordered a bottle of red wine.

Away from the backpackers and dance music, I can see a much more relaxing side to this island. This market is predominantly filled with couples meandering up and down, stopping to take in the delights of the stalls or taste the Thai delicacies, many with a cocktail in hand as they potter along (in a plastic cup I must add, not a bucket).

I imagine this is what Pete and I would have been doing had we come on holiday here together, although I couldn't think of any company I'd rather be in right now than with Joe and Sam. I watch as an older couple are picking out various wooden ornaments, in my head they are choosing these for their grandchildren. I think of how much my Dad would love it out here, he'd be trying all the different food, mesmerised by the buzz of the little street and all its sellers. I notice a family with two young girls jumping like crazy on their dad's leg in pursuit of one of the hundred balloons tied to a bicycle display and the smile on their dad's face as he hands over the money for them and ties the string around each of their wrists so they don't fly away. I picture that being Sam with his twins, I bet he is an amazing father. I could certainly see myself having children if I had someone like him as the Dad. Someone who's caring and attentive, excited by life.

Contrary to the last couple of weeks, our conversations are intellectual and interesting. We chat about the political landscape of Thailand, the impact of tourism since it's become a massive holiday hotspot and then the lapses when it isn't because of the latest disaster. We discuss Joe's career in Hollywood and every time I hear another part of his story I feel I get to know him just that little bit more. Sam asks if I've heard about the story where he was out at party with some of the biggest Hollywood stars of the moment and he nipped out the front to have a cigarette and ended up leaving them all to go to a local little spit and sawdust rock bar with the cloakroom attendant. He never ceases to amaze me - I mean really, how many people you know ditch Brad Pitt or whoever it was to go and watch some unknown rock band in a dive bar. I can tell you now, I know no one else who would do that, but if they're anything like Joe I'd like to know a lot more of them. Joe and Sam want to hear all about London and are intrigued by my funny stories of working with 17 and 18-year olds. Joe can't believe how brazen the kids in London seem to be, Thai children are so meek and mild in comparison, the thought that they would shout at me, have physical fights with each other and occasionally tell me in no uncertain times to F off.

Not brazen Joe I think, disrespectful. Thai people were very respectful of their elders and our kids, well not *always* so. I enjoy hearing Sam's stories of the dive school and I cringe inwardly as he talks about all the backpackers who came over to the island and treated it like an alcoholic playground (touched a nerve maybe?). We shared a second bottle of red as the conversations continue with ease and then Joe surprises me with a gift that he picked up at the market earlier. It's so thoughtful, he has given me a pestle and mortar, having heard me talk about how much I love cooking and that I wanted to learn everything about Thai cuisine while I was out here. You'll need this for all your curry pastes he tells me as Sam enquires if I could give 'our Sarah' some tips. I wouldn't say she's the worst cook in the world he tells us, but she's pretty far up there. Cheeky bastard, perhaps he should learn himself then.

I climb into bed that night and realise I have really missed 'adult' company, exciting conversations that don't involve one-upmanship of who's travelled to the more exciting spot or managed to live on the least money per day and therefore achieved the status of King of the hippie backpackers. Don't get me wrong, they are great kids, but that's just it, I've spent my time in Samui hanging out with kids so far. Retraction, they are not kids, but I am somewhat closer to middle age. I remember the days of inane pointless conversations, where you are so keen to impress you spend more time thinking about what your next story will be or how you can drop into the conversation that you once met Rick Astley than discussing something that is actually going on in the world, listening to people's stories, debating a subject of interest. I don't know at what point in your 20s that happens, conversations change, but I'm so glad it does.

Jamie, Gavin and Theo are slightly different, at least when they were in Bangkok they were travelling to explore, to understand the world and different cultures. I suppose that's why they travelled up to the North of Thailand when the others have come to hang out on the beach and drink buckets. Kristian was interested in these things too until he stopped thinking with his head and let his dick lead him into the line of the cheeky girls.

Anyway, it was a great night, and one that hasn't left me feeling as though tomorrow I will feel as rough as a badger's arse either. Balance, not really my forte, being easily swept up in whatever is taking place around me. Perhaps that's another step into adulthood I'm yet to take, the not easily influenced one. Who knows, maybe one day Gail's book will teach me. I still haven't got past page two. Tomorrow, I won't be hungover, so I'll get up early and start changing my life with that book.

***

I wake with a freshness I haven't felt for a while; the sun is up but has not yet seared the sand with its scorching rays. I throw on my bikini and shorts and walk along the bay. A few early birds are out enjoying the serenity, this quiet time before the jet skis and banana boats grace the water. The water is calm and as I wander along the edge it is so clear I can see the schools of fish dance along, making shapes and patterns near the surface.

'Alice.' I hear a shout and see Sam wandering towards me.

'Morning Sam, how's it going?' I reply.

'I'm good, just heading back, I have a dive tour at 1. I had fun last night.'

'Yeah me too. Nice to see you again, take care.' I give a little wave.

Sam starts wading out to his boat and appears to hesitate, his head tilted slightly to one side as if in contemplation.

'Hey Alice, you want a quick tour round the island before I head off? We can get around the island in just under an hour on the boat, and the view is pretty special?' Sam asks.

'If you're sure, yes, that would be amazing.' I reply.

'Come on then, hop on.' he smiles as I wade out to join him.

'...and that over there is the National Marine Park.' Sam points to a cluster of small islands.

We are whooshing through the water with the sun beating down on our skin. Sam steers the boat with the ease of a professional, pointing out the various landmarks and I find myself watching his profile as much as I do the scenery. No wonder this man is married with kids, he really is one of the good ones. Great company, a family dive business, a six pack that doesn't deserve a shirt, and a rugged masculinity so far removed from the hipsters who are gathering on the London streets these days.

Sam gives me hope that when I'm ready to move on, there are decent guys out there. They're probably all taken like him, but for now, I can hope some hot single gentlemen still exist, who are kind, interesting and did I mention hot?

'Thanks again Sam, that was brilliant.' I say.

'No problem, give me a shout if you make it to Koh Tao.' Sam replies as he speeds off towards the horizon, leaving me on the water's edge with the waves from the boat rippling around my ankles.

There are good guys out there. Was Pete one of them? Maybe at one point he was, but not recently. Sam actually listened when I talked, asked me questions about me, about what I think. This I realise is part of having a meaningful relationship. I may not find my Mister Perfect but throwing away what I had was not a stupid whim, I need someone I connect with, someone who is my friend as well as my boyfriend. Speaking of which, why hasn't he been in touch after my missed call. I suppose it didn't need a call back but an 'are you OK?' text or something.

I die a little inside as I think about it. Hope he's OK...no I don't. I hope he's wallowing in his own misery and cursing himself for letting me go, for being a complacent asshole who's now lost everything and is feeling like complete and utter shit.

***

Jamie and Gavin are arriving in Koh Samui today, so knowing it's going to be another big night I spend most of the day lounging on the beach, dipping in and out of the water to cool down, my mind daydreaming back to this morning's boat trip and, well, Sam.

I pop in to see Joe in the afternoon to thank him for taking me out last night, telling him how much I enjoyed it and I update him on my tour around the island with Sam this morning.

Joe raises his eyebrows and smiles, and I realise that I have been gushing about how nice Sam is. Embarrassed that he would think I'd be chasing someone else's husband I immediately clam up. I don't know why I worried, Joe knows what I've been through, I'm sure he understands that it's just a pleasant surprise to meet an interesting attractive guy, that I'm just beginning to have a bit of faith that not everyone is as useless as Pete and I'm not destined to be an old woman with eight cats just yet.

'So how's the head and the heart these days honey?' Joe asks, 'Things with Pete becoming any clearer yet?'

At the mention of Pete's name I realise that other than chastising him for not responding to my call, I haven't really thought about him much. I've thought about what I might do when I get back, where I might live, if he will be in my life. I've even thought fleetingly about online dating, and meeting someone new. Perhaps it's out of sight out of mind, or that I'm not really living my normal life right now. Pete has been something in the back of my mind nonstop, but he hasn't figured in my heart much at all. Not in the way you hear people saying that they can't go on without someone. I obviously haven't been in his mind too much either.

Before replying to Joe though, it occurs to me that he is asking this because he thinks I like Sam. Oh god, I don't want Joe to think I'm that kind of girl, the kind to shamelessly flirt and go after married men.

'Everything is quite raw.' I say.

'Hmm...you'll get there honey.' he seems to look a little disappointed.

I feel bad as I think Joe thought he'd really helped me move forward, and he really has, he's been my rock and voice of reason, making me see that I haven't lost anything in Pete. That he obviously wasn't the one for me and we're better off out of it now before marriage made it all the worse.

Poor Joe, but I can't have him thinking I'm moving on to Sam the family man, that would be embarrassing and just plain wrong. The thought of putting myself out there for anyone right now is unbearable, my heart just couldn't take it...or my head, would that mean it's definitely over, in the past with Pete?

CHAPTER 10

It's so great to see Jamie, Gavin and Theo who have arrived just in time for tomorrow's Full Moon Party and to hear about their time in Northern Thailand (these young whippersnappers and all their culture are putting me to shame). Theo tells me that he went to a temple and had a chat with a monk. It was 'spiritually fulfilling' apparently and he now feels even more than ever that he can sense the purpose of life. This is met with a couple of eye rolls from Jamie and Gavin who I think are feeling the strain of hanging out with this hippy dippy lad from Eton. Gavin tried a hundred-year old egg that was mouldy and smelt like decaying fish. Jamie visited the prison where she took the inmates some sweets and cigarettes, and she got a massage in the rehabilitation centre there where the inmates are preparing for re-entering the outside world. They all went to the elephant sanctuary and bathed the beautiful creatures and visited the white temple where you can be cleansed and fulfil a life of purity. Jesus Christ, talk about making someone feel useless.

I shared my photos with Jamie for her collection and in turn she showed me the funny images that she had also seen along the way:

No sex in toilet, prohibited 20 baht (this is about a 50 pence fine)

Be aware of invisibility

Fart in the car to add 150 baht

Our bar is presently not open because it is closed

Although I'm somewhat embarrassed when Jamie asks what I've been up to and the little of significant interest that I have to relay, I do fill her in on my escapades and, of course, on my time with Sam. I told her that he had invited me to go to Koh Tao and he would show me around. 'What are you waiting for' she asks me and I tell her that I'm not convinced his wife will be as happy to see me but I might go, I'm thinking about it for now.

The bars are heaving as the backpackers have arrived in force for tomorrow's big event. As we end the evening, well, early morning, the plans are made to go to the Full Moon Party. We'll head to the pier and catch a boat at midnight. Midnight. I laugh to myself as I head back to the hotel. Meeting at midnight, back home that was a time I rarely saw, normally mid-dream by then or more recently lying in bed staring at the ceiling trying to get to sleep. Yet here I am making plans to start my night at bedtime.

After a somewhat terrifying boat ride across to Koh Phangan, with around four times as many people on board as I think is probably acceptable, I am relieved to step off onto solid ground. The place is awash with fluorescent clothing and flashing lights. So much neon it reminds me of the acid house days and smiley faces, not that many of the people here will remember that. The Cheeky girls tell us to wait as they run to a stall, returning with luminous necklaces and headbands for everyone. What the hell, when in Rome.

Winding our way through the streets towards the beach, the atmosphere is amazing, throngs of excited people eager to reach the most infamous all night beach party, many of which have booked their holiday or planned their backpacking tour around coming.

'Two buckets each.' Kristian screams as we pass a bucket stall with the tone and volume of a frat boy, it sounds like something from 90210 - the original that is, you know, like Steve Sanders at a pool party.

'Down one now and take the other to the paaaarrttaaay.' he continues.

Cheers all round indicated that I'm alone in thinking this is a ridiculous idea with the whole night ahead of us. But not being one to be left out, I join the youngsters in what appears to be a mission to get as messy as possible. A bucket of vodka, rum and red bull later, we round onto the beach. Bloody hell, you can't see the sand, the whole beach is wall to wall people, a football stadium's worth of people bouncing, drinking, screaming.

There's fireworks and people jumping over ropes of fire (not always successfully, leading to some quick runs to the sea to immerse a burnt knee or hand). Good Will Hunting jumps in and manages five jumps before escaping with a kamikaze roll out of the line of fire.

'Come on Al, give it a go,' Good Will Hunting says, 'it's awesome.'

Feeling quite fearless now that I'm on my third bucket of god knows what concoction, I think this is a fabulous idea.

'OK, but only if you'll do it with me.' I laugh.

'You're on.' Good Will Hunting grabs my hand and leads me over just in front of the rope and counts us in - 3, 2, 1, go.

It's terrifying in a bloody exciting way, and after a few jumps we skip out of the firing line collapsing on the sand as we trip over each other falling together in an awkward jumble. Before I know it, we are caught up in the drunken moment and he's kissing me, his tongue is circling inside my mouth and I feel a tingling inside me that has been absent from my life for quite a while. That first kiss with someone new, the thought that someone finds me attractive and wants to kiss me fills me with raw animal passion. Lying at the water's edge the kissing progresses and he starts to grab my breast, which is quite enough to bring me back to reality and I pull away, getting to my feet, brushing the sand off my legs, straightening myself up and out, and generally looking anywhere other than at Good Will Hunting.

I look around and see that the party appears to have been drifting into complete debauchery around me and I hadn't even noticed the spiral. I can see people peeing in the water, lots of couples who really should get a room, some poor souls with their head in their hands and many spewing figures dotted randomly about, a sure sign that I have been at this party too long. This is the house party equivalent of still being there when there is one guy sitting in the kitchen finishing off the remains of any bottle of whisky, rum, gin, trying to make conversation and encourage you to drink with him as he desperately doesn't want the night to end. I scamper away from Good Will who is now back in the fire jump rope and stumble along the edge of the beach, sobering up instantly as I see the Cheeky Girls in a very sorry state.

One of the Cheeky's has passed out and the other is puking up next to her. I'm holding back Pippa's hair as she pukes, whilst splashing water on Heidi's face with the other hand to try and wake her up. She's coming round thank god, and in the meantime I'm looking around for the others. I need help here, someone needs to get these kids some water. Toying with the need to go and get water versus not wanting to leave them alone, I dig out my phone in the vain hope that I might be able to contact one of the gang for some assistance.

And there on my phone is the homepage I've been waiting to see for the last two weeks.
1 new message – Pete.

Before getting to read it, I hear the words of an angel, 'Can I help?' he says.

'Oh, thank god, yes. Could you get some water please?' I say without looking up, too busy trying to keep Heidi awake and Pippa's face out of her own vomit.

'Here, take this while I go and get more.' he says handing me his bottle.

'Thank you so much.' I say, as I turn to him,

'Sam! What are you doing here? Actually, tell me later could you please get some water….and if you see a man with a Superman logo on his chest can you send him this way please?'

All the guys got neon Superman logos painted on their chest when they got here. I thought it was quite ridiculous until this moment.

While Sam heads off in the direction of the bars for some water, I return to my phone. One new message. Of all the times in the last two weeks, has he got a camera on me, does he know that I've just kissed someone?? I take a deep breath and open the message.

House feels weird without you. Let's talk when you get back. Hope you're OK x

I have no time to think about this right now, as my Florence Nightingale hat is required. Half an hour later, with the two girls feeling dreadful but at least awake and holding down their fluids I sit on the beach with them and Sam absolutely done in, defeated and unable to make sense of Pete's message. Seeing the faint and familiar blue and yellow superman symbol through the now depleting crowd, I jump up and dart towards it. Kristian.

'Kristian, I'm done. Can you take the girls back to the boats please? They need an escort home.'

Seeing how drained, and let's be honest here, fucked I look, he smiles and replies with,

'Happy to oblige, you not coming?'

'No,' I shake my head, 'I just need some time out.'

'Come on you pair' Kristian picks them up with the help of Sam and me and wraps one under each arm. Their heads are lolloping around on each shoulder as they wander off towards the pier. I hope they meet some of the others on the way to help Kristian, but he's a big boy, he'll manage.

With the weight of responsibility off my shoulders, I collapse to the sand, head on my arms, arms on my knees. After three weeks of boozing, partying, kissing frat boys, nursing drunk teenagers and now reading this text - I am officially done. I am too old for this shit. And then the tears fall, and the shoulders shake uncontrollably.

I feel a hand on my back. 'Alice, what's wrong? What is it?' Sam says.

Sam. I forgot he was even here, completely lost in my own world.

'Oh god Sam, it's such a mess.' I manage.

'Is this about your ex? Joe told me you've just broken up with someone.' Sam asks, real concern showing on his face, or perhaps it's the absolute horror of being stuck with this blubbering mess and having no idea what to do with me.

'Yes, no, oh I don't know. He's just sent me a message. I don't think I want to be with him but I don't know, maybe I'm just not sure how to be on my own. I've spent so long trying to marry him, then after he didn't want to marry me, I've realised how dull and boring he was and that I deserve better, that I am better without him. And now I've just spent three weeks getting pissed like a bloody teenager. How boring is that, how stupid. This trip was meant to be about me becoming my own person again - but I'm not sure I like this person, the boring pissed person I've become.'

'And why did he text me, why now. Fuck men. They're full of shit the lot of them. Now he wants to talk. What about talking for the last three months eh? Where was he to talk and sort things out then.'

'And I'm a cradle snatcher, I snogged a college frat boy. I'm meant to teach kids, not kiss them.' I wail.

Head in my arms looking down at the sand, the party a dull beat in the background, I see my muffin top poking out the side where my shorts and vest join.

'Oh god, and all this booze has made me fat again.' I continue.

'Pom- pooey.' Sam says, starting to laugh.

I look up at him with disbelief, 'Are you now telling me I stink too? Did you just call me pooey?'

He wraps an arm around me affectionately as he laughs. 'No, no - sorry. You said fat, and one of the words for fat in Thai is pom-pooey, every time I think of it I laugh. The kids call their teacher Mr. Pom- pooey as he's a bit of a chubby guy.'

I manage a laugh, I'm not quite out of my depths of despair, but for now at least, my tantrum is over.

'Hold on a minute, what are you even doing here?' I ask, only just realising quite how bizarre it is to see him, having been too wrapped up in myself to think about it before.

'I come over here every Full Moon party, I'm part of the cleanup team that tries to get the beach back to normal the next day.' he says.

'Really, that's so good of you.' I reply.

'Yeah well, I hate seeing how the beach ends up, and all the plastic in the water is bad for the fish. Sam says, 'It's not entirely altruistic,' he adds, 'it's pretty good promo for the dive centre too.'

'But you can't start the clear up now while the party is still going?' I ask, 'You're not going to clear up while those guys are shagging over there and this lot are skinny dipping are you?'

He laughs, 'No, the clear up is tomorrow, but I drove the boat over here about an hour ago and parked up. I like to keep a look out for drunks stumbling into the water who don't have an Alice to look out for the.' he smiles.

'Not sure I was much help, sending them packing with Kristian. I should have gone with them really.'

'Ere don't beat yourself up, you helped them. You'd be surprised how few people do that here. People can be right selfish when they're off their tits.'

After a few minutes of sitting starting out to the sea (well let's face it, I'd rather have skinny dippers in my line of vision than shaggers), Sam makes a suggestion and I begin to quietly sob again, overwhelmed with his kindness. Poor Sam. He must be wondering what on earth he has done to deserve this.

'Why don't you stay on the boat with me tonight, then you can head back in the morning, well late morning once all the drunken loons are gone. Seriously, the boat ferries are a nightmare just now.'

Lying across the seats of the boat, we stare up at the stars and the full moon in comfortable silence until the booze of the evening catches up with me and I zonk out.

***

I join Sam the next morning to help with the clear up, it's the least I can do having put him through all my drama last night - only boyfriends, husbands and dads should have to deal with that shit.

Sam's presence seems to be a calming influence on me too, so anything that can prolong the time I spend with him the better. Everything about him is relaxed and funny, and I could do worse than learn to channel that myself. Does that come from being settled into family life? Or living on a paradise island teaching people to dive for a living? Who knows, but he is quite simply the most easy company, what a lucky woman his wife is.

As we trawl the beach with bin bags collecting the rubbish, I feel a lot better. The sea air is blowing the booze cobwebs away and the repetition of cleaning up giving me a pleasant sense of purpose. The team gathering up the rubbish are surprisingly jolly considering they are giving up their Sunday to clear up after a bunch of selfish bastards throwing all their shit over the beach. There's a real community feel to this group - and it's really nice to be a part of.

'How can everyone be so upbeat, spending their free time cleaning up?' I ask.

Sam raises his eyebrows, 'We're not exactly happy cleaning, but it needs to be done so what can you do. And the party each month is what most of these people live on, feed their kids from - and it brings people to the dive schools.'

'You're a very glass half full person aren't you?' I ask in awe and wonder.

'I suppose so. But look where I live?' he says, arms stretched out looking around him, 'What's not to be happy about?'

Several hours later, Sam is taking me back to Koh Samui on the boat.

'I've been thinking' he says, 'you've got another couple of weeks out here, right?'

I nod in reply.

'Why don't you come and spent some time in Koh Tao? I think you'd really like it - it makes Samui seem like a major city in comparison. Come and live on a real remote island...where electricity is scarce and shoes are most certainly optional everywhere you go.'

'My family would love to meet you.' he adds.

'That sounds great, let me think about it.' I reply.

I'd love to go over and spend time with Sam but I'm not sure I could cope with watching happy families. There is nothing that makes you feel more alone than being an extra wheel in someone else's family or relationship. I wish I'd thought about this when I was with Pete, all those nights I dragged my single friends out on couple's dinners, no wonder they didn't want to join. Oh no, that's going to be me when I get back home.

I have visions of sitting at dinner tables with my friends and their 'really great work mate', awkwardly trying to make conversation whilst everyone is half chatting and half listening to you and your dating capabilities, living vicariously through your every move. Or worse still, going to one of those dinner parties and 'someone's Dave from the gym' doesn't even turn up and then I'm left sitting with that oh so conspicuous empty seat next to me which may as well have flashing arrows pointing to it saying I have been stood up.

'Please think about it Alice, here's my number.' Sam says.

I swear he looks a bit disappointed that I might not come. That's odd.

I tell him I will think about it.

CHAPTER 11

'Oh my Buddha, look what the bat dragged in.' Joe pulls a seat out for me and I slump into it.

I spend the afternoon with Joe playing a few games of chess, I'm actually starting to get the hang of it, and relay the events of the crazy full moon. He tells me not to worry about the breakdown with Sam, he's a good guy who's more than capable of dealing with a weeping woman., but suggests I should worry about the fact that I had a breakdown in the first place. He thinks I'm letting Samui pass me by in a blur of drunken nights, and perhaps it's taking its toll.

'I don't think you are upset about Pete anymore honey, you hardly mention him, well not until today now you've got that message. I think you're upset with yourself, you haven't seen and done as much as you wanted, haven't stretched yourself to do things on your own.'

I don't reply, I don't have to. I just keep playing chess, and Joe knows not to say anymore. Shit, this man really is like a guru, no wonder everyone chats to him and comes to him for advice. I think he's right, no one likes to admit they are disappointed in themselves but that is it - I'm surrounding myself with young party people because I'm scared to be on my own, scared to go out and do things by myself.

'Sam invited me over to Koh Tao.' I tell Joe.

'Yeah? You should go. It's a great island, Sam knows all the best spots. And he'll take you diving,' Joe says, 'that's on your list isn't it?'

'I'm thinking about it.' I reply feebly.

'Look here. I think it's time that you stopped moping about feeling sorry for yourself. There are so many things to do out here, and you have a nice guy offering to show you around. Do you want to go home and when everyone asks how Thailand was you can only tell them what the bottom of a bucket looked like? Or do you want to tell them about all the things you got up to, make them all jealous?'

'I know, it's just…' I start.

'It's just what? You need to pull yourself together.

I hate to say it but you're going to have to change if you don't want to regret what you've done in these few months somewhere down the line.' He hesitates, then adds, 'No one else can do it for you.'

'I think you just did Joe.' I smile.

And so, swiftly kicked into touch and in the spirit of being a strong independent woman, I decide to go to Koh Tao.

Right. Next adventure booked, two days in Koh Tao starting tomorrow. I don't want to be too presumptuous and demanding of Sam's time, so I'll send him a text but keep it light, he might be busy anyway, but it would be nice to say hello.

Hi, it's Alice. I've booked to stay in Koh Tao for two days. Arriving tomorrow so I'll pop by the dive centre and say hello.

I debated ending the message with a kiss. I put a kiss on all my messages to my friends, but I wasn't sure and don't want his wife to get the wrong impression, so after a very long deliberation, I dropped the 'x'.

I busy myself that afternoon with booking the ferry, buying a new bikini and getting a mani/pedi. Not that I am trying to impress, I tell myself, but Sam did say no one wears shoes so maybe everyone's feet are super pretty and the nail polish acts like shoes on that island.

Ding. A reply from Sam.

Great. I'll make some plans. See you tomorrow. Dolphin Dives is half way down Sairee Beach :)

A smile spreads across my face involuntarily as I read this reply. Such a nice guy. 'Make some plans'. I wonder what that means? Maybe we'll have dinner one night, me and his family perhaps, or maybe he means he'll arrange for me to go diving. Yes, he mentioned going diving, that's probably it. And what does that smiley face mean - I never quite understood them. I resist the urge to reply, don't want to be a nuisance before I've even arrived.

Having packed a small bag for the few days, I turn down another night out which Jamie text me about and lie low, relaxing in a coffeeshop and attempting to put some of Coconut Joe's words into action by starting this bloody self-help book, again.

CHAPTER 12

The ferry slows to pull into the pier at Koh Tao, huge rocks and wooden walkways line the shore with little thatched houses on stilts settled in between them. The water is an assortment of blues and greens and as the boat comes to a stop you can see the white sand at the bottom of the water, and schools of tiny fish zig zagging through it.

My hotel is about 0.5km from the pier according to the website, so with my small backpack on (another essential purchase from yesterday) I make my way on foot. The yellow brick road type path along the beach leads the way, through a plethora of dive centres. It's like being on the set of a dive movie, nothing but scuba centres, beach and cafes. No neon signs or built up areas, just rugged beach huts, eateries and strings of twinkly fairy lights which I guess light the footpath at night.

My hotel room would probably be described by

an estate agent as a 'cosy fixer upper'. In other words, it's tiny and I'm not convinced it was ever quite finished. It feels a bit like the builders and decorators got about eighty percent there and then thought, OK that'll do. But hey - I'm not here to sit in my room.

There's something quite 1970s about everything here. The internet, I'm informed by the hotel, is 'sometimes on, sometimes off', there is a torch in my room 'for the power cuts' they say, and shoes are to be kept outside.

Showered and bikinied up, I wander down to a beach cafe for a late breakfast and look out at all the fishermen's boats lining the shore in their bright colours. Even the boats look happy, beaming out in their bright blues, reds and greens. Their owners sleeping in hammocks strung up on palm trees, waiting for some tourists to set sail for the day with them.

As it is a 'sometimes on' moment in the cafe, I pull up a map of the beach on my phone and realise I am not too far from Dolphin Dives. Well I suppose I should pop by and say hello…

Flip flops in hand, I walk along the water's edge, just deep enough to lap around my ankles as I read the dive centre names looking for Sam's spot, and then he comes into sight.

I see Sam running in circles on the beach with two gorgeous little blonde toddlers chasing after him, giggling and screaming in delight. My heart swells. Mini - Sam's, they are exactly like him, and the laughter is infectious.

As I get closer, Sam sees me and stops running, 'You made it.' he shouts, 'Welcome to paradise.' he beams, arms stretched up to the sky.

'Hey, I reply, 'and who have we got here?' I smile looking at the two blonde tots.

'This is Ben and Amy, say hi to Alice guys.'

'Hi.' they reply shyly, followed swiftly by, 'Chase us, chase us' to Sam.

'Just a minute guys.' he says, they give him all of ten seconds.

'Sarah is at the supermarket, once she's back we're free to explore the island, we have no more dives this afternoon.' Sam says.

The kids are impatiently pulling on Sam's leg to continue their game of chase, so I join the tots in chasing Sam as we wait for their Mum's return. There's nothing like a child's laughter to make you smile. Sarah appears and the game is abandoned as Ben and Amy scuttle toward her tripping numerous times on the sand in their haste. Then the most adorable sand coloured dog runs up from the water to join the party. This, I'm told is Johnny Cash the family dog, who introduces himself to me with a huge watery shake before rolling over in the sand for a tummy rub. He's such a cutie with his floppy ear and little scarred forehead.

'Hi, you must be Alice. Nice to meet you, I'm Sarah. I see you've met the tiny terrors.' she laughs as they pull at her, collapsing her onto the sand.

We all chat for a while and after Sarah insists that I join them for dinner, Sam and I take to his scooter to explore the island. What a lovely woman, and not a jealous bone in her body. I'm not sure I'd have reacted as well as that if Pete invited some female stranger into our lives to go out and play with while I stayed at home with the kids. I guess she sees it as a favour to Old Joe, looking after one of his friends while they're in town. But still, she was as cool as a cucumber.

***

We wind up and down the hills on the bike, with Sam pointing out all his favourite views, cute little bars and cafes worth a visit and generally giving me the lowdown on the island. Eventually we pull into a hidden away beach bar where we have the place to ourselves, and a little bit of private beach without a soul on it either.

As we get off the bike Sam pops the seat and produces two snorkels and masks.

'I thought we'd have lunch then a snorkel, this is a great spot and with no one else here to disturb the water, we should see quite a lot.'

Over lunch, Sam lays out his ideas for the next few days and I can't believe how much effort he's put into this. He pulls out a list of things he thinks we could do, saying that after I'd told him at the Full Moon party I was fed up with men (I don't remember saying exactly that...) and disappointed with myself for not making the most of my trip so far, he thought he'd give us a head start to make the best of my time here.

This is the list Sam had:

Diving
Flying Trapeze
Snorkeling
Rock Climbing
Yoga
Thai Massage
Meditation
Learning Fire Staff
Long Boat trip
Kayaking
Paddle Boarding

Hiking to 'two views'
Fishing

'This is amazing Sam, I can't believe you have thought of all this.' I say. Although once again I can't help thinking about Sarah. WE will do this and WE will do that...

'Well, I thought we could plan it out, see what you want to do and make the most of your time here.' he replies, with a slight blush to his cheeks, 'I've arranged for you to go out on Tom's dive trip tomorrow as I have to do instructor training with Shona.'

Tom must be one of the instructors. That's a shame I'm absolutely bricking it about the diving and kinda hoped that Sam would be there to hold my hand.

'There will be a few beginners.' he adds seeing the look of panic on my face.

'Other than tomorrow afternoon though I'm about, so we can do whatever you like.'

'Well…right now I'd like to have some ice cream.' I say, giggling, 'Have you seen that sign?'

I point to the A-board that says, I kid you not:

Probably the best ice cream on the island

'Probably'. Well, I guess they get points for honesty and modesty, no false claims here. And well, a scoop of coconut and cookies and cream later, it probably is the best ice cream I've had in Thailand so far.

Hilarious - another one to send to Jamie.

Once we've digested the best ice cream on the island we get the fins on and masks at the ready and head out to the open water. Sam has shown me how to defog the mask, with a good old spit in there - how disgusting. I struggle to get the hang of breathing through the snorkel and after the fifth swallow of salty water I'm ready to throw in the towel. With the patience of a man who's spent a lot of time with toddlers, Sam guides me through. In fact, I'm mortified with myself, I behaved just like a snotty teenager all 'oh fuck it, I just can't get it, I'm not enjoying this, it's not for me.'

I never have been good at being the learner or the beginner when everyone else is breezing through. I wouldn't say I'm competitive, but, well, OK yes, I'm bloody competitive truth be told. With everything except ten pin bowling - I think that's possibly one of the only things I enjoy that I am absolutely rubbish at. I think I'm so consistently bad that it never occurs to me to get bothered by it. Would probably be worse if I had the occasional strike and then I'd be pissed off that I can't get them all the time. Nope, not a strike in my life even when I bowled with a snazzy bowling shirt on that I found in a vintage shop in Portobello Market.

Anyway, I'm not a patient learner, when I was thirteen I had my first and last golf lesson. As a family we had been to the golf putting range many times and it appeared I was a pretty good putter. So Dad took me for a golf lesson, and not being the immediate expert in my golf swing, well, the clubs ended up thrown further than I could hit the ball and after around thirty minutes of my lesson - the game was a bogey, golf became a thing of the past.

So, about one try before the mask and snorkel were going to be thrown away as far as the golf clubs had been, I finally got the hang of it. Gliding along the surface calmly and with ease as Sam points and guides me to look at the wonders of the water, watching the fish swim around carefree, rapidly changing direction, exploring the water themselves as if it's the first time they too have been there. Maybe it is, they do say a fish only has a three second memory so perhaps to them it always feels amazing and new. Wouldn't that be nice, imagine not ever having to worry about anything for longer than three seconds - we'd all be wrinkle free, not a forehead line or eyebrow furrow in sight, no pointless arguments, no feeling permanently guilty about things you have or haven't done, no regrets. Sam taps my leg to get my attention and points behind me, turning round I see electric blue and yellow little fish, there must be about three hundred of them, so close you can feel the swoosh of air as they pass.

'That was so amazing, and eh, thanks for sticking with me.' I tuck my chin to my shoulder in embarrassment, 'I can't believe I've never done that before.'

'It's pretty amazing eh, wait till you do the diving tomorrow with Tom.' he smiles, clearly pleased to have converted another person to understand his thirst for aquatic life.

There is something so satisfying in educating someone in something you love and them feeling the same. I feel that way every time I find a new band or restaurant and take people there - thoroughly disappointed if they don't agree that it's the best thing ever.

Although why is it that when you take someone to a restaurant that you've discovered that time they always seem to fuck it up. Or an amazing bar you've found and then you walk back in with your friends only to find this time it's filled with a completely different crowd or rude nutters and twatty bar staff. 'Honestly, it wasn't like this last time' seems to be a regular retort on these occasions to my friends who I'm sure begin to doubt my ability to identify the difference between good and shit.

It's pretty attractive seeing someone so passionate about something, the way Sam talks about the sea life, works with it, understands it, he positively shines when he is talking about all things fishy. An air of confidence, a comfort in his own being, and something that surely everyone wants - a sense of knowing exactly what makes you happy and being able to live it every day AND earn money doing it.

If only I could get paid to eat in nice restaurants, drink expensive wine and shop - I might have an understanding of that feeling. Throw in playing with dogs and cooking in Jamie Oliver's home kitchen as well and I reckon I'd be there.

We make our way back to the dive centre, which is attached to Sam's home, and as we're walking towards his beach home, someone shouts out to Sam so he tells me to go on ahead and join Sarah and the gang, he just needs to speak with one of the instructors. 'Hey Shona' I hear him say as I'm wandering away.

I make my way down the path but as I glance back I see that a gorgeous girl with not much on is running up to Sam with her arms out. Nosiness takes over and I hover out of sight and watch. I don't believe what I'm seeing, this Baywatch extra runs into Sam's arms and is sticking her tongue down his throat, full on snogging. What the fuck?!

CHAPTER 13

It looks like Sam is trying to shrug this beautiful limpet off, ineffectively, as she continues to cram her tongue into any orifice available to her here in the open daylight. Once the mouth is closed off to her she's jabbing it into his ears and pulling at his t-shirt. It looks like there's a little bit of coy begging going on from her too.

Well this is not on is it? And with Sarah less than fifty feet away. Not that it really matters how close or far she is, what the hell? Men really are bastards aren't they?

It's so blatant and open that I start to wonder if perhaps they have an open marriage. Jesus Christ if that's the case and he's invited me over... has he detailed out our list for the next few days and casually omitted to add shagging me behind his wife's back, or in front of her even? With her? Of dear god, this is unbelievable.

Men are such dickheads, and here's me thinking that Sam was one of the good ones. Instructor training tomorrow afternoon with Shona he said, I have a feeling it's more likely to be horizontal and in a bed than in the open water.

I cannot believe my eyes. In broad daylight she's pawing at him, trying to pull him towards her. He looks so uncomfortable, every time he removes one of her octopus arms the other tries to devour him. He turns to see if anyone is looking and I whip my head back around the corner out of sight.

I'm wondering whether to just do a runner back to my hotel, but I can smell the food that Sarah must be cooking for our dinner and feel so bad for this poor woman. Curiosity compels me to stick around for the evening, like a horror movie you just must continue to watch even if it is through your fingers to protect you from the full brutal image. I need to work out if she knows what's going on. If she doesn't you can be sure I'll be telling Sam exactly what I think of his antics.

I take a few deep breaths and head towards the front door.

'Hello?' I gingerly shout through the open front door.

'Hi, hi. Come on in.' I hear Sarah's voice from somewhere a room or so away.

I follow the smells through to the kitchen. 'Smells great.' I say politely, because all I can actually smell is a burning pan.

'Can I give you a hand?' I ask.

'No, not at all. The guys are out on the terrace, head on out and join them.' Sarah says.

'If you're sure.' I reply.

'Yep.' she says, handing me a glass of white wine.

Poor unsuspecting beautiful Sarah.

I wander out to the terrace and there is Sam playing lego with the twins. How the hell did he sneak in there so quickly. He looks up and smiles.

'Hi Al, don't mind me.' he chortles as he has his hands full with lego bricks holding up a makeshift bridge so the twins can drive their toy cars over it.

Don't mind me. Don't mind me. Don't mind what - that you just blatantly cheated on your wife with some scantily clad twenty something girl; that you sneaked round the back to play perfect daddy afterwards without having to show your guilty face to your wife? I didn't say any of this of course, I just stood on the spot.

I just stare at him in disbelief, as he looks back at me utterly confused. I bet you're confused, didn't think anyone saw you did you? You cheating shitty scumbag.

Just as I'm contemplating exactly what I'm going to say, I hear someone else coming up on the terrace. What now I think - is the Baywatch girl coming to join the weird orgie too?

'Ere, that Shona still won't leave me alone.'

I turn to see Sam standing behind me. And in front of me. What the hell is going on, is this a glitch in the matrix or something.

'All OK?' Sam No. 2 says, looking at my baffled face.

I just stare between them both, pointing and whipping my head back and forth.

'What the…' I start, but can't complete my sentence.

'What's up?' Sam No. 2 asks.

'There's, there are two of you...' I stutter pointing a finger at each of them.

'Yeah, did I not tell you Tom was my identical twin?' Sam No. 2, real Sam laughs.

'Daddy.' The kids whine, less than pleased that their chief bridge holder is no longer undertaking his important job.

'Daddy.' they're tugging again at his sleeves.

'These aren't your kids?' I turn to Sam utterly perplexed.

'Mine? God no.' Sam laughs at the absurdity of it all.

'Ere, sometimes we wish they were though, don't we love?' Tom ruffles Ben's hair and directs his question to Sarah who is walking into the room with a couple of plates of indeterminate description.

She pops the plates onto the table and looks around at us all.

'What's going on? You all look like you're trying to answer a maths question on University Challenge or something.' she laughs.

I put my hand to my forehead in an attempt to digest what's going on.

'What the fuck…' I mumble to myself with my hand to my forehead.

'Mummy, she said a bad word.' Amy says pointing to me.

'It's OK, love' Sarah replies, now perplexed by the situation too.

'Shit, sorry. I mean sorry. Sorry.' I shake myself.

'Al, isn't it?' Tom asks me, and I nod in confirmation.

He holds out his hand to shake mine, which I shake as if on autopilot.

'I'm Tom, Sarah's husband. These are our kids, Ben and Amy, and I am also Sam's brother, the better looking twin obviously.' he smiles.

'Nice to meet you.' he finishes and we all begin to laugh hysterically as I hide my face behind my hands in sheer agonising embarrassment.

Shitting hell.

'So you're not married?' I turn to Sam.

The hysterics continue as Sam replies 'No, I'm not married.'

So just to clarify, it appears that 'the kids' and 'the family' that Sam has been referring to are in fact, his twin brother Tom, Tom's wife Sarah, and THEIR kids Ben and Amy. Tom moved out to Koh Tao ten years ago and set up a dive school, and met Sarah out here. They found out they were having twins just over three years ago and were going to give it all up and move back to Cornwall, worried they wouldn't cope with both the business and the kids on their own. Sam was also a qualified dive instructor and was looking for a change so he said that he'd move out and give them a hand, see if the three of them could make it work. It turns out they could, and he's fallen in love with the place and the kids, so almost three years later here they all are, an alternative modern family (remember that tv series My Two Dads?).

My mind's in a tizzy, I swear he said he had a wife and kids, swear Joe had said that too. Why would they tell me that? As I think back, I recall 'the kids', 'the family' being bandied about. I suppose he never said MY kids, MY wife, but come on, what else would I think. Men. Bloody men. Even the ones you're not in a relationship with confuse the hell out of you with their lack of information and half bloody stories.

I don't know why this matters to me so much, but somehow it does, things seem a little different now, and my head's in such a muddle. I just nod and smile, still silenced by the news.

It's hardly as if him not being married makes a difference, or that I'm on the market for a new man, or that this stunner would be remotely interested in me. He's just being a nice guy, showing around a friend of Joe's. But I can't help a wave of elation overwhelm me at the thought that Sam is not married, very quickly met by another wave smashing into that thought which is, in that case who was the Baywatch extra then? He may not be married, but there is certainly something going on with young Shona from the dive school. Perhaps now is not the time to ask, enough revelations for one day. Besides, I'm not sure I'd like the answer.

> But he's not married.
> And he's not a cheater.
> And I can see what his children would look like.
> And now it's time to get a grip.

***

After we all calm down and the laughter has somewhat subsided we take a seat at the table.

'Alright my lover.' Sam jokingly puts his arm

around Sarah's shoulder giggling, 'what delights do you have for us then?' he asks as the final plates are placed on the table along with the big bowl of salad, which is the only identifiable thing there.

'Stop it.' I shriek with embarrassment, 'I'm never going to live this down am I?'

'I think there's a bit more mileage in it yet love.' Tom says playfully.

Sarah confirms that as well as the salad we have chicken, falafels and potato croquettes as the boys look at each other with raised eyebrows. It's just as well I'm not allergic to any of those things because I'm buggered if I know which is which, each with a similar burnt crust around them.

'So how long are you here for Al?' Sarah asks as she passes around the dishes for each of us to fill our plates from.

'In Thailand it will be two months in total, and here on Koh Tao until the day after tomorrow.'

'I've told her she should stay longer, explore the island.' Sam says to Sarah.

'Oh, you should,' Sarah says, 'there's so much to

do here, and we'd love to see more of you.'

Dinner with Sam's family was like being wrapped in a comfort blanket after being away for over a month either pissed in company or sober on my own. They have a huge farmer's cottage style table with log benches on their terrace looking out at the water. Ben and Amy are playing at the end of the table with their lego, while Johnny Cash is sitting underneath, not so patiently waiting for them to drop any part of their dinner.

The four of us adults are enjoying a bottle of red, a tentative pick at the ensemble of dishes gracing the table, a lot of friendly jokes at my expense, and discussing our plans for the next few days.

'I'm going to go to yoga tomorrow morning, I've been trying to get Sam to come but he's having none of it.' I laugh.

'I'd pay to see you in pink leggings Sam, you'd look gert lush.' Tom adds.

'Oh shut up.' Sarah says, holding back a giggle, 'You should go,' she says to Sam, 'lots of guys go to yoga nowadays.'

'I know they do,' Sam replies, 'new age hippies and hipsters, neither of which I am.'

'Ere, I have a new one for you.' Sam says, obviously changing the subject.

'Primates from the North Pole?' he says.

'Have you heard about this,' Sarah asks, 'these two are always testing each other on these funny cryptic band names.'

'Oh yes, I have actually. He does the same with Coconut Joe.' I reply.

'Must be a guy thing.' Sarah adds.

I smile in female solidarity, but secretly I'm desperately trying to get to the answer before Tom. I love quizzes, funny facts, all this stuff. North pole hmm. Santa something? Eskimo's? The Arctic? I start to feel the clogs turning, but not in time.

'Arctic Monkeys.' Tom shouts.

Bugger, I hate being beaten at these kinds of things. See, that damn competitive streak again. You know my own family won't play Monopoly with me.

'Do you know there is a festival somewhere here in Thailand where they put on a buffet and over 600 monkeys are invited to feast on two tonnes of grilled sausage, fruit and ice cream?' I say.

'Ice cream! Ice cream!' Ben shouts from the end of the table.

'I think you've got that wrong.' Sam says with a look that suggests I've lost the plot, as Tom nods along.

'Nope,' Sarah says looking it up on her phone, 'here it is, it's held each year in Lopburi. They think they know it all Al, it's nice to see them proved wrong' she high fives me.

Sam and I clear the table and do the washing up as Tom and Sarah get the kids to bed and we all return to the terrace for a coffee, where I realise that mocking Sam seems to be the family activity of choice. All good fun, like only the closest of family and friends can manage.

Sarah suggests that we meet for a coffee on the beach after my yoga, if I can deal with the terrible two joining she adds. Of course I can, the kids are adorable.

'That would be lovely.' I reply.

CHAPTER 14

Please don't fart, please don't fart. This is the all consuming thought throughout my one-hour beginners yoga class (beginners my arse), which has five people in it. An older couple, early 70s who are annoyingly more supple than I am, a hipster with a topknot and two girls in their 20s giving it a try for the first time who thankfully know about as many of the yoga moves as I do, that being none. I mean I've heard of the downward dog and the tree, but that's about it.

The teacher is a very hippy, dippy, quietly spoken woman in her 30s who you can't help but warm to. She has the body of Elle MacPherson and even manages to pull off pink and purple leopard print leggings. I'm not sure what I expected from my first yoga session (except that I was most likely going to do an almighty loud, embarrassing trump). The moves started with stretches which felt good, balancing which I could not do, and drifted in and out of the downward dog - a surprisingly difficult move when left in position too long, and even more painful when the teacher starts pulling your heels to the floor - can't she see that just isn't possible for my body otherwise I'd be doing it already?

So yoga - well you do feel well stretched afterwards, I can't say I found the link between mind and body they are talking about, unless she's talking about the fact that my mind knows that my body can't bend any more this way or that way than it is already. I have also realised that there is a reason everyone wears leggings when doing yoga. Note to self, doing a downward dog in shorts is the most depressing thing ever, all you can see is knees that look like they belong on a hundred and twenty-year old woman, all the skin gathered and hanging towards the floor. Eugh, I've never seen anything more repulsive. Never, ever look at your knees from that angle, I could not advise against it more strongly. The image is scarring.

'I've been there my friend.' Sarah smiles, 'Yoga pants all the way, it also hides the fact that our shins and knees sweat with the sheer agony of each twist and bend.'

'I know, who knew that your knees could sweat?' I reply.

Coffee with Sarah is a real tonic. The kids are happily playing in the sand with Johnny Cash who's also come along, leaving us girls to chat. This never happens when I catch up with my mummy friends back home. More often than not I leave coffee with them having not even achieved one conversation in its entirety, between them running to bring the little rascal back from the exit or lurching up to stop them knocking over someone's coffee, every conversation is left unfinished. Here, Sarah seems completely involved in the chat, a little look every now and again to make sure Ben and Amy haven't done a bunk but other than that very much present. Beach life seems the way forward if you have rug rats, or maybe it's having twins so they can entertain each other.

We chat about her life out here, and how grateful she is to Sam for coming out. That they would have had to head back to the UK otherwise, and she really didn't want to as they love their life out here (well who wouldn't) and they couldn't have borne to give up Johnny Cash. She says she would never have wished what happened to Sam to anyone but he seems OK now, like he's in the right place for the time being.

I don't know what Sarah is referring to, but I presume she thinks I do, so I don't want to make her feel awkward and ask questions. I wonder what happened, Sam seems so lovely, I don't like to think that something awful happened to him.

Sarah asks the usual 'what brought you out here' question, so I give her the whistle stop tour with all the key points on the Pete and Al saga.

'Wow. I wasn't expecting you to say that. How do you feel about it all now?' Sarah asks.

I take a sip of my coffee as I think about how to answer that. How do I feel about it now?

'I don't really know. I can't say that I've missed Pete all that much, he hasn't been in my head very much, but I am in a kind of false reality right now.'

I don't mention that Pete wants to talk when I get back. I'm not sure why, but I just don't really want to think about it, to acknowledge it. It took all my courage to break up with him and the thought of talking about it or going through it all again is unbearable.

'The prospect of going home though does fill me with dread. I just kind of put a bomb under everything I had - my man, my wedding, my home...and buggered off.' I add.

'Sounds like you've been brave.' Sarah says, 'Not many people have the balls, or the money and job to be able to do that, so if you can why not. No better way to get over someone than distance. I should know.'

'Really?' I ask, 'Sounds like there's a story there?'

It turns out that Sarah also ended up in Koh Tao to escape a man. Sarah and her ex had been living in London back in 2008 working as recruiters for the finance sector and cashing in on fairly tasty commissions on a monthly basis; then the big crash happened. An instant recruitment freeze and needless to say - no need for finance recruitment specialists for the time being. So they thought sod it, bought round the world tickets and backpacks and took off. The idea being a year out, then once the world had calmed down and headcount freezes had been lifted they would return to London. No one would question a year's gap on the CV at that time.

They started in India then moved on to Asia. They'd been working their way around South East Asia and were halfway through the Thailand part when it all went tits up. While in Koh Tao she found out that he'd been having a fling with her friend back home before they came away - information courtesy of Facebook. It seems her friend was still emailing him looking for him to come home so they could be together. Silly bastard left his computer on and a message popped up on the screen, Sarah saw the full thing in black and white.

'I didn't want to keep travelling with him and I didn't want to go home and be unemployed or face her. So I just stayed here. I'd been out diving one day, Tom was my instructor, and we went for a drink afterwards. I think he felt sorry for me when he heard my story, offered to put me through my dive instructor course so I could get a job until I knew what I wanted to do next. I didn't really need the money straight away but I did need a focus at the time, so I thought why not. That was 8 years ago.' she laughs at the memory of how it all started.

'Whatever happened to him?' I ask, referring to the scumbag cheating ex.

'My ex? He ended up with her when he went home. They got married pretty quickly and had a kid, a little girl I think, last I heard they're now separated. I would imagine one of them has successfully not kept it in their pants again.' she smiles.

'Funny how things turn out.' Sarah adds, 'Sometimes you need to hit a low before finding out what's right for you...anyway, there are worse places to end up with a broken heart.'

Yes there certainly are I think, looking at the views around me. White sand, turquoise waters, blazing sun, giggling children and not a frown in sight.

'Especially with Sam to keep you company…' Sarah smirks.

'Give over,' I sigh, 'that's the last thing I need. Besides, he's with Shona isn't he?'

Sarah raises her eyes, 'Bloody Shona, yeah. Poor

thing.'

'Poor thing?' I ask, curiosity killing me.

'She's a sweet enough girl.' Sarah says, 'Sam hooked up with her a few months back and she's been keen to turn it into something more ever since.'

'And, has she succeeded?' I ask, trying to sound as nonchalant as is humanly possible, just a normal follow up question. All the while thinking 'please say no, please say no'.

'I think there's been the odd night. He thinks it's nothing, but he doesn't really get that she's a young girl who's taking it much more seriously than he is. I told him to be careful, that friends with benefits tends to mean different things to different people.'

I nod sympathetically, remembering how easy it was at that age to believe that someone wanted to be with you, even if all the warning signs were there, flashing and honking 'this is not going to end well'.

'Anyway,' Sarah says, 'I try to stay out of it. It's easier that way.' She shrugs, 'Now, don't you have to get back for you dive?'

***

That evening after my dive, Tom, Sam and I head to a bar where all the dive instructors hangout. It's got a great Cheers feel - everyone knows everyone, all just enjoying an après dive beer. Tom introduces me to his instructors, including Shona. I was pretty curious to meet her after the update Sarah gave me on the situation. Also, with Sam being so nice and not to mention pretty hot, I imagine he'd have his pick so I wanted to see this Baywatch babe up close.

The girls are all between 20 -25, dressed in denim non-cheek covering hot pants and playing the role of cool, relaxed surfer / dive chicks. I say playing a role as I don't get the impression they are quite as relaxed and comfortable as they are trying to appear amongst the men, who are much wider in age range. I start to get an understanding of what Sarah was implying, which is that I think there is a side dish of insecurity with this girl, and perhaps deep down a not so chilled out attitude when it comes to her relationship with Sam.

For the first time in weeks, I feel like I'm experiencing what the locals who live here do. There are loads of tourist and backpacker bars nearby, but this bar is a little bit tucked away off the main street, a place for the instructors and locals to call their own. Everyone is really welcoming, with the exception of Shona who is a little cold with me. It's like a family, a community which I guess is important when you're living abroad on your own, not everyone has actual family around them like Sam, Tom and Sarah do.

I think about my life back in London, I suppose it's slightly similar. At least, it was. My little community has been shattered into smithereens now. I'll always have Gail and Lisa, but the large group that is Pete and my mutual friends plus friends we have gathered along with way, what happens there? Do we have to share them, do they pick sides, or do we have to all awkwardly gather and then share pleasantries for the rest of our lives?

'So how long are you here for?' Shona asks, cutting into my thoughts.

'Eh, I go back to Samui tomorrow, then home in a few weeks.' I reply.

'I think you should stay here for the next few weeks. Sarah thinks so too.' Sam suddenly appears from behind my shoulder.

Sipping her cocktail, I notice Shona's eyes popping and lips pursing tighter at the mention of this. I feel overwhelmingly guilty at Sam's words. Or perhaps more so because they make me feel so damn good. He wants me to stay longer.

I know men say they don't get us, but I don't understand some girls either. This girl is half my size, has hair that obviously likes the sun unlike my frizz bomb, is most certainly the centre of attention and gets desirous looks from every man who passes her, yet she seems to resent my presence, uncertain of my being here, and nervous of me.

She's the one shagging Sam for god's sake. The joys of your early twenties I think. No idea that you have it all except the important bit - confidence and self esteem. Constantly craving attention and affirmation, jealous of every other female.

Mind you, you have just as many things to worry about in your thirties, they just happen to be different things. But thankfully the majority of the worries you had in your twenties have been and gone. No, your thirties are a different kind of concern. Just as you stop caring about the size of your boobs or the shape of your nose, you care about the wrinkles on your face or the porridge creeping onto your thighs. You care about your body clock ticking, and wonder - is this really it? Working away and living for these twenty odd days holiday a year?

Shona wraps a possessive arm around Sam and asks him if he is going back to hers tonight. Sam explains that they are due out on an early morning dive the next day but a storm may be coming so he will need to be up and out early with Tom to see how the land lies.

I look away in embarrassment at being present for

this conversation and then head towards the bar for a timely top up. I notice that Shona is giving Sam what looks like a talking to quickly followed by pussy cat eyes trying to make him change his mind.

Why is it so difficult for men to tell it like it is? Perhaps Sam does have to be up and out first thing, but going by what Sarah has told me and my observation of Sam batting away her spaghetti arms it seems more like a fob off. I mean what red blooded man turns down a night of sex because he has to get up early in the morning? None that I know, except for my ex-fiancé which does nothing to disprove my theory that if a man makes excuses about having sex with you - it ain't gonna to turn out well.

It angers me that Sam is possibly leading Shona on, angers me that Pete did the same thing to me for so long. I need to stop comparing them as it's completely different and I do know that on occasions men do tell it like it is and us females choose to hear something different. But this is touching a slightly delicate nerve for me.

I can see Shona glaring at me as if I'm to blame for all this, and I can see her point to be fair. This person turns up out of the blue and is spending all this time with 'her man'. One would not be amused. I feel like telling her she's one of the most beautiful woman I've ever seen, that she should let men chase her rather than the other way around. There must be at least a hundred deserving hunks who'd treat her like a queen for the chance to be with her, but I don't think she really wants to hear that from me. And who am I kidding, I would never have listened to the bossy bird sounding off to me about understanding the world better when you're older. I'd have told them to piss off and go home to their middle age life. Well maybe not, but you get my point.

    Funny, ten or so years ago I was jealous of so many of the girls around me, never stopping to think perhaps I should admire them, or learn from them instead. Strangely, it wasn't generally the girl with the longest legs or the prettiest face that I envied. It was all about confidence. Someone with a wacky wardrobe who would wear whatever they liked; or who made people laugh and feel special at the drop of a hat; someone who seemed so relaxed they could talk to anyone, never questioning themselves. Now that's the stuff that makes people sexy, men and women.

CHAPTER 15

Early the next morning I am jolted awake by a hammering at my door. What the hell? It takes a moment to compute it's a thunderstorm. Jesus, the rain is so loud it sounds like I'm sitting in a tent under the world's strongest tap. This is a proper tropical storm. As I open the hotel room door I see that the ground is inches deep in water, at least I think it is, I can hardly see a thing, the sky is dark gray and there is no electricity to turn on the lights. I climb back into bed, no longer scared but quietly enjoying the pelter of the rain; my only companion in this internet, light and TV free moment. I do love the sound of a thunderstorm, there's something quite romantic about it.

The storm kind of helps out on the 'should I stay longer or go' dilemma that's been going on in my head since last night. I might love a thunderstorm but not when it means me rocking about on a boat in the open water for a couple of hours. I'll stay another day at least, who knows maybe this is a sign? Hmm...old Joe did tell me to look out for the signs, follow them and you'll smile again he said. Maybe I'm meant to be here, to spend time on this island. Well, let's hope so as it doesn't look like I could get off even if I wanted to.

As the morning goes on, the rain doesn't cease, it's blasting down stronger than ever as I sit on the little terrace looking out. Not a person in sight. That is, until I see someone sloshing down the little track running between the hotel rooms. Who is this nutcase out in this? Then they get closer and make a splashing, dashing jump into my terrace for cover. Peeling off the yellow bin bag type rain mac that's stuck to their face, I realise it's Sam.

'Bloody hell Sam, what you doing out in this?' I say.

'I've come to get you. Sarah insisted, said you should come to ours.'

'You're absolutely drenched.'

'I know.' he says, peeling off the layers down to just his swimming shorts. Oh my, how I wish this was my sign. It's like something from a Calvin Klein ad, these wet abs, floppy hair all soaked, flicking his head to shake the excess water off.

'I don't know why I bothered with the clothes.' he

says.

Nor do I.

'Pack your bag, put on your bikini and we'll make a run for the truck.'

Sam says all this with such an air of command that I don't even question it. I just start packing.

'My bikini, really?'

'You may as well.' he laughs.

Once packed up, which didn't take long as I don't have much with me, Sam takes my bag and in our togs we make a run for it. Splashing through puddles and stumbling on the uneven ground below that we can no longer see, Sam grabs my hand and leads the way.

We climb into the truck and I have a fit of the giggles, looking down at myself drenched from head to toe, in my bikini. I'm shivering with the cold, or maybe it's with excitement, I'm not too sure.

'Come in, come in.' Sarah ushers us in with big fluffy towels ready to engulf us as we arrive.

'Thank you.' I smile as I wrap myself up, 'This is unbelievable isn't it?'

'It's pretty bad, even for here.' she says, 'Ben, Amy - get in here, you'll catch your death.' she screams, the kids desperate to go out bare foot and splash about in the rain.

'Now, cup of tea? Coffee? Something to warm you up?'

'Oh yes, coffee please. Have you got electricity then?'

'We have a generator for the business.' Sarah replies.

Sam rejoins us in the kitchen, 'I've put your bag in the guest room. The bathroom is over there if you want a warm shower.'

'Thanks, I will if you don't mind.'

As I'm in the shower I realise that the bathroom window is open and faces straight onto the terrace were Sarah is playing with the children, who are far from scared of the thunderstorms but are desperately trying to get down the steps to splash on the wet sand. Then I overhear a conversation.

'Will you ask Al to stay on?' Sam says to Sarah.

'Of course, I think she's lovely, but why don't you ask her yourself?' Sarah replies.

'I don't want her to get the wrong idea.' Sam says.

'What do you mean?' Sarah continues.

'Well that I have an ulterior motive?' he says.

'But you do, don't you?' Sarah says in what sounds like a confused manner.

'She says she's had it with men. So, for now no, I don't. But I just want the chance to...'

Straining to hear above the rain and the shower, I grasp onto the shower curtain, raised on tiptoes, stretching my neck so my ears are as close to the open window as I can, until, oh shit. Crash. Bang. Wallop.

'You OK in there?' Tom shouts from the other side of the bathroom door.

'Eh, yep, fine thanks, just slipped.'

And then silence from outside. What did Sam mean? What does he just want the chance to do? What does he want the chance to say?

I guess he doesn't want me to think he fancies

me, well I know that, I have seen Shona, and he's given me no reason to think differently.

But why does he want me to stay? I know we seem to get on well, but Sam's got lots of friends out here, and family. It's not like he needs the company.

Perhaps he feels sorry for me or thinks I might drift back to being the broken woman he found in Koh Phangan if he doesn't keep me on the straight and narrow. Yes, that's probably it, Sam, the Patron Saint of Messed Up Chicks, he just wants the chance to make sure I'm alright.

Feeling refreshed from the shower, yet flustered from my fall and earwigged knowledge, I join the others on the terrace and enjoy my coffee.

'I don't think any boats will be leaving today. Why don't you stay with us here for a few days, at least while the weather is like this.' Sarah says.

'I don't want to put you out. I can extend my stay at the hotel until the weather clears.' I reply.

'Nonsense.' Sarah says, and before I can protest she adds, 'We have a spare room…' she gazes over at Sam then back, 'to be honest, I could do with a hand with the kids if you wouldn't mind? They're a nightmare to entertain when we're stuck indoors and they've really taken to you.'

How can I say no to that?

***

I took them up on their offer and spent the next couple of days at the house. If Sarah thought it would help her and it meant that I was guaranteed some electricity for a hot shower each day, then I was in. They already made it clear that they wouldn't take any money so I did have one condition. I must be allowed to cook everyone dinner each night to say thanks. Tom and Sam burst into laughter.

'You can stay forever if you cook for us.' Tom said.

I was desperate for a chance to go to the food markets and have a kitchen to play around in, and to be frank, I don't think I could have handled another couple of nights of Sarah's cooking.

In the last few days I've slotted into this family like a glove that's found its missing partner. I've helped with the kids, cooked the dinners and Sam and I have looked after the kids for a full day to allow Tom and Sarah to have some time to themselves since there are no dive tours running.

After three days the storm is starting to clear, so I make noises that I should think about heading back to Samui.

'Why?' Sarah asks.

'Aren't you happy here?' Sam asks.

Wow. What a loaded question. Am I happy? I'm over the bloody moon. I am surrounded by people who are on exactly the same wavelength as me. I feel for the first time during this trip that I have a purpose, that I'm needed and useful; and that in itself is giving me the energy to make the best of my days. I've been running along the beach in the mornings, helping with the kids, spending the afternoons at food markets planning out the meal for the evening and then the nighttime is my favourite - the four of us plus the little ones sitting around the dinner table.

'Yes, I'm very happy here. You've all been so lovely opening up your house to me. But it's your home, I've already overstayed my welcome. What is it they say "houseguests are like fish, they start to smell after three days".'

'But you're not like a guest, you're like part of the family.' Sam replies.

Sarah nods her agreement and touches my arm,

'and I'll say it because no one else will. We want you to feed us.' she laughs, 'No one wants to go back to my horrible meals just yet.'

I laugh along as an inner debate goes on in my mind. I do love being here but 1) I do feel like I've just burst in on their lives and really should be moving on and 2) the more time I spend with Sam, the more I'm starting to really like him, and the sensible part of me knows that can't be good.

'Ere,' Tom says, 'Sam - think up one of those band clues. If I get it before Al then I get to keep her here as our personal chef for a few more weeks.'

I love a puzzle, love a competition. But more than that, I'd really like to stay on here, I just don't want to be the one to decide it. These guys are so nice, what if they were just being polite and here I am three weeks on driving them up the wall.

'Personal chef?' I joke, 'OK, challenge accepted. You're on.'

'OK, let me think.' Sam rubs his chin and looks at me.

'I need to try my best to think of one you'll never get and Tom will.' Sam winks at me.

Over the last few days Tom and I have been fairly even stevens on working these out.

'Right, think quick,' Sam stares at Tom, 'use some of that twin telepathy.'

They both joke about pushing their hand,s in their temples and making buzzing noises.

'What a load of bollocks,' I flick Sam on the shoulder, 'get on with it.'

I needed him to get on with it, my head was frazzled not knowing if I was going to be staying or going.

'Too many occupants in one dwelling?' Sam asks.

Oh, has he changed his mind. Maybe he's right, too many of us in one house. Well, that's fair enough, perhaps it's best I just head back anyway. I'd rather know that now than stay on and feel awkward later.

'Boom. Crowded Bloody House.' Tom shouts.

'Don't swear daddy.' Amy shouts.

'Sorry sweetie,' he replies, 'but it's worth it. Now you can grow big and tall over the next few weeks with Auntie Al's beautiful dinners.'

To which we all laugh and they all cheer. I cheer too, it's just that mine is silently.

It's so heartwarming to be wanted this much. I've never felt this sought after, needed and as much as we're basing our open discussion around the cooking I know it's more.

Sam and I are building a really special friendship, we just get each other and Sarah and I, we're like long lost childhood friends.

Turns out as much as Sarah loves her life out here, she is a bit lonely being in the house all day with mainly the kids for company, never finding time to clean the house uninterrupted, having to cook food she knows turns out to be awful for the working lads every evening. We struck a deal on me staying, as they wouldn't take any rent. I give Sarah a few hours a day to herself by looking after the little uns, we share the cleaning and I do the cooking.

Over those weeks we get right into the rhythm of things. I think Sarah is delighted to have another woman in the house, and in her life. She tells me that it's such a treat to have me here. I think she has been craving a woman's friendship, not that she doesn't have any friends out here, she's a genuinely fun person, who's very kind and everybody loves, but I get the impression she doesn't have anyone who can replace the relationships she probably has back home, her long term friends. The guys are wonderful, but let's face it, you have a different kind of time hanging out with guys than you do women, no matter how close you are to them. Then there are the dive instructor girls, nice enough, but Sarah is so different from them now, gone are the days of chasing men, downing tequila and prancing around in bikinis...and like me and my backpacker friends, there's just too much of a difference in the stage of life for a real meaningful day to day friendship. Someone you can confide in, as well as have a laugh with, someone you can cry to and ask for help from. Sarah and I just clicked, there's an immediate bond there, and I think given our past situations we both see a little bit of ourselves in each other. Sarah seeing the past situation she was in, and me, I guess I hope for things to be as wonderful for me as they have turned out for Sarah.

We quickly get into a routine. In the mornings, I entertain the kids for an hour or so to give Sarah sometime to herself. She goes to yoga or for a walk, reads a book in a coffee shop, anything really but something just for herself, by herself. Thankfully Ben and Amy have warmed to me so whether I'm on my own or with Sam or Tom, it tends to be tantrum free. We play in the pool, build sandcastles, draw and paint, and it's really lovely. Don't get me wrong, it's also a delight to hand them back, after all, that's the best thing about other people's children isn't it - enjoy the moment and then enjoy handing them back. Actually, it's exhausting if nothing else, no wonder Sarah is so happy for the break. I really don't think they could cope out here without Sam.

I've always thought that I'd have children, but have never been one to get broody or anything. It's more that I see myself as a grown up with a grown up family and grandchildren than seeing myself as a mother with a crying, shitting baby (incidentally, these guys have been potty trained thank god), but the more time I spend with these tots, the more I understand how it can become all consuming. I realise this is something I really want. 'Well, you better get a move on' I can hear my mother chirping in my ear.

Maybe it's a sign. Maybe that's why I was meant to spend time with this family, with Ben and Amy, to remind me that my biological clock is ticking, to show me the joys of family life. Dear god, is it meant to be a sign that I've made a mistake throwing everything away?

Pete and I never did discuss having children. I guess I thought that would come a little while after the wedding, but who knows, maybe he would have never wanted kids. Come to think of it, for people who were about to say yes to spending the rest of their lives together, we didn't really know much about what each other wanted. How does that happen?

So the mornings are spent around the house, or on the beach with the kids and then in the afternoon I head out and take in the island and all it has to offer. I have rented a scooter to get about and sometimes I head out on my own and sometimes Sam joins me but I'm making my way through the list Sam put together and I'm starting to feel like this is what this trip was meant to be all about. Next up, the Thai cooking lesson and Sam is going to join me. I can't help but feel relieved that at least one person in that household will be able to continue feeding the family once I've gone.

CHAPTER 16

We didn't have to travel far for our cooking lesson. There's a cafe area in the dive centre which they use to do the training, it has a fully working kitchen that's never been used. What a waste, that's like sacrilege to me. I didn't know this was here or I might have been a bit more extravagant with my evening meal choices.

Sam has arranged for Ghan to come and give us a private lesson. I tried to rope Sarah into joining us, but she was having none of it. I'm too busy she said winking at me. Now, if there's anyone who is all for Sam and me moving our relationship on, it's Sarah. She tells me on a daily basis she doesn't get why we've not hooked up yet. Give me a break I think.

Get over by getting under they say. I can't pretend my downstairs doesn't start singing 'hallelujah' every time I see Sam with his top off or as the muscles in his arms bulge when he carts all the heavy scuba tanks from the boat back to the centre each afternoon.

The problems here are plentiful however: I don't think I could see Sam as just rebound sex; he seems to have at least one other girl on the go; it's been so long since I put any effort into sex I'm not sure I still know how to do it with any pzazz; what if it all goes wrong and I'm living here; and more importantly, what if he doesn't want to.

I can feel a new electricity between us, the spark is definitely growing but let's face it, my judgement with Pete wasn't exactly spot on so maybe I'm wrong again here. Maybe he just sees me as a platonic buddy. Not to mention the last person (or at least I think the last person) to bump uglies with him was Baywatch babe Shona. That's like asking me to sing karaoke after Beyonce has just finished a song.

So back to the cooking lesson I've brought the pestle and mortar with me which Coconut Joe gave me, ever hopeful it will bring me some of his Thai cooking flair. The tables are laden with bags of exotic roots, spices, vegetables and seafood that Ghan has brought with her. The smell of it all together is somewhat pungent, you can almost taste the food already just from the fragrance of the lemongrass, kaffir lime and holy basil.

We start making a paste for a green curry by adding a million different ingredients to our mortar bowls and grinding away. It's bloody hard work turning all the roots an powders into a paste, especially when you're competing to get your paste done before Sam (shamefully and relentlessly competitive I am).

Sam has a look of serious concentration on his face as he grinds away, those arm muscles popping again with the intensity he is putting into it.

'What?' he looks up at me staring at him, 'Am I doing something wrong?'

'No, no.' I reply with a soft smile on my face, 'I was just watching your "oh so intense concentration face".'

He raises his eyebrows 'I hope it's not like seeing someone's awful shagging face.'

I'm so shocked I smack him on the arm, it's an automatic reaction, and perhaps a deflection in case he realises that was exactly what had been going through my mind.

'Sorry Ghan, paste done. What next?' I ask her, trying to get my head out of the gutter and back into the cooking class.

'This is where we turn curry green.' she says, 'With this.'

Ghan shows us how to strain the leaves to make a green liquid to be added to the pan with the paste.

'Careful,' Ghan adds, 'this green, it stain. You must wash hands quick or it stay for long time.'

I add the paste and green concoction to the wok and with the little green liquid that I have left over I can't resist and flick it in Sam's face.

'Oi.' he shrieks, 'Didn't you hear, this green stuff stay with you long time' as he grabs a pot of saffron and pinch flicks it at my face, leaving a delightful yellow streak running across my forehead.

After a stern look from Ghan we continue cooking, suppressing a fit of laughter that's taking over both of us.

'Ere, how about this one - Cinnamon Maidens?' Sam asks.

'Zig a zig ah…that, dear friend, would be the Spice Girls.' I clap at my quick achievement and flick some more green liquid at Sam for good measure.

We made another three dishes over the next hour or so, but really we were just using it as an excuse to find more colourful spices to throw at each other. By the time the cooking lesson came to an end both Sam and I looked like tribal warriors, smeared from head to toe in oranges, greens, reds and yellows.

'I give up.' Ghan held her hands up dramatically and laughed once we had finished the final dish. 'Happy this kitchen not mine.' she added.

We thanked her graciously and apologised profusely for behaving like children.

'No problem.' she said, 'Honeymoon, is it?'

'No, no, we're not together.' I replied.

Ghan just threw her head back with laughter and walked out the door.

'What a bloody mess we've made.' I look around the kitchen and it looks like a paint bomb has exploded in the middle of the cafe.

'We look like something from an African tribe.' Sam says.

'Give me your best war cry then?' I taunt him.

'Aoow-ee-ah-ee-aaow.' he shouts whilst beating his chest.

'Absolutely pathetic, this is how you do it – FFFFRRRREEEEEDDDDOOOOMM' I scream in my best Scottish accent as I make a break from the kitchen and throw my hands in the air charging towards the sea.

Sam chases after me with a much more acceptable Tarzan style war cry waving his right arm as if he's chasing me with a spear like a madman.

The water is amazing after the hot and steamy kitchen and I sink myself under the waves to cleanse my skin of the pungent spices.

'Thanks Sam, that was really fun. I would have kicked myself if I got back home and hadn't done a cooking lesson.' I say gently.

'Your welcome.' he looks at me intensely.

'What? What is it?' I ask, 'What are you staring at?'

He moves towards me and puts his left hand to my face, cupping my cheek gently. Oh dear god the feel of his fingertips grazing my face like this sends shivers down my spine. My nipples standing to attention under the water wondering what is going to happen next, as I hold my breath in anticipation.

'Hey, hey.' Tom shouts, and we turn to see that the dive boat is making its way back in from a tour. Tom, Shona and a handful of guests are there.

Sam still has his hand on my face, but the mood has changed now. What was he going to do, what was going to happen?

'You've missed a bit.' he says as he rubs a large streak of green from my cheekbone.

'Oh, thanks.' I say, dunking myself under the water to avoid his gaze. I can feel myself flustered and blushing and I need the water to cool me down with immediate effect, wash away my embarrassment and humiliation. Every part of my body thought he was going to kiss me, my loins jerking forward like they are in a race, eagerly awaiting the starter pistol.

'I, eh, should give them a hand with the scuba gear.' Sam says.

'Sure, and I'm going to clean up the kitchen before I head off to give the boxing a try.' I add.

I was glad to be cleaning up the kitchen alone as I was so confused I couldn't bear to be in company. What am I doing, here I am thinking that Sam is about to kiss me and not only does he not kiss me he, 1) clears some muck off my face like I'm a child and 2) is interrupted from clearing said muck by Shona, who I seem to forget he has a thing going on with. I feel like we are growing closer and closer but perhaps I'm misreading things, mistaking friendship for flirting.

One thing's for sure though, talk about pent up sexual frustration, I think I'll be able to knock the living day lights out of a punch bag tonight.

***

My first thought on arriving is relief that I'm not the only female there, there were around six other girls, and blow me if three of them didn't have red and pink manicured nails...I was tempted by the prospect of another ridiculously cheap manicure and pedicure yesterday but thought I'd look out of place at the boxing.

After purchasing my gloves and silky baggy unflattering muay thai boxing shorts the bell dings for us to start running up and down the side road with a slight incline. Run might be a bit of an exaggeration here, I sluggishly slogged up and down the road with the trainers shouting 'faster' at me, but at least they were doing this while chuckling. I was sweating like you wouldn't believe, every orifice was dripping, I didn't even know it was possible to be this wet without being in a shower.

After this we were given two minutes to drink

water and don the hand wraps - I'm not so pleased at this point that I've chosen to purchase a bright pink pair...you've got to be really good to carry those off I start to think. Chatting with the other girls while the trainers wrap our hands it's disturbing to discover that the others have all been doing boxing training in their own countries around the world...oh dear.

Then comes a forty-minute session of stretches and what is probably best described as boxercise mixed in with shadow boxing. Shadow boxing? I look around and everyone is practising their moves, and expertly dancing around the large space while I nervously look around and throw the odd pathetic punch. A long haired amused trainer called Noi comes to my rescue, providing his hands as a punch bag for me.

Next up, 'hit the floor and give me 20 push up'. Er, OK. So I get into position (knees on floor option) and give it everything, all the while Noi is kicking my elbows inwards, that being the much harder position to do push ups, which is not that easy when you have a pair of large breasts sitting where the trainer wants my elbows to be. I manage 14 and collapse, as Noi continues to laugh at me.

We work in partners for a while practising routines of punches and kicks and then I hear my name - I've been summoned. With trepidation, and soaked through with sweat, I grab my bottle of water and head towards the four rings where Noi is waving me towards him.

'First day here?' he asks.

'First day ever boxing.' I reply.

I'd like to tell you he takes it easy with me after this, but alas again he finds this exceptionally entertaining and has me dancing around the ring, showing me how to kick and punch and elbow for three minutes at a time. There is a minute break between rounds but that's taken up with doing ten sit ups, or push ups - so actually there is about thirty seconds to hang yourself over the ropes in sheer exhaustion before the bell dings and you're back up repeating this another three times.

I literally fall out of the ring clasping my bottle of water and stumble back towards the rest of the group in the main foam floored area where I'm then kicking the hell out of a punch bag to the loud shout of 1 to 10 keeping us in sync. Every now and again I glance around to check that everyone is going through the same pain and torture. The sympathetic look on their faces assures me that they have all been there and remember it well.

With fifteen minutes to go before the two-hour session ends I feel invigorated, I only have a short while to go - this must be coming up to the stretching right? Well yes it is, but not before doing a hundred v sits, a hundred push kicks and a hundred jumping knee movements.

'Are you coming back tomorrow morning?' Noi asks me.

Is this man kidding? It's doubtful I'll be able to walk tomorrow morning.

CHAPTER 17

I did end up with purple knees and shins within hours of the class finishing, and this morning I made John Wayne look like he's strutting down a catwalk but it was so thrilling, and the instant gratification makes it all worthwhile, a sign that you've worked hard. Honestly, I feel so powerful, roll on the next bastard who tries to nick my handbag on the streets of London, I reckon I could kick the shit out of them. Well, not quite but after a few more sessions for sure.

And to force myself to stick to it, I purchase a set of ten sessions. Move over Mike Tyson, here I come (hopefully without the arrests and ear biting that is). I'm no stranger to the latest fitness fad truth be told; zumba - lasted three weeks (the classes were at 10 o'clock on a Saturday morning); hula hooping (there's only so much you can learn before it's boring), line dancing (no I'm not kidding, one of the girls at work decided she wanted to find herself a cowboy), Pilates.

Nothing seems to stick. I did enjoy them all, but I guess it goes back to the whole golf thing, being a beginner at something just kind of sucks. Let's face it, when time is tight and you have a choice between exercise, meetings friends for dinner and lounging in front of the telly with the other half, the internal debate doesn't last long, the latter two win out. Until something else comes along for a short while and the cycle starts again, at least that's how it works with me. But out here I have loads of time, and there's nothing else to distract me. I can probably continue at home too, not that much going on there I'll be rushing home from work for now, so I may as well attempt to get those side tummy lines everyone in class had.

***

After a few weeks in Koh Phangan the Bangkok / Samui gang came over to Koh Tao for the next stage of their island hop tour. I've arranged for them all to go diving with Sam and Tom tomorrow and said that I'll take them out and show them around this evening.

Sam asked me what I reckon they'd like to do so he could give me some idea on the best places to take them. So I told him the Cheeky Girls like glitz and glamour; Kristian, Gavin, Jamie and Theo like to go somewhere the locals go, immerse themselves in the culture and Good Will Hunting likes anywhere he can take his top off and be very outlandishly American.

Sam seems to find it hilarious that I have all these nicknames for the people I've met on the trip so far. Ah finally, a fellow Brit who understands and appreciates my humour and the love we all have for a funny, non-mean nickname. He gets that it's actually quite a compliment. Not tht he knows his nickname is Patrick Swayze, or that Swayze took pride of place on a poster above my bed as a young teenager for at least two years.

With Sam's help, we settle on meeting in a pretty cool beach cocktail bar for drinks (keeping the Cheeky Girls happy), then head to a little local restaurant where they do the best Thai and Burmese food; it has the added bonus of being called Pee and Poo restaurant which I thought Jamie would appreciate for her photo collection, and then we'll head to another beach bar that has the best fire show on the island and a chance to take part in fire limbo and fire shot drinking to keep Good Will Hunting happy.

Sam was hesitant to join for the night, feeling he should leave me to it with my friends, but I managed to talk him round. I really wanted Sam to meet these people I've shared great times with, especially my time in Bangkok so he realises there has at least been some part to my pre-Sam trip that involved a bit of sightseeing and non booze related fun. I've also been emailing back and forth with Jamie, and I know that she's desperate to meet

Sam too.

The only experience Sam has had with some of these guys before is seeing the Cheeky Girls throw up at the Full Moon Party, and Kristian taking them home. Oh god, I think I told him that night that I'd snogged Good Will Hunting. Cringe. I guess he knows that they like a drink and a good night out too as I've told him that I was pretty much a piss head whilst I was hanging out with them.

I'm slightly nervous about bringing these two worlds together as I'm not overly happy with how I behaved during that first month. I didn't really do anything in particular wrong, more that I didn't really behave like a proper grown up, and I think Sam will see that these guys can be a bit immature and studenty at times. I have a chat with Sam to try to express this, and he just laughs at me. He asks if I've forgotten that he was there that night of the Full Moon and we've already talked about all this, he also adds that he hangs out with the dive instructors most of the time. We're all allowed to have different kinds of friends he says, that's what makes life interesting. And with that, I feel awful for painting such a bad picture of these really lovely, good hearted, fun people, who are behaving exactly as they should be at their age travelling the world, not to mention taking me, the old chick, under their wing. In fact, I was the only one not acting my age.

We begin the night with drinks on the bean bags in one of Koh Tao's few fancy cocktail bars. I've introduced Sam to everyone and he's chatting away with them, finding out about their travels so far, where they're off to next. Theo tells us that he joined a retreat in Koh Phangan where he was doing daily meditation, yoga and a six-day detox with colonics (too much information). He described the experience as something that 'cultivates a life that fosters awakening and supports inner growth'. Yes, seriously that's what he said - do you think he's committed their marketing slogan to memory perhaps? He's very nice but why can't he just explain things normally.

Later, Jamie and I are having a catch up slightly to the side, with Jamie wanting to know how I'm feeling about everything now and how on earth I got jammy enough to move in with Sam. She says she's delighted to see me looking so healthy and happy, and says that whatever I'm doing right now keep doing it, because I seem calm, collected and glowing. I do feel a million miles away from where I was back at the Full Moon Party, there really is no substitute for clean healthy living and making the most of life by trying new things.

Jamie wants to know how long Sam and I have been 'hooking up' for and struggles to believe that it's not the case. She says you can see a mile off that there's something between us, the way he looks at me, the way we joke about. Well I set her straight anyway, telling her about Shona who he really is hooking up with.

'I bet she loves you' Jamie says with a giggle.

'I can't say I'm her favourite person' I reluctantly admit, feeling a bit uncomfortable. I wonder if my presence is actually a real problem for Sam, I must ask him.

After dinner we move on to another beach bar, where six of the most amazingly talented guys put on a fire show where they spin, throw and juggle fire whilst contorting their bodies into shapes that would make a gymnast's eyes pop. The Cheeky Girls are pulled up by the fire guys to take part in the show which makes their night, and Good Will Hunting, not to be outdone, volunteers to take part in the next act - where he was to lie on the floor while the fire chain spun like a cartwheel to light the cigarette in his mouth. He doesn't even smoke I tell Sam, which starts the laughter that only gets more hysterical as he takes his top off before lying down. I told Sam he has a penchant for taking his top off earlier in the night and told him to look out for it - betting him dinner that it would happen. The night ends not long after this, and at a reasonably sensible hour, with everyone laying off the booze in preparation for tomorrow's diving.

As Sam and I walk home he tells me how much he likes everyone, and I feel a smugness at how lucky I have been to meet all these different people while I've been away. He did want to know if I had any idea why Jamie had called him Patrick by mistake, twice. I've no idea I told him, a secret smile to myself. Jamie has such a wicked sense of humour I bet she did that on purpose, cheeky minx.

The dive the following day is a complete success, everyone loved it and they got lucky and saw both a huge sea turtle and a small whale shark. The whole gang were singing the praises of Sam and Tom, and so thankful to me for arranging it all.

They wanted to take us out that evening to say thank you. I told Sam I wasn't up for a big night so he suggested we go to the local bar the instructors frequent and they can buy us a few beers then whenever we're ready, we can just head home. They thought this was a great idea, the guys in particular eager to be introduced to all the hottie instructors, who I have a feeling will be less happy to see the Cheeky Girls and Jamie infiltrate their turf.

Sam makes sure to introduce the gang to all the instructors, playing along with the guys when they ask to meet this one and that one in particular, all the while he's giving me a highly entertaining running commentary on who they are chasing. I'm chatting with Jamie and the Cheeky Girls and quite a few of the male instructors who I've met briefly seem intent on a long chat with me tonight, oh I wonder why, keen for an intro to my girls perhaps?

I catch Shona giving me a dirty look, one that I reckon says 'now you're bringing other people who don't belong here too, you're ruining our set up and I hold you solely responsible'. At this exact moment, Sam whispers in my ear to look at Good Will Hunting and I burst out laughing, he's once again taking his top off whilst chatting away to a few of the girls. Oh dear, that probably did not look like what I was laughing at and I swear if looks could kill I'd be dead. I wish Shona knew what we were talking about, I'm
sure she thinks we have a conspiracy going on against her.

I do feel slightly uncomfortable about it all, as other than a quick hello and kiss on the cheek, I don't think Sam has actually spent much time with Shona tonight, or any other time in general that I've seen outside the dive shop. Not that he's really spent much time with me tonight either, mainly with the guys. Maybe I am causing problems here, but Sam can't be oblivious to this and he doesn't seem to be doing too much to pacify Shona. I hope I'm not a pawn in some complicated game here.

We head home to let Tom and Sarah go out for a drink but just before we leave I notice that Shona is now talking to Kristian. She's flirting in the most overt way possible, all hair flicks, head back laughter, touching her face, mixed in with not so furtive glances towards Sam every once in awhile. Oh poor Shona, Sam isn't even noticing, too busy chatting to his buddies.

***

After Tom and Sarah have gone out, Sam plays with the kids for a while then puts them to bed as I rustle us up some dinner. I'm still experimenting with all the exotic ingredients in the markets here and the smells and tastes they create, I think this is one of the main things I missed that first month out here. I love visiting all these fabulous food markets and bringing it back here to play around with the produce. Not having a kitchen in Samui and being unable to cook is such a shame. Now I can hear it already, poor me, I have to eat dinner out every night and not cook or clean up, but really, I've just loved cooking for the family, and they seem pretty pleased with the food too which is a bonus.

We take to the sofa with dinner and a bottle of red to watch a movie. 'Enjoy your Netflix and chill' Tom had shouted back to us as he closed the door on his way out. Now, I work in a college, so I know what a Netflix and chill is, and so did my blushing cheeks. It pretty much means that date where instead of going out for dinner or to a bar you stay in and shag. Ha ha, thanks Tom, not awkward at all. Tom seems unable to understand that Sam and I have had no romantic dalliances and isn't shy to comment. I suppose the circumstances are quite odd, Jamie thought the same, but as the one in the situation, our relationship seems completely natural. Not that it doesn't make me want to scream out loud to each of these nosy observers 'I know, and I really thought something was going to happen too, but alas it seems not'.

'Thanks for arranging everything today.' I say.

'No worries, your friends are great. And Good Will Hunting is fucking hilarious.'

'Yeah, they're a good crowd, I think you got extra brownie points from the guys for introducing them to all the dive girls.' I say.

'I noticed,' he smiles, 'and what is he all about taking his top off at every occasion?'

'I've no idea,' I laugh, 'but I told you, I'm not exaggerating, every excuse, and even those that are not excuses. Must be about 5-6 times a day.'

'What is his real name anyway?' Sam asks.

I stop, mid fork-to-mouth action to think, then smirk, then laugh, 'You know, I have absolutely no idea.'

And we both crack up.

'And I think Kristian and Shona seemed to be hitting it off.' Sam muses.

I didn't think he'd noticed, he didn't seem to react at all to it in the bar. Shit, what am I meant to say here. Playing for time I pretend I didn't hear him.

'Huh...'

'Shona and Kristian. They were pretty flirty when we left.' Sam says.

'Oh, oh yeah, Kristian flirts with everyone, I'm sure it didn't mean anything.' I say.

'You don't have to say that for me. I don't care. In fact, it would be quite a relief if she got with him tonight.' Sam says.

'Really? But you and Shona are kind of together aren't you?' I ask.

It's one of the few things we haven't really talked about, but Sam's never brought it up so I've never really felt it fair to ask him too much about it (especially when I can ask Sarah instead).

'Eh no, I wouldn't say we're together. We've had a thing in the past, nothing serious, she knows that.' Sam says.

'Yeah OK.' I reply, with raised eyebrows and a tone that leaves no doubt that I think otherwise.

'What does that mean?' he asks.

'Oh, come on, you know she thinks there is more to it than that. That outrageous flirting with Kristian tonight was for your benefit and god knows she can't stand you hanging out with me.' I reply.

I continue, 'whether she thinks you're together because of something you've said or done, or because…' I pause.

'Because what?' he asks, curiosity spreading across his face as I'm not normally one to hold back on words.

'Nothing. Not my place to say.' I reply.

'No come on. You've started now.' Sam says, 'I won't take offence, what were you going to say?'

'Well, sometimes girls think that "hanging out" a few times means that you are now automatically theirs, hands off everyone else. Ever heard the phrase actions speak louder than words.'

'I'm just putting it out there, but have you by any

chance told her that it's a casual, friends with benefits, no strings attached thing and then the same evening gone home with her?' I ask.

'Well, probably. But not in a long time. At least not in the last couple of months.'

'Right, well first of all, you can't have that conversation and hook up that night. That's just bloody confusing for anyone, let alone a youngish girl who obviously wants more than you do from this. And secondly, have you spoken to her about the fact that you haven't hooked up recently and what that does or doesn't mean?'

'Not really, I thought by nothing happening it would just fizzle out.' he reluctantly admits.

'For fuck sake Sam,' I put my head in my hands, 'fizzling out happens when you've been dating and then you don't date anymore, when you only see someone by arrangement and then don't arrange to see them anymore. You can't be working and going out in the evenings around someone and not say anything. No wonder the girl looks like she wants to kill me.'

'Oh fuck. That is exactly what's happened. Ere do you think I need to have a word with her?' he asks.

'I think if you've no intention of taking it further,

the sooner you put her out of her misery the better. She's hardly going to be stuck for alternatives but she needs to know that it's time to consider them.' I say with a finality that suggests that the subject is closed.

'Now, what are we going to watch...Single White Female? Fatal Attraction?' I ask.
I don't get any more suggestions out before I'm hit in the face with a flying cushion.

'Sorry, couldn't resist.' I snigger, whilst another cushion lands square in my face.

So, it turns out Sam has got himself in a bit of a pickle. Well at least Sarah will be pleased they're not serious. I hold nothing against Sam for having a bit of fun with Shona, but hey, you've got to be straight with people, let them know where they stand.

Sam says he's going to speak with Shona, let her know that he really likes her, but that it's not going to turn into a relationship and he's sorry if he gave her the wrong impression. I've told him already what she will most likely say, 'hey, I don't want a relationship, so let's just continue as we are - friends with benefits and all that'. I've also told him don't be fooled, that's the last ditch attempt to hold onto you in some way.

'Sadly I say that from experience.' I add, 'You need to find someone who is equally not into you if you want a 'friends with benefits' situation. Someone who is just as keen NOT to be in a relationship as you are.'

'You offering?' he teases.

Now it's my turn to return the cushions at record speed across the room. Three in a row, knocking him back into the sofa, and covering his face just long enough for my flushed red face to return to a semi-normal shade.

At that point, I could have gone on for a while about not leading someone on if you had no intention of being with them, but I realise I would have been thinking more about Pete leading me on with marriage than Sam and Shona's situation.

I thankfully didn't say anything more. I don't have a problem with Sam or what he's doing, so I just keep schtum, shut my mouth and settle down in front of the telly for a movie. Not Fatal Attraction or Single White Female.

'Duke.' I scream mid movie.

'What?' Sam looks at me perplexed.

'Good Will Hunting. His name is Duke.'

CHAPTER 18

I am more than half way through the Koh Tao to do list now and Sam is going to join me for today's activities. I'm glad because they are two of the scariest one's to me. Flying trapeze, which I am only aware exists thanks to Carrie in Sex and the City; and a Thai massage. A massage, scary? Yes terrifying, I have heard that they hurt like hell, and the masseuse twists you like a rubix cube and they giggle and talk about you all the way through it. And I hate going to salons for something I don't fully understand, they leave you in the room to get ready but never really tell you what 'getting ready means' - are you meant to keep your underwear on or take it off, should you cover yourself up with the towel or does that make you a complete prude.

I shudder at the memory of my first spray tan experience. I had been escorted into the little room where the spray tan booth was, and the therapist said that she would let me get ready and would be back in shortly.

She handed me a tiny plastic pocket which had a throw away shower cap in it. So I stripped down to my knickers, popped the shower cap on my head and as she knocked to see if I was ready I folded my hands over my boobs, sticking my fingers under my armpits and called her in. The look on her face was one of perplexed wonder, whilst she was desperately trying to purse her lips together to hold back a smile. What on earth, my body can't be the worst she's seen I was thinking. Then she ever so politely passed me another plastic pocket and suggested that I popped these pants on instead of my own ones so that they don't get stained from the tan and she turned and walked out. I'd only put the bloody throw away pants on my head. She had the courtesy to not tell me I was an eejit, just gave me another pair to put on as she left the room to no doubt tell all the others what I'd done. I didn't know whether to remove the pant hat or not, so instead I ended up standing in a booth double panted trying to make small talk with the therapist about my impending summer holiday.

Needless to say, I'm not a massive fan of anything that involves stripping off in salons but it's on the list and I have vowed to be adventurous, take risks and step out of my comfort zone this trip, so a Thai massage it is.

Sam and I pulled in on the bike to the rather amusingly named 'Weiner Massage'. After he had assured me that although the name suggests otherwise this was not one of the 'happy ending' massage places, we went inside and asked for two Thai massages.

They obviously thought we were a couple as we were led through to a beautiful room with two beds low to the floor, candles and rose petals all around. Oh dear, am I now meant to get naked in front of Sam? In fact, how many clothes am I meant to take off here exactly, I can't bear getting this wrong again. The ladies tell us to get down to our pants (at least this time I'm informed and not offered any confusing plastic pockets) and then leave the room for us to get ready.

I remove my outer layers and then fiddle about in a ridiculous fashion trying to remove my bra and get myself face down on the bed all in one move. I could hear Sam laughing at my peculiar shuffle and turned to see the sparkle in his eye as he was trying to hold back any further outbursts.

'Well this is awkward.' I give him a funny look as I cock my head to the side.

'Nothing I haven't seen already.' he laughs.
s
His laughter continued as my eyes popped out my head with pain when she first attacks my back, and I even join in myself when they start walking on our backs. It seems to go on forever this pushing and jabbing at my back, my breasts getting flatter and flatter under me until I'm sure my nipples are peeking out from under my

armpits giving Sam a salute.

Then she puts her foot alarmingly close to my lady parts and yanks my leg, she throws me above her head by kicking her knees into my back. She twists me in every possible way only stopping the stretch when I actually scream out loud, to which she says sorry, Sam laughed, the masseuses laughed and then they proceed to chat in Thai, most probably talking about what a wimp I am, or how much cellulite I have on the back of my thighs.

Walking out the door I almost feel like I'd been abused, dazed by the pain, but I have to admit also feeling extremely relaxed and satisfyingly stretched.

'Oh my god, why didn't you tell me what was going to happen?' I asked Sam, half giggling, half serious.

'Well that would have taken away half the fun now wouldn't it?' he replied putting his arm around my shoulder mocking me.

***

Next up. A flying trapeze class. Holy Shit.

'I hope you're doing this too mister.' I ask Sam.

'Yes, I am, don't worry.' Sam laughs.

'Have you done it before?' I ask, wondering if he is already an expert and once again I'm going to be the beginner.

'No, I've thought about doing it seeing as it's here, but have never got around to it,' he says.

So with a mixture of trepidation and excitement, we head off towards the circus (at least it's a circus in my head). It's on the other side of the island, and I take in the beautiful views as I sit behind Sam on his scooter. I smile as I realise that my hands are now fairly relaxed resting on my own thighs, a far cry from my initial trips on the scooter when I would be crushing the driver's abs as I clung on for my life. Hell, I've even learnt to drive the damn things myself. Not something I'll be continuing on the streets of London right enough, but I've mastered it for out here at least.

I've come a long way I think, done so much and really settled into this life out here. I mean who thought that Alice from t'up north would be doing the bloody flying trapeze in the middle of a tropical Thai island that she disappeared off to on her own. Not me, that's for sure.

Standing at the base of the large circus nets, we

receive a ten-minute theory lesson on timings to jump for the bar and well, that's about it other than don't worry the net will catch you so just enjoy it. That's it - really? The only instruction we get and now we are deemed ready to go?

Looking up at the podium I am now apparently 'ready to jump from' it suddenly seems very high. There are platforms on both sides with an almighty huge net running underneath and three swinging trapeze bars between the podiums. I climb up to my podium slowly. I look across and Sam is climbing up at the same time. A look of fear flitting between us, in fact it's the first time I've seen any form of nerves from Sam in all the activities we've done. And so I decide to play with him a little.

As he's looking across at me, I pretend to miss a rung on the ladder.

'Al!' he shrieks.

'Just joking.' I shout back.

As I get to the top and we look across at each other, a smile as wide as the net below spreads across my face. The trainer obviously realises that I'm up for a bit of joking about and finds Sam's reaction amusing too, so decides that we will play another little trick on him.

And so when it's my turn to try and swing for the

bar first, the trainer counts me in: 1...2...and just after two I fall off the edge straight into the net.

'Whooaa.' I scream.

'Jesus Christ Al, you OK?' Sam shouts.

'I am AMAZING.' I shout up, flinging my arms around.

Suzy, the trainer, had suggested that I fall straight into the net, she said it's the best way to lose the fear of falling, she also said it was very sweet to see how worried my 'boyfriend' looked when I did the whole pretend to fall off the ladder and should we wind him up a bit more.

Talk about a look of fear, Sam looked terrified. Suzy was right, that was both hilarious and the easiest way to get over falling. Jumping for the bars was easy after that, all fear of falling lost. Catching them, not so easy, but I kept going, and the thrill when you finally catch the next bar and swing, well that's some form of freedom.

Sam has almost an extra foot on my piddly five-foot three stature, so managed to get to grips with it a bit quicker than me. But when we've both finally got the hang of it, Suzy ups the anti and suggests that Sam hangs upside down, wrapping his knees around the bar and I swing and jump into his hands.

Seriously? They think we can do this already, I can't go home with broken bones I tell her. After some reassurance that no harm will come to us even if we can't do it and that Sam is more than strong enough to catch me, I think what the hell. It's not like I'm trying to hide my weight from him, he's seen me in a bikini often enough, hell he's seen me in just my pants at Weiner massage.

Jump one - and straight into the net for me.
Jump two - our hands touch but no grasp, and back in the net for me.
Jump three - one hand hold, almost there but not quite, and I pull both of us into the nets.

On jump four, Sam grabs both wrists as we swing back and forth cheering in celebration, until we bundle onto the nets. I feel like a sodding superstar, maybe a circus star really, but a star nonetheless. Now this is really one thing to add to my dating profile if I end up doing that online dating malarkey when I go home.

'Well done us.' I hold my hand up to high five Sam.

'Pretty good going for a shorty.' he says to me, 'So, quick shower and change then dinner? I owe you after not believing you about Good Will Hunting's stripping capabilities.'

'So you do, yeah, let's do it.' I reply.

***

Sam told me he had picked one of his favourite places and he took me to the most quaint wooden restaurant nestled high up in the hills that looked down almost all around the island. We arrive early and are able to catch the last moments of the sunset which cast the deepest pinks, reds and oranges across the skyline.

The restaurant is filled with twinkling lights, candles and lanterns hanging from the trees. I'm glad I made an effort with my appearance, as unlike the rest of the island this is a place you feel you should be looking a bit done up at least. As we sit in a corner table looking out at the horizon we talk about our lives back home, our childhoods, our mutual love for James Bond. I can't believe his favourite Bond is Pierce Brosnan, who can like him over Connery, I mean really?

As we talk about our friends, Sam seemed to have a lump in his throat. After enquiring if he was OK he told me that his best friend James had been a firefighter back in Cornwall. They shared a flat together, spent most of their time together and had been inseparable as kids. James had been called out to a house one evening where a mother and a little boy were upstairs in a house fire. They had managed to get the mother out easily enough, but when James went back in for the young boy, the fire had escalated. He managed to get the boy out of the window to safety, landing him on a large sheet held taut to catch them now the downstairs had become an impossible exit, but James never followed.

Sam tells me that life kind of lost all meaning for him after that, he couldn't get his head around the fact that one day everything was fine and the next, he was just gone. After a few months of depression, his brother had suggested that Sam should come out to Koh Tao, that they could really do with the help, and he thought 'why not'. He had really missed Tom too, especially now that James was gone.

After a while out here, Sam not only enjoyed himself again, but made the decision to live the best life that he could for both James and himself. That he would grab life by the balls.

'Which is why I'm so keen for you to enjoy yourself out here.' he said, 'Life can be short so you've got to go for it, enjoy it and only settle for the best.'

I'm tortured by the sadness that Sam feels when telling his story and talking about his friend and I'm in admiration at his approach to getting on with things, making sure he is living a life worthy of both of them. I'm so touched that he feels so keen for me to make the best of things too. I guess I'm starting to understand the inner workings of him a little bit more.

I finally understand what Sarah was talking about when she said that Sam had had a difficult time. I couldn't imagine losing your best friend so young, and I could completely understand how this would make you so disillusioned with life. Kind of makes my problems pale into insignificance.

Moving the conversation on from his past tragedy, I asked Sam what he would love to do in the future, what would be the most fulfilling job and way of living. I told Sam that I'd always wanted to run a cafe, no more sitting behind a desk at a computer all day, which Sam completely understood as that is exactly what he was doing before he moved out here. Sam told me that he has always wanted to drive Route 66 across the states and go to Las Vegas, he plans to go there in the next few years, but as far as day to day living, he wasn't sure it got much better than it is now.

We shared our funny teenage memories together. Our first kiss stories, mine was in the back of the bus on a school trip during a game of dares and I vividly remember he tasted like spaghetti bolognese, Sam's was down on the beach during a game of spin the bottle where he purposely landed the bottle on Suzie, the girl that all the boys in his class fancied. Our first boyfriend / girlfriend, mine was a chap called John who I played in a table tennis after school club with. We played doubles and then snuck round the back of the school afterwards for a quick smooch. Sam's first girlfriend was Suzie, he obviously made a better impression on his first kiss than I did with old Spag Bol boy.

'Go on then, you know what's coming next.' Sam said smiling, 'First time you had sex?'

'You first.' I say, slightly giddy with wine and enjoyment of our conversation. It's like that night where you stay up all night with your new boyfriend just talking, when you really get to know them and realise just how much more you want to know. That clicking moment, THE night.

'My first time was a bit of a shambles. We were at a party and I had sneaked a few of my Dad's cans of lager, so I had the drunken confidence of youth. The party was one of those first ones where everyone gets pissed, you know what I mean?'

I nod along, I know the kind of party he meant.

'Anyway, everyone had disappeared into various bedrooms and I thought I'd best do the same with the girl I was going out with. One thing led to another and we just kind of fumbled into it and muddled through' he laughed at the memory.

'Now you?'

'Oh, do I have to' I cover my face with my hands, 'It's so cheesy, I had been with my boyfriend for about a year and we had arranged to have sex on fireworks evening as we knew we would have the house to ourselves with everyone out at firework shows. God it's so cringey.'

'And, were there fireworks then?' he smiles.

'Well there were outside.' I laugh. 'It's quite sweet really when I think about it.'

'You're quite sweet.' Sam says, looking at me seriously.

I look away in embarrassment, not quite sure how to take this.

'I, erm, I spoke to Shona this morning. Made it clear that nothing was going to happen again.' Sam says, looking straight at me.

'Oh, well that's good. How did she take it?' I ask, trying to seem much more relaxed than I was.

'Funnily enough, she said exactly what you said she would, that we could just keep it relaxed, no strings blah blah blah.'

'Told you.' I smiled and nodded my head to the left, cocky little shit that I am (see, I still need to be right).

'I ended up telling her I like someone else so she understood I meant it.' he added.

I nodded in agreement that that was a good way forward.

I was a little light headed all of a sudden. Between the wine, the atmosphere and the intense conversation and looks between us I was washed up in emotion, but still completely unsure of what to make of it all, not willing to trust my own judgement.

We noticed that everyone else had now left the restaurant, bloody hell we must have been there for over four hours, and we started to make a move. As we left the restaurant and wandered out to the bike, Sam grabbed me and turned me to face him, placing his hand on my cheek.

'What is it, have I got something on my face again?' I ask, brushing my hands over my cheeks to shake lose any crumbs hanging around.

'No.' he said, 'You don't have anything on your face. Nor did you last time when we were like this.' he added, staring straight into my eyes.

Oh god, he remembers that moment in the water too. I thought it was just me.

Sam begins to stroke the side of my face gently with his thumb as he moves towards me. We are so close I can feel the warmth of his breath on my face, although I'm not breathing at all. I'm frozen stiff from the head up. The lower half not so much as everything underneath my skirt starts to stir. Sam moves towards me slowly, as if he is giving me the chance to turn away if this is not what I want. Are you kidding me, I'm going nowhere, and I try and illustrate with my eyes that yes, this is fine. This is fucking fantastic, please please just do it.

I tilt my head and he kisses the side of my mouth softly, then he bites on my bottom lip just enough to make me silently groan. I put my hand on the back of his head, fingers working their way through his hair as I pull him closer towards me. The kiss is strong and powerful now.

We finally pull apart and I look to the floor coyly.

'I've been wanting to do that for weeks.' Sam says, holding my hands.

My voice is absent, my legs are like jelly and my heart is thumping in my chest. Sam likes me, he really likes me. I just stare at him.

'You want to head back?' he asks me.

I just nod, still unable to find my words, floating on kisses. But then I am overcome with panic about what will happen when we get home. Is he going to expect me to sleep with him? God knows I want to but not right now without any preparation. I need to have a bikini wax first, I need to be wearing my matching underwear, I need to moisturise from head to toe, I need to remember how the hell to do it, and what about the others in the house, I can't begin to think about them hearing us.

I sit behind Sam on the bike as we ride home, I'm on the brink of orgasm already thinking about our kiss, now wrapped tightly to him my chest against his back, my arms circling his waist and resting gently in his lap just above the part of him that I am desperate to have inside me.

It's times like this that I wish I was one of those high maintenance girls who has a bikini wax scheduled in every three weeks like clockwork, who doesn't leave the bathroom without exfoliating and slathering on creams every day. But alas, I am not, and this lady garden is not fit for public, let alone a night of sex with the man of my dreams. Think of something else Alice, calm yourself down here.

As we reach the house, I jump off the bike and run into the house, straight into the bathroom to gather my thoughts. I splash my face with water for a while and then head back out to the terrace where Sam is talking with Tom.

'Hey.' I say.

'Hey,' Tom says, 'want to join me for a beer?'

'Sure.' I say quickly, not looking at Sam and heading into the kitchen to get us both a beer from the fridge.

I drink my beer very quickly, the fastest I think I've ever drunk a beer beyond my teenage years, yawn loudly and make my excuses as I head to bed.

As I come out of the bathroom from brushing my teeth, Sam is there outside the door

'Night you.' he says and plants a soft kiss on my lips, 'Don't make plans for tomorrow, I have a surprise.'

I lie down in the dark, my head swirling with happiness. Every part of my body is screaming and shouting in joy, like it's been woken from a coma and I start to make a mental to do list in my head for tomorrow. Surely his plans can't be all day, but I better get up early just in case and plough through my list of essentials:

- Bikini wax (I must research what is the current thing - Hollywood, Brazilian, something else I've no idea about)
- Buy condoms
- Buy fancy moisturizer
- 200 squats and sit ups in the morning
- Locate one and only set of fancy matching underwear

I wonder if I'm getting carried away as I make my list. Maybe this was a one off kiss, if he was just caught up in the moment, the restaurant was pretty romantic with all the candles and twinkly lights. But for now, I will stick to the list. I'm not having this opportunity come up again and not being able to do anything about it. One night of exciting anticipation and frustration is enough, but it's not happening again.

CHAPTER 19

I wake up with the birds, eager to get my to do list under way. First things first, where the bloody hell is my matching underwear, I have a black lacy bra and knickers set somewhere. Not that I tend to wear this as a set, I'm one of those just grab whatever knickers are on the top of the drawer and whatever bra works best with the top that I'm wearing. Gail always gives me shit for this, can't understand why I don't wear matching sets all the time. Really, is this what other people do? I'm not so sure.

I find the knickers in my washing pile and head into the bathroom to hand wash them, then place them on my window sill to dry. Next up, I get my phone out to work out what kind of wax I need. What on earth do you put into google to find this out. Pubic hairstyles? Vagina hair trends? How much bush should you have in your lady garden?

Google wastes no time in confirming that the

options are endless with regards to prune or let your garden flourish, eight types no less: Au naturale, bikini line touch up, full bikini line wax, French wax: the landing strip, Brazilian wax: the Bermuda triangle, Brazilian wax: the desert island, the love heart, the Hollywood.

Jesus Christ, who knew? And that's not even going into all the vajazzle options (been there, done that, not doing it again thank you).

I sneak out before anyone is up and head down the main road until I find a salon that is open and head on in. On the wall there is a sign that says:

Bikini wax 600 - 1000 baht

What the hell does that mean? Does the price depend on how hairy you are down there, how much work they have to do? Please, please, please don't let me be a 1000 bahter, I couldn't live with the shame, and it wouldn't exactly spark my inner sexy diva getting ready for a night of hot passion.

'Bikini wax?' I ask the therapist.

'Yes, through here.' she says and ushers me through to a small room and points towards the bed for me to get up.

Another of my horrible fears is realised. I never

know whether you are meant to keep your knick knacks on and just pull them to the side, or to take them off. I decide to leave them on and climb up onto the bed as the therapist is turning on the wax pot and getting all her tools in order.

She turns back round and points to my pants 'off' she says and then turns back to continue with what she is doing.

Once I'm lying down on the bed again, stark naked from the waist down she turns back to me and puts her head down very close to inspect what she is dealing with, no doubt calculating the number of hairs so she can work out what to charge me.

'What style?' she asks

'Erm, Brazilian, the triangle one please?' I ask. I've decided this is the one that makes me look like I'm not trying too hard. I've no idea how I've come to this conclusion, but I have.

She begins to strip away the hair as I silently bite my lip and yelp in pain inwardly. Perhaps I should have cut the hair really short before coming here, might have made it slightly less painful as each strip is yanked from me pulling at the skin as if it wants to come off with the strip too.

God I hate this.

Just as I thought I was finished, she asked me to turn over. Turn over, what for?

I turn over and she then asks me to hold my bum cheeks apart. Oh my god, this is so awful. Now I've heard of a sack and crack wax, but I thought that was just for men and really kinky women. Why don't women talk about these things, for all we spend hours and hours examining what's going on in our lives to the nth degree no one ever sits down and tells you how you're meant to manage your bush and if you should be including an arse wax in your bikini routine or not. Seems like I don't have an option anyway on this occasion.

'Whoa,' she says, 'I think this first time for you.'

Holy mother of god, not only am I sat here holding my bum cheeks apart, I now also have someone implying that my bum looks like something from Harry and the Hendersons. Ground, please swallow me up now.
And if I thought the front wax was painful, that was pure pleasure in comparison to this.

All this effort had better lead to some serious action, that is as long as I don't look like a skinned chicken for too long, these bumpy red bits can do one asap.

'700 baht.' she says. Well, at least I'm not a 1000 bahter. Imagine what her reaction to one of those would be if my arse got that reaction and it was only a 700 bahter.

I make a final stop on my way home at the chemist to pick up some vanilla and coconut moisturising oil and a pack of condoms, do you ever stop getting embarrassed buying condoms?

'Ah there you are.' Sam smiles as I return to the house.

'Yeah, just had to do a few errands.' I reply, feeling like my pruned bush has a flashing neon sign pointing at it saying, 'I was the errand, check me out.'

'Cool, right if you want to pack an overnight bag and then we'll head off.' Sam says.

'Oh, OK.' I smile and make my way to my room to get packed.

Overnight bag. My shaven chicken starts to cluck with excitement.

'What are we up to?' I ask.

'We're going to Koh Samui, but that's all I'm telling you.' he cocks his head smugly.

***

Sam and I are doing our best to act our normal selves on the boat over to Koh Samui. I can't help sneak a few peeks at him as he expertly maneuvers the boat through the water. He really is a beautiful specimen of a man. He pulls me close to steer the boat for a while, telling me it's amazing to feel the power of the boat in your grasp, that there's nothing like it. I hold the wheel as Sam stands behind me, his hands over mine helping me steer the way. That's it, he says, brushing my hair to one side and kissing my neck, sending shivers down my spine.

I had wondered how we were going to manage the transition from friends to, well, to this. I didn't want to make the first move in case it had been a one off, but now it wasn't, I allow myself to be fully engulfed in the moment, moving my head to the side and letting out a small gasp.

As we dock in Samui and clamber off the boat, Sam tells me that he hopes it's OK for him to commandeer the day, that he's pretty sure I'll enjoy what he has planned.

'Sure, where are we going?' I ask, tugging on Sam's arm with excitement.

'It's a surprise, be patient.' Sam replies.

'I can't. I don't possess that virtue. Please tell me? Can we walk there?' I ask.

'No, Joe's giving us his bike. Now that's all you're getting.'

As we near Joe's place, Sam tells me that he's booked me into my old hotel for the night.

'I can stay at Joe's.' he says.

'Really?' I say, my painful morning was not done for nothing.

'Well I didn't want to presume?' he says.

'Give me your bag.' I smile, making it clear that Joe's sofa will not be needed for the evening.

Check me out, where has this confidence come from. I'm like a total horn dog.

I head off to get checked in and Sam wanders on to Joe's, where I'll meet him shortly. It's funny being back in a hotel room after sharing a family home with Sam and the gang. Feels like I have 'dirty weekend' tattooed all over my face.

'Honey, how are you? Welcome back.' I hear Joe's familiar drawl as I walk into Coconut Joes.

Oh, I've missed Old Joe. Such a lovely man. Spending time with Joe is a bit like getting to visit your favourite Uncle as a kid, you get excited with the anticipation of a day of fun with him, and he never lets you down - always a day filled with games and adventures and of making you feel really, really special. Joe has the ability to make you feel like you are the only person in the room, that you are the most interesting person in the world, as if everything else has turned silent to him, and you are the only thing that matters in the moment.

'You look great. Koh Tao life obviously suits you.' Joe Says.

'So Sam, here's the keys, have fun at the…' Joe adds.

'Stop.' Sam playfully clasps his hand over Joe's mouth 'It's a surprise, Al doesn't know where she's going.'

'Feel free to continue Joe.' I smile in as charming a manner as I can manage.

'My lips are sealed.' says Joe.

So we head off towards the South of the island,

for a secret activity, but I'm struggling to concentrate on anything other than WE ARE GOING TO HAVE SEX THIS EVENING.

I lean into his ear to ask from the back of the scooter, 'Give me a hint?'

'What do you think it is?' he asks playfully.

'Well the last thing you planned involved me swinging from a trapeze, so could be anything, swinging from the chandeliers for all I know.'

Oh my god, where did that come from. I didn't mean to say that, it makes me sound like I'm from the 1970s and does that have connotations of wild sex, I don't actually think I know what that means, let's hope Sam doesn't either. I just meant to say it could be something bizarre like bungee jumping, yet somehow I've mixed up my phrases, come out with the wrong thing.

'Did you just say swinging?' Sam asks me, not quite sure he heard me right.

Oh my god, it gets worse. Swinging. I'm glad he can't see how red my face is. In fact scratch that I'm positively flushed from head to toe.
'
'What did you just say?' Sam repeats, a hint of amusement in his voice.

'Nothing. Just you concentrate on the road.' I reply, slapping him in the ribs.

I swear he thinks I'm talking about swinging, knows I'm embarrassed and I can feel his shoulders shaking as he's trying to hold back the laughter.

We finally slow and turn down a little dirt track leading to our intended destination, and as we get closer I can hear lots and lots of barking.

'What is this?' I ask.

'You'll see.' replies Sam.

And then the sign providing the '100 yards this way' arrow tell me that we are going to the Samui Dog Rescue Centre.

Oh I can't believe it. All these dogs and I get to play with them all afternoon. This is the most amazing surprise. One of my favourite things about Thailand has been all the dogs that roam the streets, they're not like pitiful strays, they're mainly looked after by the community who I guess have them collected by the rescue centre as and when it's needed.

I jump off the scooter and wrap my arms around Sam in thanks for arranging this - he knows me so well.

He takes my hand and leads me in through the gate.

'And I have an extra surprise for you, Sarah has said that we can pick a dog to bring back so that Johnny Cash has a buddy.' Sam says.

'Are you serious?' I ask, in a far higher voice than intended.

'We get to choose one?' I ask, my voice only slightly dropping back towards a normal level.

'Yeah. Well you do. I'll have a veto, but unless you pick the craziest dog here I'm pretty happy to go with your choice.' Sam replies.

So we spend the afternoon playing with the dogs, helping to feed the puppies, washing and brushing others, all the while keeping an eye out for a little buddy for Johnny Cash.

Sam has really pulled it out the bag here, I couldn't have asked for a better way to spend the day than with both him and all these four-legged adorable beauties. I look across and see Sam kissing the top of one of the puppies heads, and realise that he is smitten with these little guys too. You gotta love a man who kisses and cuddles dogs.

But choosing one? Oh this is going to be tough,

and it's like they know I'm doing it, each one vying for my attention in the cutest way possible. Then I notice a little sandy coloured guy, with little scuffs and scars on his elbows and knees, or whatever the equivalent dog term is for the knuckles on their legs. He is almost invisible as he's sleeping on a similar coloured pile of sand, only noticeable by his twitching, he's obviously having a little dream.

'He looks like he could be Johnny Cash's brother. Let's ask about him?' I say.

John, the Manager tells us that he has been there for a couple of months, he had a big cut on his head and that's why they took him in. He's really placid and would be fine around children and with another dog in the house. He's not too demanding of attention and as long as he is near sand like this pile here, he's a happy guy. He doesn't have a name which breaks my heart so I decide he's definitely the one.

No veto from Sam thankfully. They ask for Sam's t-shirt to leave with the dog so he can get used to his smell, they'll make sure all his jabs are done, chop off the poor fella's balls and he'll be ready to pick up next week.

'Do you have a name in mind?' asks John, 'We can start calling him it this week if so, get him used to it along with your smell.'

Sam nods in my direction, 'Over to you.'

I'm shaking with excitement, I've always wanted to have another dog, but a flat in London doesn't exactly make the ideal dwelling, and Johnny Cash is quite possibly the coolest dog's name I've ever heard, so the pressure is on.

'Well, he'll need to feel as cool as Johnny Cash, so how about...Elvis.'

'There you go John, next Saturday Elvis will be leaving the building.' laughs Sam.

As Sam takes his top off to leave with Elvis (how clever is that, so the dog gets used to your smell), I can't help my eyes wandering towards his chest and abs. My, my, Sam - a taster of what's to come later. Give me that horse, I'm ready to jump back on.

I am positively ogling him but it's getting me far too frisky for public...think of him in fluorescent speedos Alice, think disgusting fluorescent speedos. That's done it, momentary objectification over, not even Sam could pull off speedos.

As we head back towards Joe's, Sam now topless, I can't help noticing that I'm leaning in to him and he's sitting much further back than normal on the bike, his hot and sweaty back pushing against my nipples. Now,

I'm not being dirty here, he really is hot and sweaty, it's over 30 degrees.

Check out this six pack, I giggle as I think what would have happened if I was on one of those dating websites back home and I requested a six pack like this. I'd probably get replies of people holding a six pack of Stella or something, balancing it on their rotund middle. I've never really cared about muscles on men before...perhaps it's like that phrase 'once you go black you don't go back', or in the case of abs it's 'once you go solid the alternative is horrid'. Oh yes, it's been a tricky few months but I am most certainly now ready to move on. Pete who? I've definitely moved past the 'I hate men, don't touch me with a barge pole' phase into the, well based on the way this sweaty back is making me feel, the horrendously horny phase.

It's been quite some time since I've had a bit of a rumble in the sheets, and an incredibly long time since I've been with anyone other than Pete (the brief fumble with Good Will Hunting doesn't count). The whole thing fills me with excitement and terror all at once. Maybe I should have slept with Good Will Hunting just to get it out of the way I think, become a one time cougar to conquer that first time with a new person fear. I giggle at this preposterous thought as we wind our way down the hills back towards Old Joes.

***

'Oh Joe, honestly it was so embarrassing. I thought Sam was cheating on his wife.' I cringe at the memory.

'I can't believe you thought this one had a wife and kids.' Joe pats Sam on the shoulder affectionately.

'You are both to blame,' I laugh, 'all this chat about the twins and Sarah, and not one mention of Tom.'

The night continues with the three of us sharing a few beers, eating Joe's Pad Thai and with me trying to impress Joe with my changed ways, telling him about all the activities that I've been up to.

Joe cocks his head to Sam 'Seems like you're a good influence.'

I realise that Joe tactfully doesn't ask me any questions about the Pete saga, and concentrates more on the company at hand.

Joe has had quite an eventful month too. Since I've been away, he has discovered the world of Facebook. He has got in touch with a lot of old friends, but it seems to be one in particular that he is most pleased about - a lady called Goya from his home village. She and Joe were an item back in the day, and although he doesn't give me the full run down, I'm sure this is the person he was thinking about before when we were talking about there only having been one person he came close to settling down with.

Goya still lives in the same village, she has two grown up children and an ex-husband. His eyes are sparkling as he talks about her, I see the fire and excitement of a teenage boy in them.

'And are you going to see her?' I ask Joe.

'Well, yes actually. That's the funny thing, she saw on Facebook that I lived here and got in touch to say she was coming this weekend to visit her son who lives here too.' he says.

'Oh Joe,' I clasp my hands in joy, 'that's only a couple of days away.'

'Yes, it will be nice to see her.' he says, calmly, playing down what I sense is something much more to him than he is letting on.

The bar starts to fill up later in the evening with the club promotion guys vying for a bit of Joe's attention before they head on out to the neon street to sell their bars to the tourists. To give Joe the chance to chat to everyone else, I suggest to Sam maybe we take a wander along the beach, visit another bar.

'Don't lose your clothes this time.' Joe smirks.

'What's this?' Sam smiles, 'Ere, I thought I knew all your Koh Samui stories.'

'Nothing, come on.' I say, 'See you in the morning Joe.'

'Night honey.' Joe replies wandering off to join the boys.

As we wander along the beach, dipping our feet in the water, Sam takes my hand and I feel like there's a sunburst inside of me.

'Thanks for today.' I turn to him.

'You're welcome.' Sam replies, and kisses me.

'Do you want another drink?' Sam asks.

No, I want you. Now.

'Not really, you?' I look into his eyes.

No.' he replies and we walk back towards the hotel in silence.

As we close the door behind us, Sam pulls me

close to him, my chest pressed to his and he kisses me hard on the mouth. Gripping the back of my hair he tilts my head to the side and kisses his way down the side of my neck, while removing the straps of my sundress from my shoulders allowing the dress to drop to the floor circling my bare feet.

He turns me around so he can undo my bra and cups my loose breasts in his hands as they are released from their black lace casing. My head is leaned back into his shoulder and I can feel him hard against my lower back and I let out a moan.

His left hand continues to pinch gently at my nipple as the right traces its way down my body, making its way inside my last remaining item of clothing until I can take it no longer. I let out a slight cry and turn around to face Sam desperate to have him inside me. He lays me onto the bed, revealing his glorious hardness and we move together until I shudder and pant in euphoria.

CHAPTER 20

I wake up early with the sun streaking through a gap between the curtain and the window and bathe in its heat and the memory of my evening. I turn on my side and admire sleeping beauty next to me, his hands behind his head and his mouth slightly open, and there is a gentle purr escaping in a rhythmic manner (god, I must still be in the first throws of passion, who in their right mind describes someone snoring in a bed with them like that.).

I creep out of bed careful not to wake him and nip to the bathroom. Looking in the mirror I whisper 'OMG Alice' to myself, unable to stop smiling. I grab my make-up bag and do a quick early morning touch up job, you know the one, the 'really this is what I look like first thing in the morning' routine - top eyelash mascara, face serum, pinch of cream blusher, a messy top bun, brush teeth, mouthwash and fast as you like lie down again and pretend you've just woken up.

As I climb back into bed Sam stirs.

'Morning.' he smiles, pulling me into him.

'Morning you.' I reply with a kiss.

'Don't you look lush in the morning.' Sam says.

'You don't look too shabby yourself mister.'

Sam folds me into his arms for a recap of last night and my heart skips a beat - he still wants me in the morning.

We pack our little bag just as it's nearing check-out time, having made the most of being on our own. Heading over to Joe's to say goodbye I realise how much I've missed him and I decide to stay an extra day in Samui. Sam has to get back with the boat and will be out on dives all day so I will follow on tomorrow on the ferry.

I wade out to the boat with Sam, and give him a discreet smooch before he heads off. I don't know why I'm trying to be subtle it's not like Joe doesn't know where Sam slept last night.

'You sure you don't want me to come back for

you in the morning?' Sam asks.

'No, it's fine. I'll probably have a lie in and come back in the afternoon anyway.' I reply.

I wave at my gorgeous man as he drives the boat out of sight and then make my way back to Old Joe's.

'Well, well, well.' Joe smiles.

'Game of chess?' I reply.

'Sure honey.'

As Joe sets up the chessboard he tells me how pleased he is to see me looking so well. Jeez, I must have seriously looked like shit before as that's both Joe and Jamie who've made quite a deal out of this transformation. Like a proud daughter I tell him about all the things I've been doing - the cooking, boxing, trapeze, yoga and how Sam has helped me work my way through the list, making sure I do everything possible before I leave.

Ugh, the thought of leaving. It's less than two weeks away. How am I going to leave all this behind? I keep reminding myself that this is just a lucky escape from my normal life, that Sam and I are a whirlwind holiday romance, but my head doesn't always want to compute that.

'And, eh...things seem close with you and Sam?' Joe drops in casually.

'We've just been really good friends.' I say.

'Been. Not are?' he smiles.

'Well yes, things have kind of progressed in the last few days.' I tell Joe, shyness creeping over me.

'I think that's ace, a holiday romance, just what you need to put the past year behind you.' Joe says.

'Yes, obviously I'm off home soon, but it's nice to be wanted, a little fling to move me on.' I force a smile.

Although, I don't feel like this at all, Sam is no rebound shag or holiday fling. I suppose he is a summer romance but I've let myself fall much deeper than that. I'm pretty sure he has too, the way we are together seems much closer than you would expect given the length of time we've known each other.

'Speaking of the past. Any word from home?' Old Joe asks.

'I got that text saying he wanted to talk when I got back on the night of the Full Moon party, but I haven't heard anything since, that was almost a month ago.' I shrug.

'That's odd. And you feel OK about going home?' he asks.

No I never want to leave Sam, I want to live in Koh Tao forever.

'Yeah, I feel OK about it. I still have no idea where I'll live or what's next, but I'm not terrified of being alone anymore.' I say.

Because I can't see beyond being with Sam right now.

Joe tells me how much admiration he has for me. He applauds that I've pulled myself together so well given how I was only a month ago. He pats me on the hand as he lists through all the activities I've done, how well I look and emphasises how great it is I've done all this for myself. As always with Old Joe, there is an underlying message here. His admiration is tinged with fear that this new positive person is party built upon the foundations of Sam, reliant on Sam, rather than completely down to me. He has an uncanny way of not saying everything out loud but somehow conveying what he's thinking enough to get the cogs turning.

I do now what Joe is trying to say. It's great that Sam and I are 'having fun', but we live on different sides of the world so let's be realistic here, and in the meantime let's concentrate on ensuring my happiness can continue without Sam in my life, which will be the case before I know it. Oh I know it can, but god I don't want it to.

'Tell me Joe, what are you going to do with Goya tomorrow? How is she getting here? Are you going to pick her up?' I finally stop for a breath.

He laughs at my excitement, 'Typical girl, you'll be asking what I'm going to be wearing next. Her ferry gets in late morning and her son is picking her up. She plans to come over here with him and his family early afternoon, so the grandchildren can play on the beach.'

'And?' I ask.

'And what?' Joe asks.

'What will you be wearing?' I reply.

'Oh my Buddha, my three-piece suit what do you think.' he nods down to his current attire.

He's' wearing cut off denim shorts (very casual but he does have good legs) and his tank top (a little on the tight side and it has been through the wash too many times to still be considered white).

**

I wake up early in the morning and get the first ferry over to Koh Tao not wanting to wait any longer to see Sam. Besides, Goya arrives today so I want to be out the way and give Joe some space. Before I leave I pop into Coconut Joe's and place a new white vest top on Joe's chair, just to give him the option.

I daydream my way across the water as the ferry rocks gently over the waves. A cheeky smile spreads as I think about the whoop of joy Sarah will give when she hears the news. Where will I sleep now I wonder, will Sam and I share a room or will we be carrying out clandestine activities after dark as the rest of the family sleep. Oh, it's all so dramatic.

Perhaps low key is the best way, given the recent Shona scenario. No need to upset her when I'm leaving so soon anyway. Gulp, I can't bear the thought of leaving. I push that to the back of my mind, that's a problem for future Alice, let's not think about that just now.

I make my way back to Sam's house via the food market. I'm going to cook up a storm tonight for the family, an afternoon in the kitchen sounds idyllic, maybe Sam will join me and help too.

Shopping done, I meander back to the house smiling at all the early birds getting ready for a day of diving. And then I hear a familiar voice that makes me turn. I arch my back to look down the little side street I've just past and freeze.

The street is lined with little huts and it's where I think a lot of the dive staff live. On a doorstep around half way down the road is Sam. It looks like he is saying goodbye to someone although I can't see who it is because Sam is hugging them and his frame is hiding them from view. What the hell? Has he spent the night with someone else? How bloody dare he, and who is this slut? Move Sam, move so I can see the tart.

I crawl along the wall remaining out of sight so I can get a better view and hopefully hear what they're saying.

Oh dear god, this wasn't wise. The huggee is not someone I know, but she makes a damn good young Demi Moore lookalike. Now would be a good time to leave, but instead I take a step closer to hear what is being said.

'Thank you so much, you were amazing.' she says, putting her hands on each side of his jaw and planting a smakeroo on the lips.

Jesus Christ. I run quickly to get out of the street and I don't stop running until I'm almost home.

Maybe it's not him I think. Maybe it's...well the only other person it could have been is Tom and even I don't want that to be the case, he has a wife and kids for god's sake.

I climb up onto the terrace and see Tom, Sarah and the twins having breakfast.

'Hey.' I say, 'Morning.'

'How was Samui? We've heard about Elvis.' Sarah says.

Elvis? What? Oh, I forgot about the dog, so much has happened in the last 30 odd hours.

'Eh yeah. He's lovely. I'm just going to pop my bags down.' I say wandering into the house.

As I pass Sam's room I check no one is looking and creek open his door. Nope, not still in bed, and nope, his bed doesn't look slept it.

I lie on my bed and digest what has happened here. I know I have been guilty of a mistaken identity situation with Sam before, but alas I have not repeated the error on this occasion, that was Sam on young Demi Moore's front step.

It seems I have got carried away and thought our

hook up meant something more than it did. Just because I don't go to bed with people willy nilly doesn't mean others don't. It's not as if the clues weren't there, what was this Shona situation, and didn't I almost mock her for taking the whole thing too seriously? What a bloody fool I am, carried away again, just like the situation with Pete. Am I incapable of seeing things as they are? Always falling for the charm offensive.

I can't even take it out on Sam, he'd think I'm an absolute nutcase going mad when we've only spent one night together (and one morning). And I'm going back to London in less than a fortnight.

I need to get a grip, I came out here to get my head around being single, to get over my break up with Pete, not to find myself in some fresh drama. Jeez, lost my fiancé, lost the sexy diver dude, lost his amazing family - good going Al, perhaps the problem is closer to home than I think. The tears roll gently down my cheeks and the pillow beneath my head gets wet little puddles on either side of my ears.

What am I going to do? I can't stay here now, it will be torture. Sam will no doubt be his usual flirty self, but I can't be one of a few flings he's having, I just can't.

Of all the bad things that Pete did to me, at least he never did that. There was no cheating, no playing away. I wonder what he's up to now. I haven't had any new messages from him, 'that's odd' Joe said.

Let's talk when you're back.

His text comes back into my mind. Should I have responded? Maybe having someone like Pete isn't such a bad thing. At least his lack of charisma makes him less likely to be chatted up by other woman. Oh Al shut up, you're being ridiculous - and mean.

I dig out my phone and bring Pete's profile up on Facebook, he never puts much on there, but I can't help but have a look. Oh. Status update to 'single'. Oh.

I scroll down to see that he's been tagged in a photo. In the photo, he has his arm around someone called 'Daisy'. I zoom in on the photo to get a good look at this Daisy. She looks like she is early twenties, it must have been a sunny day as she is not wearing much on the top half, a little white vest with no bra on. She could be pretty if she stopped doing one of those stupid trout pout selfies.

I try to see where they are in the photo, it looks like some kind of park or field, there are stalls, stands and stages in the background and people dressed in festival garb.

A wave of nausea hits me. Pete's moved on, he's going to festivals with girls called Daisy - what happened to talking when I got back?

What the hell do I do now? Everything is crumbling around me. My chat with Joe hits me like a slap in the face, his fear that my happiness is linked to a man... hmm, could have a point there, Pete never even entered my mind until this shit with Sam happened.

'Hey, you're back early?' Sam pops his head around my bedroom door.

'Yeah, I caught the first ferry.' I reply wiping a tear with the back of my hand.

'What's the matter?' Sam sits down on the edge of the bed.

'Me? Nothing, something in my eye. Sorry I've got to run, I've got a boxing class.' I jump up from the bed and grab my trainers.

'OK, I'll see you later then?' he moves towards me placing his hands on my shoulders.

'Yep, I'll do dinner for everyone. I've got to go or I'll be late.' I give him a quick kiss on the cheek while shoving my feet in my trainers.

I leave the house and start to run.

CHAPTER 21

I'm half an hour early for the boxing class so I just keep running. No, I don't suddenly think I'm Forrest Gump, but I do have to keep busy and not think too much, and right now running seems to be fulfilling that need, maybe Forrest was onto something after all.

I punch and kick the living daylights out of the punch bag at the boxing. Noi keeps giving me the thumbs up 'Good, good power' he says.

At the end of the class he asks me, 'Same time tomorrow?'

'I can't,' I reply, 'I'm leaving tomorrow.'

I only used six out of the ten lessons I bought, some things never change. I decided at some point during the class that the best thing to do was move on.

I'm not in a good head space, but I know I have the capability to get there if I do the hardest thing I can. Walk away from Sam and his family in Koh Tao. It was going to happen in just over a week anyway, perhaps this is a better way, before I get myself in
any further.

After the boxing I nip back to the house, thankfully it is empty so I leave a note for everyone saying that dinner will be at seven. I get on my scooter and for the last time take a drive around the island. Stopping at points to take in the views and commit them to memory or to think about the things that I have done there.

What a magical place, I have completely changed as a person out here, I've experienced so much that I never imagined possible. I want to let Sam and his family now how much they mean to me, and how grateful I am for everything they've done, so I stop to run a few errands on the way back.

I have decided to make a big lasagne for dinner. Well, three ginormous lasagnes to be exact so I can box them up and freeze them for Sarah. I was going to cook Thai food, but I figure they can get take away Thai when I've left or maybe even Sam will cook for them. Lasagne on the other hand with just the right tomato to meat ratio that Tom likes, not as easy.

As I'm running around the cafe's kitchen Sam comes in.

'Hey, I've missed you today.' he says, putting his arm around my shoulder

'Oops, 'scuse me.' I duck out of his arm to open the oven and look at the lasagnes that don't yet need to be checked.

Sam steps back slightly put out, unsure of this sudden change from the person he shared a room with in Koh Samui. He doesn't know I saw him with Demi so can't quite get his head around it.

'Is everything OK?' he asks, his eyebrows knitted together like a confused cartoon character.

'Yes fine, but we need to have a chat Sam.'

I've had all day to think about how to deal with this situation, and although my heart feels like someone has ripped it out my chest and stamped on it, it's not Sam's fault. I've twisted this into something more than it actually is, and I don't want him to feel bad. He's been such a massive part of 'fixing me' for want of a better explanation. Making me enjoy life again, bringing back my confidence. He's taken me to the edge of my comfort zone and beyond and for that I'll be forever grateful. So he's broken my heart too, big deal, least I know it can beat with passion again. And Sam deserves to find the person he's looking for, not to feel guilty because I found out he was hooking up with someone else. He owes me nothing, so I'm going to lay this 'chat' at his door.

'Sure. What's going on?' Sam asks, concern in his eyes.

'I really appreciate everything you've done, and I had a wonderful time in Koh Samui with you.' I start my practised verse.

'Sounds like there's a but coming?' Sam says with raised eyebrows.

'There is,' I say with a sad smile, 'I'm just not ready for all this, only two months ago I was planning my wedding. I think I just need to be on my own for a while.'

'OK, let's just go back to being buddies then?' he suggests.

'Actually, I've decided to head back to Koh Samui in the morning, spend my last week or so there.' I look down, unable to look in Sam's eyes.

'I see. And I can't change your mind?' he playfully elbows me in the ribs.

'Not this time.' I nudge him back.

'Now, would you go and get some wine for tonight's dinner please, while I finish everything off?' I ask.

'Sarah's going to be gutted you know.' Sam is staring at me.

'Off, go get the wine.' I order as I turn towards the oven to hide the tears welling up in my eyes.

***

I've gone to town with dinner tonight, with the table on the terrace spilling over with plate loads of food to accompany the lasagne. To the side, a smaller table is filled with wine coolers and beautifully chilled bottles of Sauvignon Blanc.

Just as we are about to sit down in our usual spots, the girls one side and the boys the other, with Sarah and Tom in the middle to look after the kids, I realise how normal this setup has become, how beautifully familiar. Tom takes a bottle from one of the coolers and Sarah appears with a tray of chilled flutes.

'A toast to our favourite house guest before we eat.' Tom says, producing a bottle of Champagne that must have been hiding behind the bottles of wine. There's cheers all round as Tom successfully pops the cork and fills the glasses. Oh shit, I'm going already, I can feel my eyes welling up with the emotion of it all. How can I say goodbye to these special people?

'Why are you crying Alice?' Amy asks me.

'Oh, I'm not sweetie.' I reply, embarrassed. Out of the mouths of babes and all that, when everyone else was kindly turning a blind eye to my glassy eyes.

'Yes you are.' Ben says, 'Your cheeks are wet. Have you hurt yourself?'

'No Ben,' I crouch down and wrap my arms around the twins, 'I'm the happiest I've been in a long while.'

'Can't you stay a bit longer then?' Tom winks.

'Leave it Tom.' Sam butts in.

I'm grateful for Sam's interruption as I'm not sure I could deal with a re-hash of why I'm leaving, especially from Sarah who I have feeling is not convinced by what she's heard.

'So, a toast.' Sarah says, bringing us all back on track and raising her glass.

'To our good friend Alice. You have been a

breath of fresh air in our lives, part of our family and we will miss you so very much. Wishing you all the happiness in the world for your future and have a safe trip back. Please come and visit us again soon.' Sarah finishes, with a lump in her throat and a tear in her eye.

'And cheers for all the cooking and showing us what real food tastes like.' Tom adds, getting a playful slap on the arm from Sarah.

The evening continues with talks of the last few weeks, funny stories of our lives and many promises to keep in touch. My heart swells at the warmth of these people and tears have been shed on and off throughout the evening. Sam has been fairly quiet, the usual barrage of abuse is being thrown at him from his family but he doesn't seem to be retaliating tonight, just the odd wry smile in response.

'Back in a sec.' I say.

I return from my room with a bag, I've got each of them a little gift to say thank you and goodbye.

'Just a little something silly to say thank you.' I say to the table.

For the kids, I have a couple of pairs of wellies with frog faces, so they don't have to stay inside next time a storm comes, they put them on straight away and get the hose out to soak each other's feet.

For Tom, I've bought a case of ketchup, the only thing he says that makes Sarah's food bearable, thankfully this is met with laughter.

'But hopefully you won't need it.' I say handing Sarah her gift, a voucher for a Thai cooking class and a book called 'Cooking with Poo' (this is not a joke, this is the name of an actual cooking book in Thailand, I promise).

'And for you.' I hand Sam his gift.

This was the hardest one to choose, but I settled for having a t-shirt made that says *Patron Saint of Messy Chicks* on one side and *My Hero* on the other.

'Honestly Sam, how I went from a wailing woman on your shoulder to living here, feeling this happy and carefree is a minor miracle, and very much down to you.'

This time, it's Sarah who is trying to hold back the tears, as she says, 'Sometimes it just takes the right person to get you out of a funk.'

'Now, who's for another glass?' Sam suggests, embarrassed by the conversation I think.

We finish the bottle and then as it's time to put

the kids to bed, Sam and I take our leave.

We head down to a quiet beach cafe, and settle into a couple of big bean bags on the water's edge. As I look around and see the palm trees lit with fairy lights, the water glistening and lapping softly on the beach, I turn to see Sam, he's in a world of his own. Silent again, only the sound of the water and Bob Marley in the background.

'You OK Sam?' I ask.

'Hmm, sorry, yeah I'm fine.' he replies unconvincingly.

We've had so many conversations Sam and I, shared so much, talked about everything in our lives, our families, our past, yet tonight we don't seem to be connected. It's pretty upsetting. After a little pushing on my part with the conversation we're back on track, I think we're both just sad that this friendship is coming to an end, and for me, well I feel like I've lost the love of my life all over again.

People say that when you travel, when you're away from home, your friendships develop so much quicker, that they are so much more intense during that time. Truth be told, I always thought this was a kind of wanky thing that travellers said to cement their whole -

you find yourself, you wouldn't get it if you haven't done it, wouldn't understand persona. But, I have to eat my words, now I get it.

'You ready for home now?' Sam asks.

'As I'll ever be.' I reply, 'I have a couple of weeks when I get back before starting work, enough time to find somewhere to live and start afresh...uch, and a wedding the weekend after I get back that he will be at. Oh joy.'

'Yeah, I'll be fine.' I continue, 'Tough gig though, knowing you'll all be out here living this life.' I say, elbowing him affectionately.

'So stay then?' Sam says.

'If only.' I reply.

What are you doing to me.

Neither of us really seem ready for the night to end, but it is 2am and the bars are calling it a night so reluctantly we do too and make our way home.

CHAPTER 22

I check into my hut next to Coconut Joe's (thankfully the reception has checked me into a different one than I shared with Sam). It seems terribly quiet after living with the kids and the dogs. I know I have to get used to this given I will be on my own when I get back but the silence is disturbing for now, so I quickly get into my bikini and head for the beach.

I'm bobbing up and down on the waves and I remember that Joe was meeting Goya yesterday and wonder how he got on. I glance over towards his bar and it doesn't take me long to find out. I see a crowd sitting on a beach table just outside Coconut Joe's. There is a little boy of about four building sandcastles with the help of his dad, and a girl of around nine playing dominoes with her mum, her grandmother and Old Joe (who is wearing his new white vest top by the way).

I can hear Joe's laugh from here mixed with the

excited screams of the young girl as he plays games and tricks with her. Goya seems to be sitting back watching her family around her with pride, under the umbrella she's holding over her head to protect her from the sun.

As I get out the water, the heat of the sand makes me run for a shaded part of the beach. Really, you'd think by now I'd have learnt to bring my flip flops down to the water's edge with me.

'Hey.' Joe yells.

I guess he saw me running up the beach. I was going to leave him to it, but now that he said hi, well it would be rude not to go over wouldn't it? Not that I'm a nosy beggar at all. I wrap myself up in my sarong and head over towards them.

'Hiya honey.' Old Joe says, 'Can't stay away eh? I swear I took you to the pier yesterday…Everyone, this is a good friend of mine Alice.'

'Hi.' I wave around the table at everyone.

Always the perfect host, Joe does the introductions, 'This is Goya, her son and his wife Po and Noo and their children Som and Nan.' He smiles the smile of a very happy man.

'Lovely to meet you. How long are you here for?'

I direct my question to Goya.

'I leave this afternoon, but I'll be back again soon.' she casts a subtle glance at Joe and squishes her grandson's cheeks, 'yes I will.'

'And we live here, on the other side of the island.' Po adds.

'Well enjoy the rest of your day. I'm off for a lie down in the air con.' I say fanning my face with my hand.

I hope I didn't seem rude or short, but I'm just not up for socialising right now, truth be told I'm feeling very sorry for myself and downright miserable.

At least someone's relationship seems to be going well though from the looks of it. Talking of new relationships, I decide it's about time I had another look at Pete's Facebook page to see if darling daisy has posted any more pictures of them frolicking at festivals, just as there is a knock on my door.

I open my door and sitting on my little terrace bench is Old Joe. He pats the spot next to him, and I take his cue and join.

'Goya is sweet, is it going well?' I ask enthusiastically.

'Yes, it's going great. Now, why are you back here?'

'Talk about making me feel welcome.' I laugh nervously.

'You know what I mean, what's going on? Only yesterday you couldn't wait to rush back to Koh Tao. Come on, out with it.'

'Everything's fine really. I just realised I need to be on my own just now. I'm not quite ready yet for anything else.'

'Hmm.' he nods his head.

'You said it yourself,' I add, 'it's got to be about me just now, just me.'

'I didn't say that.' Joe shakes his head.

'No, but it's what you were thinking.' I look over at him.

He laughs and sighs, 'you're a smart biscuit you are. You going to come back and join us?'

'No, I'm fine here. I'll catch up with you later though. I want to hear all about your weekend.' I lean my head on his shoulder.

Joe looks at the open suitcase on the floor with everything scattered around it and points at the book laughing, 'you still pretending to read that bloody book?'

'Maybe,' As usual, he's managed to make me smile, 'I'll be round in a bit.'

Joe and I are halfway through our first game of chess for the evening and he's been telling me all about Goya and her life. She's had a good life he says, blessed with her two boys and now two grandchildren. The ex-husband doesn't sound too nice Joe says, but he was gone years ago and she's done just fine without him.

They wondered what life would have been like if they had stayed together, not that Goya would ever have wished to change the life she has with her boys.

'That's quite full on talk isn't it?' I ask.

'When you're our age honey there's no point in holding back.' Joe tells me.

'So what now, will you see her again?' I ask.

'Yes, she's going to be over here lots to spend time with her family, so I suppose I will.' he says, his eyes sparkling.

'So, are you going to tell me what happened then?' Joe changes the subject abruptly, 'Why are you really back here?'

'I told you. I'm not ready for anything new, I wanted to spend the last week on my own, get prepared for single life back home.'

'As good as that sounds, I don't believe you. Tell me what's going on.' he asks sternly.

Bugger, why can he read me like a book.

I tell Joe that he is correct and the opposite is indeed the case. It's not that I'm not ready to move on and put the past behind me, but in fact I feel like I am completely falling in love with Sam and given that I leave next week no good can come of this. I see no need to tell Joe about catching Sam with Demi Moore, they are friends and it's not my place to say bad things about Sam. Besides, that bit is not really essential to understand my reasons for wanting to leave. I won't be with Sam this time next week, Demi or no Demi, and that is my problem.

Nothing more can happen I tell him, so I thought I should get away. Two broken hearts in one summer is quite enough, least this way I get a week's recovery time before returning home.

'I guess I'm not very good at this holiday romance, summer fling stuff.' I laugh at myself.

'You'll be fine.' Joe says.

'Yes, perhaps I'm destined to a life of solitude instead.' I snort.

'That's not such a bad thing.' Joe muses.

'I'm not so sure' I reply.

'I think you're muddling your words.' Joe says

Pot. Kettle. Black

'Loneliness and solitude. Loneliness expresses *the pain* of being alone and solitude expresses *the glory* of being alone.' he says.

Wow. Fair enough. Perhaps I was using my words incorrectly.

'That sounds like something you read in my 'bloody book'' I giggle.

'I just think you need to learn how to be happy in your own company for now. Eight years you have shared your life with one other person, compromised, made choices for both of you. You need to learn who you are again, what makes you happy, how to enjoy your own company. Then you will be ready for who knows what.' Joe takes my hand.

'I have been doing that.' I reply defensively, 'I've done so much more than when I was staying here.' I add.

'I know, I know,' He pats my arm gently, 'and that's fantastic, I'm really proud of you. But how much time have you spent alone, getting to know YOU?'

I sit silently while I digest this. Quite honestly, not much time on my own at all.

'Why don't you go somewhere for a few days on your own, relax, read that friggin' book, find some inner peace…' Joe continues, but I start to zone out.

Inner peace, where have I heard that recently, or was it inner growth I'd heard about?

'Ah.' I say out of the blue cutting Joe off, 'Cultivate a life that fosters awakening and supports inner growth.'

'Sure.' Joe smiles, 'I wouldn't have gone that far but whatever floats your ferry.'

.No sorry,' I appear to have developed jazz hands to help me explain, 'A friend I met went on a six-day retreat in Koh Phangan - yoga, meditation, detox and all that mindfulness hooey.'

I remembered the phrase as Jamie and I kept joking that they'd turned Theo into a walking marketing material. God, we laughed so much and here I am, not only quoting the marketing but considering going along myself. Believe me, the irony has not gone unnoticed.

'Have you ever been to one of those retreat things Joe?' I ask.

'No, not exactly, but I have spent a lot of time on my own and I'm certainly the better for it. Why not give it a try?'

'I'll think about it.' I say nodding.

'Let me make some calls. Find out what options there are on Koh Phangan for you, one of my friends is a yogi over there.' Joe says.

Of course one of his friends is a yogi, this guy knows everyone.

CHAPTER 23

Spurred on by a gigantic ego boost from Joe regarding my bravery so far, I'm now on my way to Sky High Happiness Retreat in Koh Phangan. For the next six days I will be detoxing, meditating, yoga(ing?) and learning how to change my inner space...whatever that means.

Once I'm in the taxi at Koh Phangan we climb the mountainous roads and career down the other side. No danger of forgetting I'm in the jungle here, surrounded by huge trees, elephants and buffalos all visible from the taxi, oh and there are no barriers along the cliff edge roads just to add some more adventure.

I arrive at Sky High Happiness and am welcomed with a carrot and ginger juice and given a million forms to fill in about my health, diet, usual exercise regimes and state of mind.

As I'm completing in the forms I take my phone out to look up the postcode of my doctor's surgery and ask the receptionist for the wifi code.

'Oh sorry, we don't have wifi here. We find our guests welcome it once they're used to it.' she smiles, 'A digital detox if you will.'

She adds, 'if it's for information on the form you can just leave blank what you don't know.'

This is one of my pet peeves, it annoys the hell out of me - 'if you don't know something leave it blank' - in that case you don't fucking need it, just leave the question out. Form filling, unnecessary form filling - that's what I would put in room 101, never to see the light of day again.

Calm down Alice, it's only a bloody form - bit nervous are you?

Forms completed to a fashion, Era my dedicated SPIE shows me around the retreat. SPIE, Spiritual Person Invested in my Enlightenment, yep - that's really what they just called her and I'm beginning to wonder if I've made a big mistake and have unknowingly enrolled myself in some cult programme.

'Six days you're here is it?' Era asks.

We'll see.

'Yes, that's right.' I smile.

'Great. If you just want to place your phone, shoes and any other electronic items you have in this box then we will get you settled in.' Era proffers a wicker box at me.

Huh? My phone? The only reason I didn't panic when they said there was no wifi was because I thought with it being my last week I could treat myself to a 4G overseas wifi package. Seeing the look of panic on my face Era tells me that Sky High likes to focus on disconnecting from the outside world, allowing the guests to unplug and reboot, to go back to nature.

'If you leave your bag there we can pick it up on the way to your room.' she tells me.

I thought she was going to say the porter will take it, I have paid a fair whack to be here after all. No doubt there is something very 'back to nature' about breaking your back carting your own luggage up hills in your bare feet.

The retreat is spread out over three levels, nestled amongst the rocks and the hills with wooden bridges and steep steps guiding the way through jungle paths to each area. At the lowest level is the beach, Sky High has its own private cove. The beach has a scattering of sunbeds and some hammocks hanging between palm trees. Kayaks and paddleboards (shudder) are resting against a beach hut, and next to that is a large bamboo sala with cushions and throws where Era tells me some of the healing sessions take place. That must be for the people who didn't pass the state of mind check-in form correctly I reckon.

Moving up a level are the main communal areas. There is a raised platform where many of the group activities are carried out like yoga, pilates, and special classes from visiting therapists. There is a Relaxation area where guests enjoy reading, writing, watching a movie or 'being at one with themselves' she tells me. Each evening a movie starts at 7pm, unless there is a guest lecturer or special event taking place. The room is filled with plants and cushions and candles and windchimes, like a mood board an interior designer would use to show "hippy shabby chic".

The cafe is also on this level Era explains, although you don't need to think about that (really, is it room service for me then with my fabulous detox meals).

We finally collect my bag and make our way up to my room. I don't think it could be any further away, jeez it was about 150 barefoot steps to get up here.

The room is pretty rustic (basic actually but I'm

trying to be positive here). There is a single bed made from bamboo with a mosquito net around it, a wicker chair, a writing desk and a small wardrobe.

Where's the TV?

I poke my head into the bathroom while Era is arranging another pile of paperwork on my bed.

It's quite basic, but fine. Loo, shower, sink and some contraption that looks like a baby bath with various tubes.

'So here's your schedule.' Era says.

'Take your time to go through it and if you have any questions just ask. I'll be your dedicated SPIE, but all the SPIEs will be able to help you with anything.'

'OK, thanks.'

'Great, so we'll see you in,' she looks at the schedule, '30 minutes in the main sala for your intro session.'

Era floats off leaving me to study my schedule. There's a lot of items on here, mainly juice - supplements - juice - supplements. Is this going to be my diet over the next six days. Where is lunch and dinner detailed on the itinerary? Eh? I thought my detox would be hummus and vegetable dips or spiralised courgette pasta - not just bloody juice, juice and more juice. I really should start paying attention before jumping in at the deep end with things.

***

I arrive for the intro session and join two others who are already sitting on either side of Era.

'Come.' she welcomes me, guiding me with her arms to sit in front of her to complete the circle with the four of us. This is all a bit hippy dippy for my liking.

Era guides us through the detox programme that we are on. The three of us here have gone for the 'juice detox' (I based my decision on length of time and cost truthfully, I hadn't really looked at the finer details). It's not quite as extreme as fasting at least.

Over the course of the next six days we may experience headaches and mood swings as we adjust to the different diet. This is our body saying goodbye to evil toxins she tells us. Good god, with the toxins in my body after the last few months I must be heading for a whole world of pain.

The sunrise yoga sessions start at 5.45am she tells us, and the sun rises during the session. Sounds idyllic other than it's in the middle of the night.

'You look concerned Alice?' Era asks.

'I'm just unsure how I'll wake at that time without my phone as an alarm clock.' I reply.

'Just let nature take its course, and it's not mandatory but I guarantee once you've done it once you will be there every day.'

This woman clearly has no idea about my sleeping capabilities.

Slotted into the day there are various optional activities; colema (no idea what that is); healing therapy; massage and reflexology; lunchtime guest lectures and in the evening there is sunset yoga from 6-7pm on the beach, followed by relaxation time. Many use this time to write in their 'journal of future intent' to end the day. The retreat closes around 9pm each evening.

'Now if we could just share a moment together to thank our bodies for all the work it does for us, and to let it know that in the next six days we will be showing our gratitude through cleansing, calming ad re-energising the mind, body and soul.' Era says softly with her eyes closed.

I'm looking around our little group to make sure that everyone else is wondering what the fuck she is talking about and quickly realise that the others also have their eyes closed and are nodding along solemnly. Oh dear, what am I letting myself in for. I can't even text someone to say if they don't hear from me in six days time I have been captured, brainwashed and swallowed into a cult in the middle of the jungle on Koh Phangan and can they send a search team for me, I will send smoke signals for them to find me.

Era takes the hands of the two people next to her and I realise that we are all to form a kumbaya circle. Oh no, no, no, I can't bear it, it's just so cringey.

'Now, to focus the mind, I'd like you all to join me in a humming buzz.'

A what?

'Touch your tongue to the top of your mouth and buzz like a bee.'

BZZZZZZZ - Everyone has started doing it.

'That's great, tell the anxiety to buzz off. A little louder Alice, buzz that panic away.' Era says in between her own buzzing.

Is she kidding me, the thought of sitting here buzzing is what's giving me anxiety. I buzz for a short while, after all I have voluntarily signed up for this gig, so I should at least give it a try, although I can't stop looking around for the hidden camera show that just might be filming me.

'Finally, as there are only a few hours of today left I suggest you start your journals by setting out your intentions for the next week. Committing them to paper allows you to focus the mind.' Era says.

So, what are my intentions while I'm here. Well the first one was not to contact Sam or Facebook stalk Pete so mission accomplished there as I have an enforced digital injunction on me.

OK, second intention. Now, why am I here? What do I actually want to get out of this? I want to adjust to my new life I suppose, being on my own, I'd like techniques to help me enjoy solitude now that I'm single.

Final one, what else. Well, I'd like the courage to continue to embrace new things like I have done on this trip, to keep learning and evolving rather than returning to a dull boring life when I return to real life.

Oh, and an extra one, I'd like to be able to stick at something, Thai boxing for example or yoga if it finally grabs me in the next six days.

So there we go, three intentions:

- Learn to enjoy solitude

- Be brave, live a life of adventure and new experiences
- Commit, make goals and stick to them

Realising I have around 45 minutes before 'bedtime' I pop my head into the relaxation area, maybe there's something going on. No, some people reading, some watching the end of a move, and some sitting cross-legged in a trance like state. It doesn't look like anyone's up for a chat so I best start giving this 'enjoy solitude' lark a go then and head off to my room to ready my book. Although, by the time my head hit the pillow I was out for the count.

***

I wake with a jump, what the hell is that noise. 'Fuck you. Fuck you.' it sounds like. Then I hear a scuttling on the roof and there it is again, 'Fuck you. Fuck you.'

If you can imagine an owl doing its "twit two" noise, it sounds a bit like that but much louder and deeper and instead of "twit two" it's saying "fuck you." Well fuck you too, you daft bird.

What time is it anyway? 5.15am!

Just as the fuck you bird stops, the crickets start in

mass, then the whistling birds and for good measure a morning breeze sends the wind chimes hanging from my balcony in a spin.

Morning it is then. I jump in the shower to wake myself up properly and make my way down to the beach for my first sunrise yoga session (this time in full length leggings - no more granny knees during the downward dog move).

'Morning, you made it then without your alarm clock?' Era winks at me in amusement and I laugh.

There are around twenty people on the beach, some stretching in anticipation for the class to start and others sitting on their mat 'ohm'ing. Oh Christ, I hope I'm not going to have to buzz like a bee again. Stretching I can deal with, pain I can deal with, but ohming and chanting I'm not so sure.

'Namaste.' the yogi clasps his hands together and presses them in front of his heart.

'I see we have some new people today.' he nods and bows in our direction.

'At Sky High Happiness we spend the morning yoga session carrying out the art of yin yoga. This focuses on relaxation, stretching and clearing the mind.'

Ah, now this I know. Yin and Yang. Yang is about movement and Yin is stillness. So, watch the sunrise while staying still and doing nothing - sure, sounds good to me.

Well what a surprise, I am not hating this like I did the last time. The yoga class I did before I struggled to keep up with the pace, unable to flow from one move to the next at the same speed as the others. But this is far less about movement, and there is more time to get into the pose and hold it. It is still tough but a different kind of tough, and I can see how you have to clear your mind to focus on staying in one position for four or five minutes at a time.

We finish with the meditation seat move, and as I am sitting there contemplating life (well actually wondering when I get my breakfast juice) the sun pops up in front of me, bathing the lower half of the sky and the water's reflection in a dazzling yellow and orange glow. The sounds of the birds and crickets a welcome addition to frame the picture in my mind - jungle paradise sunrise.

During the day I relax on the beach with my book (yes, the very one), I take a swim and I attend a lecture on nutrition. By the afternoon I am ready for a lie down since I was literally up with the birds.

I re-enter the relaxation room after a quick nap, although there's only a couple of people there.

'Where is everyone?' I ask a man with dreadlocks, pale pale skin and a large number of wooden beads around his neck.

'Colema time.' he replies.

'Pardon?' I begin to wonder if I'm meant to be somewhere that I don't know about.

'Colonic cleanse time.' he says.

'Oh, I see. They do everyone at once do they?' I ask, very intrigued and slightly disgusted.

'No, they're self-administered.' he tells me.

Hmm. Oh, that must be what that baby bath thing with the tubes is all about in my room.

Good god, the only thing I can think of that's worse than colonic irrigation is having to do it yourself. Surely you want an expert in charge of that kind of shit, no pun intended. And now all I can smell in the retreat is shit. Is this my imagination or a natural consequence of everyone 'cleansing' at the same time?

Am I the only person in this place doing a normal poo?

***

My last activity for the day is sunset meditation.

'Be aware of your bottom.' she says.

Is she serious? Who the bloody hell isn't aware of their bottom - has she never heard the phrase does my bum look big in this?

'Be aware of your thighs, focus all your thoughts on your thighs.' she says.

So that they squish even more into the sand beneath me...I thought this meditation stuff was meant to be relaxing.

'Clear your mind of everything, concentrate on your breathing, push all thoughts from your mind.' she says.

Oh no, oh no, I'm getting the giggles. I sneak open one of my eyes and look around to see if anyone else is laughing too, alas not, everyone has their eyes closed, their faces poised in concentration.

Come on, we're being asked to be aware of our bum, yet she's trying to relax us, I can't be the only one who finds this an odd technique! OK giggle over, embrace the challenge Alice.

'Focus on clearing your mind.' she tells us. But my mind won't quiet, the events of the last few months clicking through like pictures on a slide show, like my own personal film, horror movie more like.

I find it quite emotional sitting in silence (it's been thirty-five minutes since she asked us to think about our rear-ends). Sitting alone with all these thoughts overwhelms me and as the session finishes I realise that I have tears streaming down my face. I didn't even notice it happening, had no idea I had been crying. That's weird, it's like I had been in a trance or something although I thought I was completely with it.

CHAPTER 24

Over the week, I begin to look forward to most of the activities and fall into a regular routine. Morning yoga starts me off, there are worse ways to start your day and hey, if it's good for me too then even better. And the meditation sessions in the evenings, well this is the biggest surprise to me. I love it, taking the time to be still, to focus on clearing my mind, not to constantly have that slide show of life whizzing through my mind behind the scenes - well that really is 'learning to find inner peace'.

I've also attended a bikram yoga session - never again unless it's an emergency weight loss necessity - gone to pilates, attended various lectures on Buddhism, nutrition, spirituality and being your own cheerleader.

The only thing I'd never put myself through again was the 'creative dance' session. I'm not shy to shaking my stuff to a bit of Stevie Wonder, but this, well this is something else.

The class was held by a "spiritual guide" called Claude. He was about seven-foot tall, dressed head to toe in white linen (trousers far too short and shirt far too open) and he had shoulder length bleached blonde hair that belonged on someone at least thirty years his junior.

Claude encouraged us to let ourselves go, allow the body to decide on the direction it wants to move, not the mind. I can assure you that my body wanted to move as far away from there as possible. He seemed to be channeling the Pink Panther as he crept and pranced around the floor. Thankfully I found some fellow skeptics at this particular session, a necessary camaraderie to allow me to have my 'expressive experience' in the middle of the circle. I went for the 'surprised genie emerging from a bottle' display. Honestly, never ever again.

Surprisingly the main joy of the retreat was just being by myself, enjoying my own space and not being distracted or interrupted by anyone or anything else. It took me a while to learn to occupy my free time, but now I welcome my own space and am happy to deliberate over how to spend my time. I think that means I've reached solitude over loneliness Joe.

On the last morning I have a catch up with my SPIE Era just after the sunrise yoga session.

'Well, how has it been?' Era asks me.

'It's been really.... Interesting.' I reply, 'You know, I was a bit unsure to begin with.'

Era laughs, 'I know. I wouldn't go taking up poker anytime soon.'

'Oh no, was it that obvious?' my face crinkles in embarrassment.

Era continues to laugh, 'Your facial expressions tell a thousand stories. Including the fact this place began to grow on you?'

'It really did. I'm not sure some of the stuff is for me, like the creative dancing,' I roll my eyes, 'but the yoga at sunrise has been fantastic and I really found the meditation helpful, just need to deal with the sideys.'

'The what's?' she smiles.

'The sideys. I don't know what else to call them. I can sit and focus on nothing, clear my mind but then all of a sudden a thought or image shoots into my vision from the side and it takes me a while to get rid of the bloody thing.' I explain.

'Ah yes, that's normal. It just takes time and practise to control the sideys.' she smiles, 'I might steal that expression, I like it.' she winks.

'So, just before we finish tell me again what your intentions were?' Era asks.

'They were: Learn to enjoy solitude. Be brave, have adventures and new experiences. Commit, make goals and stick to them.' I tell her.

'OK, and do you feel you have the skills to live as you intend?' she muses.

I pause for thought before replying. But realise this doesn't need a grand analysis. Just take being here for example: I've enjoyed being by myself, in fact I've kind of grown to like me; I've tried all the weird and wonderful activities, and I didn't throw in the towel and leave on day one even though I felt like it at the time.

'Yes. I need to really focus on continuing to live this way, but I certainly know I'm capable.' I nod.

'I'm very proud of you Alice, thank you for sharing your journey with me,' Era bows towards me, 'Namaste.'

'Namaste.' I bow back gratefully.

***

Rejuvenated and invigorated I head back to Coconut Joe's for my final few hours in Koh Samui.

The solitude has been great, but I can't wait to talk to someone about my experiences, the good the bad and the ugly.

'Wow. You look bright as a zipper.' Joe tells me as he throws his arms in the air to welcome me.

'It was quite something.' I smile.

'Tell me everything.' Joe says, with that wonderful way he has of making you feel like you are the most interesting person in the world.

I fill him in on everything from my panic when they told me I was cut off from the world to the bizarre creative dancing, all the other activities and my new found joy from meditation.

'Oh, and I think I kind of like my own company.' I finish.

'And so you bloody should honey,' Joe taps my hand gently, 'you are wonderful.'

'One for the road?' Joe asks.

'Absolutely.' I say and we play a game of chess

and eat a plate of Pad Thai.

Joe takes me to the airport and we promise to stay in touch. Joes says he will update me on Facebook about how things progress with Goya and I promise to do the same with my life.

'Have you heard from anyone' Joe asks.

'I haven't turned my phone back on since leaving the retreat.' I tell him.

Joe laughs heartily, 'Well honey, that's what I call progress.'

'Thank you Joe, for everything.' I hold him tight as we say goodbye at the airport, not wanting to let go.

CHAPTER 25

'Ladies and Gentlemen, welcome to London Heathrow. The time is currently 6.40am.'

It's close to 10am by the time I've schlepped across London at rush hour with my now overly stuffed wheely bag to Lisa's North London house. Upon arrival, I clambered down her side path to locate the key 'under the plastic frog that's sitting on a stone lily in the back left corner of the garden'.

Lisa and Rob are already at work so I take my case straight up to my room, which is stacked with my worldly possessions. Unable to deal with organising it all right now, I head downstairs for a cup of coffee and half an hour of morning telly - I love a bit of Philip Schofield.

There's a note on the fridge from Lisa that makes me smile:

Hey stranger,
Welcome back, bacon, eggs and croissants in the fridge for you. Help yourself to anything and make yourself at home. Can't wait to see you, usual dinner spot booked for 8.

L x

What a sweetie, I can't wait to see the girls, it's been years since we've gone this long without seeing each other. I make myself a bacon croissant smothered in ketchup (Tom would be proud) and get up to speed with the news, the soaps, the weather and 'what to wear in the autumnal months' courtesy of daytime telly.

By mid-afternoon I've loaded and unloaded the washing machine twice, and managed to sort through the boxes and bags in my room to try and dig out everything I might need for the next few weeks. Autumnal clothes, work clothes and toiletries all finding a handy spot. Then there's the rest of the stuff here - life's gatherings of books, nik naks, photos, summer clothes, winter clothes, what the hell was I thinking clothes, shoes and bags all finding a spot in boxes on top of the wardrobe or tucked under the bed.

How sad, I can pack up my whole life's belongings into someone's spare room. I suppose that's quite normal for Londoners, more people on the rental market than not, most places fully furnished and your biggest purchase is a painting, or maybe a rug that you've picked up to decorate your current abode along the way.

The bonus however, is that I did manage to move out of our flat in one afternoon. There you go, people ask how long it takes to change your life forever, a split second I'm sure many would answer - but for me I'd say one afternoon.

Ah Pete - I wonder how he's doing living there on his own. God knows what kind of state the place is in, when I left I don't think he even knew where the mop and hoover were kept, what day the rubbish is collected, where the spare bedding is so you can put the other in the wash. The wedding. Ten days time and I will see Pete at a bloody wedding, how ironic.

I'm not sure yet if we will have a lot to say to each other or nothing. We've not been in touch again since the text at the time of the Full Moon Party. Ten weeks is a long time to not see or speak with someone if you've seen them pretty much every day for the previous seven years. Maybe I should have been in touch again, but I don't think he'll be that fussed with Daisy to keep him company.

I hope I don't completely lose my tan in the next ten days. My floaty dress purchases will be perfect for the wedding but not if I've returned to that transparent milk bottle colour I'm usually sporting. Not that I care if he still fancies me, it's more I want him to see me glowing, ask about my travels and hear about how adventurous I've been - that I've actually been out in the world doing things - not living a dull, monotonous life for once.

I think about Sam still out there, and Sarah and the kids. I can even visualise what they're up to right now, so much a part of their lives they allowed me to be. The emotion is exhausting and with jet lag setting in too I pop to bed for a couple of hours before heading out to meet the girls after they finish work at Balhams.

***

Slightly dazed and confused after my nap, I wake still exhausted and wonder what the time is. God, I haven't turned my phone back on yet. I reach for my handbag and tune back into digital life. Shit, I've got to be in the West End in less than an hour, I jump up as the phone is still winding back into action.

I take a quick shower and don the required post sunshine holiday outfit - jeans and a white t-shirt, the 'don't I look healthy and yes, I have been on holiday' clothes. The weathers still pretty mild so I fling on one of the floaty cardi purchases and my beaded sandals and with a touch of mascara, I'm good to go.

'Dahling, you look fabulous. Come here, this table here.' says Davidos.

'Hi Davidos, how you doing?' I reply.

'Oh me, I'm wonderful. But you - how are you? They tell me you broke up with your fiancé - but this cannot be, you look glowing dahling?' Davidos says.

Loves the gossip he does.

I smile, 'Yes, no more wedding, I've spent the summer in Thailand and it WAS fabulous dahling.'

Gail arrives next and we order a bottle of wine as I catch up on Gail's news. She says she can't wait to hear about my trip but we must wait for Lisa too for that. In the meantime I encourage her to fill me in on the plans for her wedding.

'Sorry I'm late, we've so much to finish off for next week's event. Alice, come here you, you look amazing.' Lisa wraps herself around me.

'Thank you. What's this event next week?' I ask.

'Oh shit, I haven't told you. Rob and I are off to drive across the states, well Route 66 for a month promoting rock and roll's next big thing. We leave on Monday, could you look after the cat? I assume you're staying with us for a bit anyway?' Lisa replies.

'Sounds like a hard life eh, how fab.' I reply, although I can't help visualising Sam in a chevvy driving Route 66 instead of Lisa and Rob.

'As if you can talk Miss two months in Thailand.' says Lisa.

'Correction,' adds Gail, 'two months in Thailand, not working and living with a sexy dive instructor to be precise. We. Need. More. Details.'

I share the stories of my summer with the girls, who ooh and ahh at all my adventures and go through the ups and downs of the trip with me as I give them a stage by stage account. We debate over the wasted time of my first few weeks out there, and the girls agree that it was expected, of course you're going to get pissed, be a bit useless - hell you'd probably have done the same here but wouldn't have had the sunshine or space to clear your head too and would have had a lot of hungover days at work.

'I almost fell off my seat when I saw that picture of you outside the strip club.' Lisa tells me.

We chat about the people I met along the way, giggle at my snog with Good Will Hunting, muse over the amazing life Old Joe has led, laugh about my misunderstanding of Sam's wife and kids and I get quizzed incessantly as to my 'relationship' with Sam.

'I was a complete mess when I met him.' I reply, 'He was just a nice guy looking out for me. We became really close, good friends. We had a one-night stand but that was it, he's a bit of a ladies' man really.' I try to keep my voice light and fluffy.

'But that body Al, show me the picture again, the one you text through to us with him driving the boat with his top off.' Gail pleads.

I dig my phone back out to oblige, it's not like Sam's abs belong to me so there's no harm in sharing the eye candy. As I pull the phone out I see that I have a few messages.

From Sarah:

Elvis has arrived, great choice. We all miss you very much. Stay in touch xxx

From Sam:

Hope you find what you're looking for. Safe flight home x

From Lisa:

Running late, but I'll be there soon x

'You going to show us this body again or what?' Lisa asks.

'Oh sorry, I had some messages.' I say, finally looking up from the phone.

'From?' asks Gail.

'From Sam actually, just saying safe trip back, and Sarah with a picture of their new dog.'

'Uh huh,' says Lisa, looking from Gail to me with raised eyebrows, 'and that's why you have gone all doe-eyed. And I don't mean the picture of the dog.'

'Oh shut up you pair. It's not like that. Besides, I was out there to deal with the whole Pete fiasco, wasn't I.' I say.

'So did you deal with the Pete fiasco?' Gail asks with trepidation, following what has been a fun, jovial catch up so far.

'Yeah, I think so. It still hurts, and it's still a bit scary, but I know I did the right thing, know that it would have been a disaster to go ahead with the wedding. I just need to start a new life back here now, a new way forward and I'll be fine.' I reply.

'Well, it doesn't sound like we should be worrying about you on your future tinder dates anyway. You will kick and punch the shit out of any assholes after all that kick boxing training.' Lisa ends this with a terrible, terrible rendition of Kung Fu Fighting.

'How is Pete anyway, has anyone seen him' I ask.

'No, not really. Rob saw him out in Soho the weekend after you left, he could hardly string two words together he was so smashed, but nothing other than that.' Lisa replies.

'Oh dear.' I respond.

'Hey, it was a week after the break up. And you were the same by all accounts and look at you now. I'm sure he's just fine.' Gail says.

'Yeah.' I say, pensively.

'Have you been in touch with him much while you were away?' Lisa asks.

'No, he sent me a message a few weeks after I left saying he missed me, wanted to talk, I replied saying thanks for the message and we'll talk when we get back, but nothing more.' I say.

'What do you mean 'talk' when you're back?' Gail asks, 'Does he think you'll get back together?'

'Oh I don't think so. I think he was maybe hopeful at that time, it was early days, but we haven't been in touch again since so I'm sure he knows it's over. Besides, I think he has someone new, I saw pictures of him at a festival looking pretty cosy with some girl called Daisy.' I say.

I haven't really thought about whether Pete is still expecting a talk, I suppose at the time I thought it might mean something, perhaps thanks wasn't the right reply but I could hardly say I was missing him too, as I wasn't. We didn't have any further communication after that so I thought we'd just drifted out of touch. And now that there is a Daisy on the scene I'm pretty sure we won't have to really talk about it again.

'God I'm dreading this wedding. Everyone there will have only heard Pete's version of events over the Summer, how I lost the plot and buggered off to Thailand just after breaking off the wedding.'

'Well, you can bail out early if it's awkward. Besides, look at that toned, tanned body of yours - you've got to want him to see that...see what he threw away.' Gail says.

'Eh lost, Alice left him remember.' Lisa adds.

'And if he's a prick to you, you can show him the picture of Sam and tell him that's who you've been shacked up with in paradise for the last month.' Gail laughs.

'I won't be there now.' Lisa tells me, 'We'll be halfway across route 66 at the time.'

'But I will.' Gail assures me, 'Although I think I'll be the one needing the support, you should see the state of the bridesmaid dress she has me wearing.'

'Now, wait till I tell you guys about Sky High Happiness.' I continue, 'Gail you will be so proud and Lisa, well you won't believe it...'

Once again the neighbouring tables are split between joy and annoyance at the volume of shrieks and laughter coming from our table.

CHAPTER 26

Lisa and Rob are manic getting ready for their big trip, so I decide to get out of their way before I begin my house / cat sitting and I head up North to see Mum and Dad for the weekend.

The train whisks me through the countryside as I take in the greenery and drift in and out of a daydream of my time in Thailand. I can't help noticing that this journey is a million miles away from my last trip up here. My shoulders are no longer attached to my ears and my brow isn't sitting as if my eyes have been stitched together. There's no après work people this time as it's too early, just a young mum playing snap with her two little ones, they remind me of the twins, all noise and giggles. She tries to quieten down the kids, giving me a look of apology at the same time.

'Please don't worry, leave them be.' I smile back.

'Koowee, Koowee, Alice.' Mum waves towards me as I climb off the train.

'Hey mum.' I wave back.

As I reach her she touches my face then steps back to take a good look at me.

'Sweetie pie, look at you, you look so healthy.' Mum says.

She touches my face and says my skin is radiant, strokes my hair and comments on my natural sun highlights, oh and she loves the beaded sandals, very glamourous apparently. Home, a place that makes you feel a million dollars.

'Your Dad should be back from work shortly.' Mum tells me on the car journey home,
'He suggested we might go to the pub for dinner if you like? Sit in the beer garden since the weather is nice?'

'Sounds good to me.' I reply.

As we enter the house Sean's little legs run as fast as they will allow him nowadays to say his hello, before returning to lie down in the hot spot created near the back door where the sun beams through.

I pop my bag up in my room, and when I come back downstairs Mum has poured a couple of glasses of wine and set up the garden chairs in the little suntrap out the back.

'Cheers.' Mum raises her glass, 'To my brave girl.'

'Cheers.' I reply, clinking our glasses.

'Thanks Mum, I wasn't too sure how you felt about everything now.' I say.
'

'Nor was I,' she says, 'but seeing you now, I can just instantly see my beautiful, fun, carefree girl is back. That a huge weight has been lifted off your shoulders. I'm sorry I doubted you, I should have known you were unhappy. I did know you were unhappy - I was just worried you were being rash in throwing everything away.'

'And now?' I ask.

'I haven't seen you like this in years - so bright, so revitalised and I very proud of you sweetie pie.' Mum replies.

'Thanks Mum, that means a lot.' I reply giving her hand a squeeze.

'Am I interrupting?' Dad says, as he appears by the back door.

'Dad, hi.' I jump up for a bear hug.

'Doesn't she look amazing John?' Mum says.

'Lookin' good kid.' Dad replies, winking at me.

Mum disappears upstairs to get ready to go out, giving me time to chat to Dad about Mum's new view on my life. He tells me he knew she would come round as soon as she got used to it. Two of the young girls in the village got divorced over the summer he tells me which I think helped her see that even here things have kind of changed.

I asked how she dealt with delivering the news to the village that the wedding was off - it can't have been too bad if we're going out in public tonight. Dad chuckles and tells me that after she realised you weren't going to change your mind she just bit the bullet and told people you had left him, changed your mind and taken a sabbatical to explore the world. I think you have your brother to thank he adds, they polished off a few bottles of wine one night and Adam filled Mum in on how many people in the town had settled and were actually miserable, he perhaps shared his own thoughts on Pete's behaviour too, and convinced your Mum that having doubts and being brave enough to acknowledge them was a good thing.

Thank you Adam.

Settling down in the beer garden with our drinks I fill Mum and Dad in on my travels, the abridged version of course, more emphasis on my daytime activities, Old Joe and my beautiful Koh Tao family. Dad can't get enough of the stories, living vicariously through your children I think it's called, wanting detailed descriptions and explanations of everything - the food, the water, diving, the temples.

'I'll cook some Thai food for you tomorrow, I took a cooking lesson out there.' I tell them.

'Oh, if you're sure. I was going to do Shepherd's Pie?' Mum says.

Who cooks Shepherd's pie when it's still summery out? Back to the feeder in her, or maybe the fear of the spicy food.

'Why don't I cook Thai, I won't make it too spicy, and you can do the shepherd's pie for Sunday lunch?' I suggest.

'Deal. But you can make mine as spicy as it should

be.' Dad says, before Mum stops me invading her kitchen.

As Dad is flicking through my phone looking at the photos I can see in the corner of my eye someone sidling up to the table. Oh great, it's the couple that own the local restaurant. They have two daughters also in their thirties and are the 'go to' people if you want the local gossip or want to know anything that's going on in the town.

'Alice, hi. I thought that was you with your Mum and Dad. How are you?' the nosy woman asks.

Here we go. Cue - inquisition on marriage status, jobs and kids, or lack there off.
'I'm great thanks, just up for the weekend. How are you? How's Claire and Sarah?' I reply politely.

'Oh, we're great. Busy, busy over the summer. Claire's expecting baby number three and Sarah has just moved into those big houses on Woodland's Avenue with Sam and the little ones.' Nosy woman replies.

Sam, just hearing the name makes me want to fabricate my Sam into my boyfriend just to reduce the inquisition slightly. Why are people so concerned with what everyone else is up to, especially people like me that they see but once every two years or so.

'You've been away haven't you I think I heard?' nosy woman continues.

I think I heard, yeah right, I bet she was positively revelling in the news of an abandoned wedding and a runaway bride.

'Yes, I spent the last few months travelling in Thailand.' I reply.

'On your own? Like a student backpacking?' she asks, with a look of horror.

Now, I can't make out if she is just clarifying how I was travelling and with whom, if it's utter shock that someone my age is still gallivanting about like a student, or just down right rude and judgemental.

Just before I get the chance to reply, Mum decides to do it for me.

'Yes, Alice took a sabbatical from work to broaden her horizons and see the world. Few others have a job to allow it, or money to afford it independently. We're just looking at the photos now, such a truly rich experience.' Mum says.

That shut her up.

'Yes quite. Eh, well enjoy your meal.' nosy woman

replies.

Thank you waitress, the food couldn't have appeared at a better moment.

Dad and I exchange glances and start to laugh.

'That told her eh?' Dad says.

'I'm sick of all these judgemental people. And it's true, it is a brave thing to go and see the world by yourself.' Mum says.

'That's not quite what you meant by independent though is it? You said who can afford it independently.' I say.

'You know what they're like here, talking about her kids all moving into fancy houses - their daughters wouldn't know a day's hard work if their life depended on it. Sometimes it doesn't hurt to remind her of that.' Mum says.

Clearly my Mum has had a brain transplant while I've been away. Maybe I'm not the only one who has changed, who would have thought my big life shift would have had a knock-on effect on her.

I chat with Dad after Mum has gone to bed and enquire where that came from earlier in the pub. Dad tells me she's always like that when it comes to me and Adam. She's really very proud of both of us and only mentions her fears with us personally.

She is also sick and tired of the local gossip and all that keeping up with the Joneses shit. Last month our neighbour's son was arrested for drugs, it was just a bit of weed Dad tells me (odd words to hear from my father 'it was just a bit of weed'), but you'd think he was selling heroin to toddlers he says, the way the chinese whispers escalated around town. Poor Joan (the naughty kid's Mum) was beside herself, didn't go out for weeks and everyone kept asking your mum about it, looking for more news, if she was worried about living next door to a drug dealer, blaming the parents until mum told them all to shut up and leave the poor family alone.

Dad continues to tell me that Mum had to go around to Joan's and force her to go to the shops with her. When they were out lots of people started whispering and staring so your mum quite loudly told them all 'if you don't mind, could you please kindly fuck off'.

Way to go Mum.

I guess Mum really doesn't give a shit about the town chat, or conforming to 'the norm' in how you live your life. I guess it was me who felt I had to conform and assumed this was more from nurture than nature. Until recently that is, when I've finally taken steps to do what's right for me, not what I think I should be doing, but what I want to be doing.

***

I spend the next afternoon at the supermarket, taking Dad's car to the big one a bit further away to pick up my extensive list of ingredients for tonight's meal. Such simple cooking, yet so many ingredients. All set up in the kitchen, I rest my iPad on mum's cookery book stand to get my recipes the cooking school emailed to me. As I go into my emails I see one there from Sam entitled: Elvis has left the building.

Hey Al,

How's it going? All is good here, I went to Samui last week (Joe says hi by the way) to pick up Elvis and thought you'd like to know he is now successfully relocated to Casa Madhouse. He and Johnny Cash are getting on well - well they're sniffing each other's arses a lot at least.

How's things with you? You staying with Lisa and her fella (sorry, can't remember his name). Have you seen Pete yet?

Take care and speak soon, Sam x

P.S Attached, a photo of the dogs sniffing each other's arses.

'That's delightful, where on earth did you get that from?' Mum says, wandering into the kitchen and looking over my shoulder at the photo.

'Hi, aren't they cute? This is Elvis and Johnny Cash - Sam and his family's dogs.' I tell her.

'Why on earth have you got a picture of them sniffing each other's bums...anyway, can I give you a hand?' Mum asks.

'No that's fine thanks. You just relax.' I reply.

'What we having anyway?' Mum asks looking through the bags of herbs and spices, 'It smells very, eh, pungent.'

'I thought I'd do quite a few different things for you to try.' I tell Mum. As she continues to hover around I add, 'Really Mum, I'm happy to do it all, you put your feet up.'

Really Mum, I am. Besides I want to get my email backup and re-read Sam's message. Isn't it weird that Sam's email pops up as I'm cooking Thai food? I smile remembering the cooking lesson we shared. The mess we made at the back bench of the class chucking spices at each other, what we must have looked like running into the water like tribal warriors at the end of it. I wonder if he's cooked again, cooked for the family, or maybe for someone else? Someone special?

I better not make the same mess today in Mum's kitchen, she'd have me lynched. I lay out all my herbs and spices and get to work. Pulling up my recipes on email and turning on some reggae to set the mood. I always listened to reggae in Sarah's kitchen whilst cooking dinner - it just seemed right with the view straight out onto the beach.

'Right guys, dinner's ready.' I shout.

'Smells wonderful.' Dad says wandering into the kitchen.

'If not a little spicy.' Mum adds.

'Don't worry, I have all levels of spice going on here.' I tell them.

As I bring the plates one by one over to the table, I think my parents are in quiet awe at both the volume of food and variety of dishes I've produced over the last couple of hours.

'I've made a selection so you can have a little taste of everything.' I say.

'It's like a banquet, what have we got?' Dad asks.

'We have a Thai green curry with chicken, pad Thai with prawns, pad ka pow - be careful of that one Mum, the spice really is like a 'ka pow'. Some fried rice, and a chicken satay dish here.' I say.

Each dish is met with oohs and aaahs, and as we make our way through the feast I tell them about the cooking class I attended. Mum gazes over towards the kitchen discreetly as I reach the part about Sam and I having our spice fight. No mess this time thankfully, well not thankfully that day was so much fun.

I notice Mum and Dad smiling to themselves during my story, I think they can see the memories glistening in my eyes, the happiness on my face, that I don't give a toss if I'm married or single, just that I'm happy. I can see that she and Dad are genuinely over the moon to hear me so full of beans and excitement.

'You must have cooked this stuff more than once, it's fantastic.' Mum asks.

'Yeah, I cooked quite a lot in Koh Tao, Sarah wasn't a great cook so I helped out a lot. Although, it really is an easy style of cooking - I can teach you if there's any of these you want to do, give you the recipes?' I say.

'The green curry, learn the green curry.' Dad nods

at Mum.

As we linger around the dining table, grazing on the food and enjoying a glass of wine we chat about what's next for me. Have I spoken with Pete at all they enquire.

I update them that I haven't been in touch with Pete, that's all now in the past. They nod in understanding and agreement and I don't feel the need to tell them that I'll see Pete at this wedding next weekend. As for the rest, I start back at work on Monday which will be a shock to the system, and I'm house/cat sitting for Lisa for a month so will look for a flat to rent during that time. I'm going to have to move a little bit further out of Central London I tell them, so I can afford a place of my own but that's definitely the preferred option to flat sharing again at the moment if I can manage it.

'And then when you're ready you can get back out there on the dating scene sweetie pie? Shame that Sam boy doesn't live in London, he sounds like a lovely young man.' Mum says.

Oh, my heart whimpers a little.

'Mum, he's just a friend. And yes, at some point, it's a horrific thought though. Everything is online dating nowadays and all pictures of di...I mean people scanning through your pictures, judging how you look.' I say.

Bloody hell, I almost said dick pics to my mother, and in front of my father.

'Whatever happened to approaching someone in a bar?' Dad asks.

'I don't know Dad, I really don't know.' I reply.

'Everyone uses that Facebook thingy now to meet new people, don't they?' says Mum.

'No, not that one, but similar things yes. Dating apps that you can get on your phone.' I reply.

'Just you be careful,' Mum adds, 'there's lots of disgusting people out there who send you pictures of their willies on those things.'

I almost choke on my wine. 'Mum!'

'What? You don't think I see this stuff on the telly. They had a whole segment on it on This Morning.' Mum says.

'Well, on that note I think I may finally have quenched my appetite.' I giggle.

I start to clear up the plates but Mum insists that she and Dad will clear up and I should just relax. I settle in the sofa and pull Sean up onto my lap 'you'd love Johnny Cash and Elvis' I say to him 'and splashing around in the water, rolling around on the sand'.

We watch an hour of mutually consensual telly - that being, nothing anyone thoroughly enjoyed or hated, before I hit the hay. As I climb into bed I dig out Sam's email, what is Mum like, never even met Sam and she's hoping he'll be the new man in my life.

Hey Sam,

Elvis has left the building. He looks so cute in that picture with JC, even if it is a picture of a couple of arse sniffers.

Yep, I'm back staying at Lisa and Rob's now. They are actually going away for work for a month, so I'll be there looking after the place until I get somewhere sorted.

Up at my folks this weekend, just cooked them a big Thai banquet. You practised your cooking again yet? Cooked for anyone special?

Back to work on Monday, euch. Why am I not a dive instructor like you?

I haven't seen Pete yet, but I will see him at a wedding next weekend - oh joy.

Take Care, A x

CHAPTER 27

The week has flown by and the day of reckoning is here. The Wedding. The day I come face to face with my past. Why, when you're looking forward to something does it take forever to arrive and when you're dreading it, it appears instantly, dramatically like a bolt of lightning.

I keep thinking back to Pete's text:

House feels weird without you. Let's talk when you get back. Stay safe x

The thought of having to re-live the break-up all over again hangs over me. What if he still wants to talk? What if he thinks we've got a chance of getting back together, thinks this has just been a break, not a break-up? I'm finally happy with this outcome, flat hunting aside, adjusting to being on my own, thinking about what I want to do, how I want to spend my time.

I even went out for dinner on my own this week, and enjoyed it after realising the rest of the restaurant wasn't staring at me, judging me or whispering about me being stood up, truth be told, I don't think anyone even noticed. I started yoga this week too, went two evenings and had another night out with Gail, how would I even have time for anyone else in my life.

Then I think about the pictures on Facebook of him with Daisy. Maybe he has no intention of rehashing things, perhaps he's moved on and that's that. That somehow makes me feel uneasy too.

Dressed up and as ready as I'll ever be, I take a look in the mirror and see a pretty different person staring back than I did when I was going to our last wedding together. I see a happy person, and for once I'm in my own dress.

As I step out the taxi I see Pete straight away, hovering by the church doors chatting with one of the ushers. He's lost a bit of weight I realise, he looks well.

As I wander up the steps to the church he catches my eye.

'Hi Al.' he says, shifting from side to side uncomfortably.

'Hey.' I manage.

Thankfully, just then a couple of older ladies I don't know arrive at the church needing assistance, so Pete offers to show them to their seats, leading the way down the aisle with an old dear on either arm. I sneak off and settle myself near the back of the church.

The wedding is beautiful, but I can't help thinking what a waste of money it all is. The amount they must have spent on this wedding they could have had six months travelling the world together. Funny how quickly your perspective changes eh? It's not that I'm now suddenly against marriage, not at all, but I'm no longer assessing the atmosphere, the food, the dress, but more the couple.

What makes a wedding special? The marriage. Like Sam, I'm looking for perfect, not 'this'll do', and when that happens I couldn't care less if the cake has two or three tiers, if it's raining or the sun is shining - just that I am walking down the aisle to the love of my life, my best friend, the person I want to grow old and grey with. I want a marriage, not just a wedding.

After the meal I take a time out and wander to the terrace for a breath of fresh air. Everyone has politely ignored the conversation of Pete and I breaking up, however this seems to include my trip away and consequently I have very little to say to anyone, so a break from the inane forced chit chat is a pleasant relief.

As I look out over the terrace I feel my phone vibrate in my clutch bag and take it out to check my messages.

From Lisa:
Good luck today. Here if you need me x

From Sam:
Thinking of you today. Hope you show the bastard what he's missing! X

As I'm composing a reply to Lisa, I hear that familiar voice.

'Well this is déjà vu.' Pete says.

I take a deep breath and turn around slowly, 'Hi Pete.'

'You look good.' he says, as he wanders towards me.

'You too.' I reply.

And I mean it. He does look good. I wondered all week how I'd feel when I saw him, whether I'd get butterflies in my stomach, be racked with regret. But I didn't feel either of those things when I first saw him at the church and I don't feel them now. I feel a sadness, a dawning and realisation that this is now a man of my past, but no doubt or regrets on my decision.

'About your message.' I begin, I've just got to get this over with, remove any thoughts he has of us returning to where we were before.

'I did miss you Al, didn't know what to do with myself.' Pete says.

'Pete, let me stop you there. I'm sorry, I know it's hard being on your own, but I think we made the right decision.' I say.

'It is hard being on your own…' Pete says.

'I'm sorry, we're not getting back together.' I interrupt and blurt out.

'Al, eh, I think you're misunderstanding me. What I mean is, I'm not on my own anymore, I've met someone.' Pete says.

Good god, what an ass I've just made of myself, thinking he wanted me back, was miserable without me. But the way he started the conversation I thought he was telling me it was hard being without ME. I know I saw pictures of him with someone, but I thought that was a date or something, not an "I'm with someone".

'Oh, I see.' I say, trying to recover quickly.

'I did want to get back together when I sent that message. I did. But then, well I met Daisy, and we just kind of clicked. In fact, I wanted to tell you because she is coming today, tonight I mean, to the evening bit.' Pete says.

'I, well, that's great. I look forward to meeting her. Will you excuse me, I need to pop to the loo, too many of these.' I say, raising my champagne glass.

And breath. Safely sheltered in a toilet cubicle I take a few deep breaths and digest this latest revelation. Pete has properly met someone. He didn't waste any time did he? And she's coming here tonight? Does that mean it's serious already? Now I know why I didn't get any more messages from him, any more requests to talk on my return.

I dig out my phone, *I hope you show the bastard what he's missing* Sam's message says. He's not missing anything by all accounts.

I text Gail's number, as a panic rises in me.

Gail. Emergency in toilet. Cubicle 3. Come quick.

Three minutes later Gail is knocking on the door and lifting armfuls of pink taffeta in the air to get the dress into the loo.

'Hi, what's going on, you spoke to him?' she asks.

'Yes and it was going fine. Then I told Pete we were definitely not getting back together, you know because of his message.'

'He didn't take it well?' Gail asks.

'No, he took it just fine. He's met someone already, and she's due here any minute for the evening reception.' I tell her.

'Oh god. You OK?' Gail asks.

'I don't know.' I reply, and then the tears come, 'Oh Gail, why am I crying? Why is this bothering me?'

'Right. It's just the shock hon. Do you feel like you want to be with him?' Gail asks.

'No, but…' I start.

'Exactly. It's just shock. No one likes to see their ex move on first. For god sake stop crying, you look so hot right now, you can't meet the new girl all red faced.'

Gail giggles.

'I know, I know. But do I have to meet her? Can't I just do a bunk now?' I whine.

'No. Redo your make-up, return to the party and if it all goes tits up leave your phone open with Sam's photo on it.' Gail says.

'Now there's a thought.' I chuckle, 'Thanks you.'

'No probs love, I'll be right out there, but bridezilla has me on a short leash so I better go. Ta ta.' Gail ends.

I re-enter the ballroom once I've trowelled on the make-up and join some of the girls I know in the middle of the dancefloor. My eye constantly wandering towards Pete, looking out for his new woman to arrive. The ballroom is getting busier, so I assume the evening guests are starting to arrive. I notice Pete answer his phone and leave the bar to go out to the hotel foyer. Shit. Shit. Shit. I don't think I want to meet this person. Please god let the dance floor swallow me up. And then Pete re-appears with his new lady, oh wait, that is no lady, she is positively a child, I don't think she'd even get served a beer in the states, this kid looks like one of my students.

They're standing at the bar and I feel I really need to get this over with. So I put a brave face on and make my way to the bar, standing just a couple of people to the left of them. As my wine glass is topped up I feel a tap on my shoulder.

'Al, hi, this is Daisy.' Pete says.

'Hi Daisy, nice to meet you.' I say.

'Hiya.' Daisy replies, all bouncy, perky, 'Your tan looks amazing, where did you get it done?'

'Done? Oh, eh, I've been in Thailand.' I reply once I've digested and understood the question.

'Oh wow. I thought you'd like, found an amazing tanning place. Mine's the St. Tropez mud tan.' Daisy replies.

'Eh right, great.' I smile.

'Babe, come on let's dance.' Daisy says, tugging on Pete's arm.

I raise my eyebrows knowing she has more chance of getting him to rip his own arm off than to dance.

'Maybe later.' he says, 'You go, you know those guys.' he points towards the ushers and their girlfriends.

'OK.' she plants a kiss on his cheek and bounces off.

'She's sweet, when's her curfew?' I ask.

'Al, come on.' Pete replies.

'Sorry, but seriously, how old is she?' I ask.

'She's 22, but very mature.' Pete replies.

I look out at the dance floor where she's bopping along to the music and I smile inside. This man is so far away from being a grown up, from settling down. In fact, it's just as well he's leaving the woman in their 30s alone, they don't need a Peter Pan in their lives. And neither do I. This man wants a girl, not a woman.

'I'm sure she is Pete. Let's hope she's not too mature though, wouldn't want her to scare you with thoughts of a 'future' together. I'm glad you're happy. Take care.' and I give him a kiss on the cheek goodbye.

I don't feel the need to stay an extra hour to save face, it's time to go home. I weave my way through the crowd to find the bride and say my goodbyes.

'Louise,' I tap her on the shoulder to get her attention, 'thank you so much for today, it's been great and you look stunning.'

'Al, I'm so sorry. I didn't know that Pete was bringing someone. I just asked Gordon and he said last night at the stag do for her to come to the evening bit, but I didn't know. Really I didn't.' Louise says.

'Lou, don't worry about it. I met her, she seems nice. I've just had a really busy week and I'm shattered. Thanks again, enjoy the rest of your night.' I say, taking my leave.

And that my dear, is closure.

***

Back to work, 983 emails in my inbox. Jeez, that's today sorted then, let's hope half of them are the usual irrelevant drivel that circulates through the college's cyberspace - has anyone seen my mickey mouse mug, can you give me some charity money for running a couple of miles, can we please tidy up after ourselves in the kitchen.

I hear a couple of students talking about what they did that Summer, sounds like they were in Greece or Ibiza or something - stories of DJs and boys and booze. They remind me of Gabs and Mads, bet they're also talking about their trip away, and I smile at the memories of the Bangkok gang. I wonder where they are now, I wonder what this bunch of students would think if I told them I had a fairly similar Summer to them - snort incredulously with laughter probably. I must have a nose on Facebook and see what they are all up to at lunchtime.

The day drags on, clearing emails and generally pottering, not quite back in the swing of things until the clock finally hits 5 o'clock, begrudgingly it seems. Lisa's house is less than an hour's walk, and as the tube station is once again closed due to overcrowding, I take advantage of the nice evening and walk towards home.

Around half way, I walk past a cute little pub on a corner, it has a wide pavement and various tables and chairs dotted around outside. I stop and look back, there are a few free tables, and a strange thought enters my head - I have nowhere to be, no one who needs me to cook them dinner except the cat. So I retrace my steps a little, enter the pub, order a Sauvignon Blanc and sit myself at one of the outdoor tables. It's a strange feeling sitting here alone, knowing I'm not waiting for anyone or that no one is waiting for me, wondering where I am. Strange, but not unpleasant.

I take a quick picture of the grey office buildings, rush hour traffic and pissed off people in suits trying to make their way home from work and send it to Sarah:

Look familiar? Miss any of this? x

You kidding? X

Comes my instant reply, including a pic from Sarah's terrace of the beach with the kids and the dogs all mucking about in the sand. Bitch. Just teasing. Well it's back to reality for me now. Not too bad really, I can do anything I like, my time is my own.

I take a notepad out and jot down the things I'd like to do with my free time, and the things I need to do:
- Find a kickboxing club
- Find a flat
- Clear out my wardrobe (remember the fashion police memo?)
- Visit more art galleries
- Got to the ballet at Sadler's Wells

These last two are on every 'things I should be doing in London' list I've ever made. I feel like I'm missing the culture bone in my body, everyone raves about the V&A Museum and the ballet, it just seems monumentally dull to me. How do people stare at one painting for so long - what are they looking at? What do they see that I don't see? Maybe my eyesight's much better than everyone else's, because really a couple of seconds on each painting and I'm done, seen all there is to see. And the ballet? I prefer my men like Sam, in board shorts rather than ball hugging tights and leggings.

I scan the internet and find various kickboxing

clubs around the area. Oh look, here's one - Fight Club in East London, that sounds interesting if not a bit menacing. Classes are 7.30pm every evening - perfect.

Next on the list, let's check out what kind of shoebox I can get myself on my budget. Scanning through the various offerings I realise my options are somewhat limited. How do people live alone in London, some of these places are more than my whole monthly salary, and they're still tiny. I expand the search another five miles wider than where I want to be. At least these places are a bit more affordable, only just though. I guess I took for granted the difference two salaries makes instead of one.

Well that's two items on my list underway already, commit and stick to things - perhaps Sky High Happiness has changed my life after all I laugh to myself.

***

The next few weeks pass in a blur, the summer feeling like a distant dream, like someone else's life other than the Thai food I'm cooking and my new found obsession with Thai boxing as a reminder that it was indeed me.

The thought of Pete with his teeny bopper now graces my face with a smirk rather than a grimace, he may have escaped the tightening grasp of marriage, but I can foresee a different kind of pressure lurking in the mist. Who knows, maybe I'm wrong but I can't help feeling that Pete's nonchalance after the initial honeymoon period has the ability to send anyone crackers.

Sam and I have been in touch, I told him about the 'closure', he's told me that Shona has finally moved on to a new instructor, thankfully. We've teased each other about tinder and online dating and joked that we'd even write each other's profiles.

Lisa is back next week and I've finally found myself a room in a shared flat in East London that will do just fine. It's not too far from Tarquin's flat and I text Gail to let her know. She calls to say she's meeting Tarquin tonight near my work and do I want to join. Do I? Of course, this is what I do now. Take advantage of having nowhere to be and going with the flow.

I wander into Soho weaving my way through the suits and the creatives until I find the little pub tucked away down a side street - I'm delighted it's not one of those pretentious bars that takes hours to get served at and makes you feel like your elbows are glued to your ribs as people bump their way past you. I see Gail and Tarquin at a small table in the corner and make my way over. We say our hello's and Tarquin heads to the bar to get me a drink.

It's great to see how happy they are, they have all

their little jokes, they're constantly touching each other's hands, legs, face - that time at the beginning of a relationship when you still get butterflies and can't wait to see each other again, even when you're still with them, but these guys are not at the beginning of a relationship. They just have something really special.

Like all couples they think everyone else needs to be in love to be happy, so it doesn't surprise me when the topic of me dating again comes up.

'Maybe in a bit. I'm quite enjoying being single for now.' I say.

'It's just, Tarquin and I thought you might really get on with his friend Jason?' Gail says.

Here we go.

'He's a sound guy.' Tarquin says.

'Please, can we all just go out? See if you get on? No pressure.' Gail says.

'I don't think so. Sorry.' I reply.

'OK, well how about you have to go out on two dates in the next month, and if you don't then you'll meet Jason? What do you say? You've got to get out there at some point?' Gail says.

For the sake of ending the conversation and moving on, I agree. Adding a caveat that the month doesn't start until my birthday which is only the weekend after next anyway.

'What we doing for your birthday this year?' Gail asks.

'I found a glitz and glamour free flow champagne night.' I say.

'Let me guess, where you can dress up as a Bond Girl.' Gail says, then turns to Tarquin to explain, 'Alice here is somewhat infatuated with the Bond movies. Loves any excuse to throw on some gold sequined effort and hide a plastic gun somewhere on her body.'

I roll my eyes, 'Not quite infatuated, but yeah, I guess it's safe to say I'm a bit of a Bond fan.'

'You're coming aren't you?' I say to Tarquin, 'Lisa and Rob will be there too.'

'Sure, sounds fun.' Tarquin says.

'And there your month of dating starts. Deal?' says Gail.

'Deal.' I reluctantly reply.

CHAPTER 28

As my birthday comes round I feel at a bit of a low, another year older, where on earth is the time going. Pretty soon I'm going to be checking the next box up on surveys. If I had a proper address I'd be receiving life insurance letters and saga tour brochures I reckon.

Then I remind myself that it's not all bad. I was asked out by a guy at the boxing last week. I'm not remotely interested but at least he was. Anyway, I told the boxing chunk that I'm very busy just now, can I take a rain check knowing that I might need him to help me fulfil my two dates in a month deal.

I start my birthday with a coffee in Lisa's garden. I'm due to move out next week, so I'm taking advantage of the outdoor space while I still have it.

Checking my emails, I find one from Sarah:

Happy Birthday Miss,

How you doing? So jealous you're going to be glitzing it up with champagne tonight at some bar. Sounds fab. What's it called? Not like we get much of that out here.

Hope you have an amazing night. Birthday hugs and kisses from all of us. Who knows - maybe you'll find your James Bond!

Lots of love,

Sarah and the gang xxx

Dressed up and almost ready to go, my phone dings and I see it's from Sam:

Happy Birthday. Hope you have a great night x

Bless, Sarah must have reminded him it was my birthday.

***

'Cheers, Happy Birthday.' Lisa says, as the five of us chink our champagne flutes.

I take in my group of friends, Lisa and Rob so at ease with each other, his hand resting comfortably on the small of her back; Tarquin and Gail sharing discreet kisses, his arm draped protectively over Gail's shoulder.

Looking at my best friends and their men, I can feel the warmth, can see that they are each with the right person, their Mister Right. I gaze around the room at the glamourous gang of thirty-somethings. A few groups of women are dancing, a few first dates are going on. Not that many people are as dressed up as me, but hey it's my birthday, I can do what I want.

We'd been chatting for an hour or so and were starting to get a bit tiddly, telling jokes, the girls pointing out various men to me that I may be interested in and reminding me about my dating pledge. I was listening to stories of Lisa and Rob's US road trip when my eye caught someone on the other side of the room by the entrance.

Stood on the other side of the room in a tux, with a bowtie undone hanging around his neck, holding a bunch of roses and looking around the bar is Sam, who locks eyes with me.

'Who is that Al?' asks Rob.

'That's James Bond.' says Lisa, a grin spreading across her face.

'That's her Patrick Swayze.' says Gail at the same

time.

'Sam. What are you doing here?' I ask as he walks across the room.

'I thought the birthday girl might need a James Bond.' Sam says, handing me the roses, 'Brosnan obviously, not Connery.'

'You look stunning.' Sam says, as he moves his head towards me.

He kisses me on the lips tentatively, then leans back out of the kiss and says, 'is this OK?'

I lean back in and grab the back of his head and pull him toward me, the kiss leaving me tingling from head to toe, butterflies let loose in my tummy. I feel the flowers being taken out of my hand by one of the girls and I pull Sam even closer so his chest is cemented to mine.

As we pull apart Sam says, 'I haven't stopped thinking about you.'

'Eh, hem.' Rob coughs as Lisa playfully hits him.

'Oh, sorry guys, this is Sam. Sam, this is everyone - Lisa, Rob, Gail, Tarquin.' I say.

Tarquin leans over the bar and produces a glass of champagne, handing it to Sam.

'Here you go mate, looks like you might need it.' Tarquin says.

'How did you know I was here?' I ask.

'Sarah.' he smiles, 'I asked her to find out where you'd be.'

We enjoy the rest of the evening telling the gang about our tales of Koh Tao. We, did I just use 'we' about Sam and me? Calm down Al, let's not get carried away again.

As the night goes on, Sam's arm closely secured around my waist, I see the looks and giggles from the girls, they're whispering to me about how amazing this guy is, this gesture is.

'So how long are you here for? Why are you back in the UK?' I ask.

He tells me he's here for ten days, going to see his parents tomorrow for the week, but he wanted to see me, hoped it would be a nice surprise. He also tells me he's staying in a hotel around the corner tonight.

'Wanna join me?' he asks.

As we close the hotel room door, Sam starts kissing my neck from behind and pulling me passionately towards him. One hand is holding my head as he continues to kiss down towards my breasts and the other is unzipping the back of my gold dress. Once the dress is undone he removes his shirt and turns me around, slowly taking the straps from my shoulder and releasing them so that the dress drops and hangs from my hips. We move towards the bed and he pulls the dress slowly down off my body. Teasing me with his breath on my nipples, and delicate strokes to my tummy, my inner thighs until I can take no more and demand that he is inside me right now and I explode with sheer happiness.

***

I wake in the morning to see Sam staring down at me.

'Morning gorgeous.' he says, as I'm still coming round.

'Morning.' I smile.

He kisses me and then props himself up on the bed, as if he's been there a while waiting for me to wake.

'I have a proposition for you.' he says.

'I think you did that last night didn't you?' I reply.

'OK, so I have another proposition for you.' he says.

'Does it involve coffee?' I ask, stretching and still waking up.

Sam jumps up to pop on the kettle sitting on top of the mini bar.

'You know we've got the empty cafe at the dive centre? Well, we thought you might want to run it?' he says.

'What are you talking about?' I say, a look of confusion spread across my face.

Sam wanders round to my side of the bed with a coffee as I sit up.

'Sam, you're not making much sense.' I say.

'Look, you don't have to answer me straight away, but think about it. You loved it out in Koh Tao, you said you'd love to cook for a living and we just thought - maybe you'd consider it. Living in Paradise, living with us, being with me?' he says, taking my hands,
'Just think about it.' he says, kissing me tenderly.

What the hell has just happened? I'm in utter disbelief. Am I still dreaming? Me, with Sam, living in Thailand. I can't, I have commitments here, I have a job, I move into a flat next week...and, well everything else is up in the air, but I can't just up sticks for good can I? Sam cuts into my thoughts.

'Let's go for a walk, you can be the tour guide this time.' he says.

'I can't go out in that.' I laugh, pointing to my discarded sequin dress.

'Here,' he throws me a shirt and a pair of his jeans, 'you can roll up the sleeves and legs.'

We are pretty close to the river so I decide to head towards the South Bank, cutting own a few side streets until we come by the river opposite Big Ben.

'Wow.' says Sam.

'Have you never been here before?' I ask.

'Yeah, I have, but it was a long time ago and I forgot how impressive it is.' he replies.

We hold hands and wander along, taking in the street artists, listening to the buskers, and filling each other in on what's been going on in our lives, although we tend to know most of this already.

As we pass the Gallery of Modern Art I ask if he wants to go in.

'Sure.' he replies.

See, I knew I'd end up in a gallery one day.

'Ere, I just don't get it, isn't that just a pile of bricks?' Sam says.

I laugh. I'm not alone.

'Yes, it's just a bloody pile of bricks. Shall we get out of here and go to the aquarium?' I say.

'Now you're talking.' he says, grabbing my hand to lead us out of the museum.

I watch Sam as he wanders around the aquarium, his face glowing as he pulls me from one tank to the next explaining what each fish is and where you'd normally find them.

As we leave we grab a coffee and find a spot on the grass to relax. I haven't mentioned Sam's proposal again since this morning, but it's all that's going through my head, that and an insatiable desire to relive last night's sexual re-awakening.

'Did you mean what you said this morning?' I ask, lying flat on the ground and staring up into the clouds.

'Yes. I did.' Sam says, lying on his side staring at me.

'I've never met anyone like you Alice. I think you're amazing, and I want to be with you. I know you have your job and your life is here, but will you at least think about it?' he asks.

'Yes, I'll think about it. I'm just in a bit of shock right now. I didn't know you liked me like that though.' I say.

'What? After that night we had together, of course I did. I was devastated when you said you weren't ready and you left.' he said.

I turn to face Sam, 'Come on. I saw you the next morning with Demi Moore.'

Sam looks confused, 'The morning you came back from Joe's?'

'Yes, look it doesn't matter now. You obviously feel different.' I grab his hand.

'No wait a minute. Nothing happened then. That

was Shona's cousin, she had arrived to tell Shona about something that happened back home and Shona broke down, so we both helped look after her.'

'Oh, what happened? Was everything OK?'

'Yeah, kind of. There was a fire back home and all her childhood belongings were burnt to a crisp, and her home was gone. None of her family had been in the house so that was OK, but her cat was... Obviously I have a history with fire stories as you know so I helped her realise that belongings really don't matter, at least all her family were fine, well other than Duffy the cat.'

'Is that why you said you weren't interested? Why you buggered off?' Sam looks shocked.

'Well, yeah.' I nod. 'Poor Shona, why didn't you tell me that had happened?'

'I don't know, I didn't really want to start talking about Shona when we were just getting together, and I didn't know you'd made up an alternative story in your head, did I? You and your bloody hot headedness, why don't you think before you do things?' he asks, amused and frustrated at once.

'Well, if I didn't behave like that I would never have been in Thailand in the first place.' I reply cheekily.

'Oh Sam.' I say, before pulling him into me.

'Get a room.' I hear some teenagers shout as we move away from each other like naughty kids.

'I'm heading off to my parents tonight for a week, but will you think about it while I'm away?' he asks.

I walk Sam to the station so he can get the train to Devon and we kiss goodbye as I promise to digest what he has asked me. I begin walking in a daze down the street, my head cloudy as I try to understand what has happened in the last twenty-four hours. Me and Sam? Me and Sam in Thailand? Me running a cafe? It's like something from a movie. I've always fancied Sam, I mean who wouldn't, I'd hoped I would find someone like Sam ever since I met him. I just never thought it would actually be Sam.

First I thought he was married, then he had a kind of girlfriend, then straight after we hooked up I thought oh well, I was one of many. All these conversations we've had when he said he doesn't want just anyone, they must be perfect. Does this make me his version of perfect?

Somehow I walk myself all the way back to Lisa's, and as I walk in I hear Lisa bounding down the stairs to see me.

'Oh my god Al, talk about romantic.' she screams.

I smile, 'I know, and you won't believe what has happened.' I say.

'The way you were groping each other last night when you left I'm sure I have a pretty good idea...and so will everyone else Miss, walking about in your heels and oversized men's clothing screams dirty stop out.' Lisa laughs.

'No, wait till you hear the rest of it.' I add.

And so I explain Sam's proposal to Lisa, and with each sentence her jaw drops a little further.

'And what are you going to do?' she asks.

'I have no idea, I'm meant to be moving into that flat next week.' I say.

'Bugger the flat, that's easily sorted. I mean, what do you want to do? We all knew there was more to you and him than you were letting on.' she says.

'Really there wasn't. I had no idea he liked me like this. Thought we were just mates who'd had a night together.' I say.

'Well there's no doubt now. Great friends who fancy the pants off each other, isn't that the perfect combination?' she says.

'What do you think I should do?' I ask.

'Only you can answer that. Selfishly, I'd absolutely hate to see you move to the other side of the world, but bloody hell, he's turned up dressed like James Bond and pretty much declared his love for you - this is the shit from fairy tales, I think you have to at least think about it.' she says.

Ding.

Email from Sarah:

Hey hun,

I hear he's finally told you how he feels. Hope you don't mind I told him where you would be, it was about time he told you how he felt. Please, please, please come out here, we can't deal with him moping about missing you anymore.

Seriously, you could make a good business with the cafe and Sam's already looked into the best way to sort out your work permit and visa.

I vote yes.

Lots of love,

Your Koh Tao family who misses you dreadfully x

I drift through the day with a giddy sense of euphoria, floating on Sam's confession and suggestion.

CHAPTER 29

The next week at work seems like a conspiracy to drive me away, I want to tell the rude students to take a hike, then my twat boss Jonesy has me complete a very long report in a very short period of time, only to tell me when I submit it he no longer needs it and sorry he should have told me - eh, yeah you fucking should have.

Is this a sign? Someone trying to tell me something about the one thing that is potentially keeping me here. Old Joe did tell me to look out for the signs.

Aside from the frustrations of work, Sam's messages I'm receiving every couple of hours are seeing me through, sexting, a whole new world of exciting.

I've told the new flat I've had a delay on moving in by a week while I stay on at Lisa's which they seemed O with. I suppose a week's loss in rent beats going through the horrific meet, interview, show the house to randoms all over again.

And today I've bunked off work to head up to my parents. It's a Friday anyway and other than completing an irrelevant report, my mind has been a little full this week for me to make any significant contribution.

I'm due to see Sam again tomorrow, and I'm trembling with excitement at the thought of it. So I take the early morning train up and by midday I'm sipping a coffee in the kitchen with Mum.

'How you doing sweetie pie, you in the new place now?' she asks.

'No, not yet. I'm due to move in next week, but I'm not sure yet.' I reply.

'Oh, I thought it was a done deal. What happened?' she asks.

A grin spreads across my face that only says one thing - I'm smitten, in the first throes of love or lust.

'Oh, you've met someone haven't you? Tell me all.' Mum says.

I giggle an embarrassed giggle as I tell Mum about

Sam turning up for my birthday dressed as James Bond and carrying roses.

'I knew that boy sounded lovely. How fantastic, I didn't know he'd moved back from Thailand?' she says.

'He hasn't. He was coming over to visit his family, so surprised me.' I say.

I didn't go into detail about the fact I spent the evening in his hotel, some harmless editing is often necessary for your parents, but I think she gets the gist something special happened.

'So it's just a flying visit. That's a shame.' she adds.

'Yes it is. But he had a proposition for me. He wants me to move out to Thailand and run the cafe in the dive centre.' I say, raising my eyebrows to show I too am in disbelief.

'Oh, for goodness sake, does he think you can just up sticks like that?' she says.

'Well, it's quite an opportunity, and it's not like I have lots keeping me here that wouldn't be here when I got back.' I say.

I realise for the first time this really is true. How

many people dream of the opportunity to live abroad, doing a job they've always wanted to do. Throw into the mix an almost declaration of undying love from the person who lives in said place and I'm not sure most people's dreams would be much further beyond this.

What's the most important thing in life. Being happy. And what makes me happy? Sam, his family, cooking, dogs, beach life... and here it all is on a plate for me.

As Dad walks through the door, he hasn't even got his jacket off before mum is talking to him ten to the dozen about what's going on, the words coming out her mouth so quickly Dad is struggling to keep up.

'That's quite a week you've had love.' he says, after a long pause.

'Yep, pretty surreal.' I say.

'And you really like this Sam guy?' he asks.

'Yes, I really do.' I reply.

Dad looks at the floor and rubs his chin in contemplation. After a moment, he looks up at Mum and says, 'I guess you better get online and start researching our next holiday.'

Mum looks at Dad confused.

'Have you ever known this one to make the boring, maintain the status quo decision?' he says, 'And it seems like she may have met her spontaneous match here.'

To be fair, yes I do like spontaneity, I love it, and maybe there's a reason I've been thrown this opportunity. I keep thinking back to Old Joe and his view that everything happens for a reason, that you should look out for the signs.

'Oh darling, is your father right? Are you going to do it?' Mum asks.

'I'm still thinking about it.' I reply, with a subtle glance at Dad who knows that decisions are best drip fed to my mother.

***

The next day I head back to London, opting for a train that will get me back in time to meet Sam off his train. Lisa's said he can stay with us for the next two nights before he heads back, a combination of generosity and curiosity I'm sure.

I nervously await the arrival of Sam's train, pacing back and forth, dizzy at the thought of seeing him, the butterflies doing a dance in my tummy.

As I see Sam walking down the platform, my body shivers with pleasure, my heart explodes with desire and I'm left in no doubt about what I have to do.

'YES!' I scream, throwing my hands in the air, as he walks through the gates.

A smile stretches across his face as he runs towards me, picks me up and spins me around in delight.

'Really?' he asks.

'Really.' I reply, nodding.

There's cheers and claps around us as I've obviously drawn attention to myself with my shriek. Sam looks around at the observers, and takes a bow.

'Old Joe always told me to look out for the signs, and all the signs are pointing towards you.' I say.

Sam is bent double with laughter at this.

'What is it? What have I said?' I smile at him.

Sam replies, 'Old Joe always says that. The signs will make you happy. You know he's talking about all the misspellings on the actual signs don't you? The sign shop that has a huge banner outside saying 'sing shop'; pee and poo restaurant; wiener massage...but I'm sure he meant the signs that said I was your James Bond too.'

EPILOGUE

It took me six weeks to pack up my London life, work my notice and move my stuff to a more permanent storage spot, my childhood bedroom where my dreams of a life with Patrick Swayze began. That was ten months ago.

The cafe has now been open for eight months and is going well. I didn't move in with Sam and the family straight away because you know what, I quite like my own space nowadays. However, we have just found our own house to move into and well, that makes sense seeing as we are getting married in two days time.

The wedding is taking place at Coconut Joe's and Joe has got himself ordained so that he can perform the wedding for us. Goya is now living at Coconut Joe's too having finally moved to Samui six months ago after the visits got more and more frequent.

The wedding is a pretty low-key beach affair. A big wok of Pad Thai, a relaxed cream sundress, and no tiered cake - but most importantly this Saturday is about a marriage not a wedding day. We've spent the money on our honeymoon instead – we're taking a month to drive Route 66.

This morning I picked up my parents, my brother, Lisa, Rob, Gail and Tarquin from the airport and having checked in they are now at Coconut Joe's meeting my Thailand family.

I look over at Mum as she is chatting with Sarah and playing with the twins and the dogs, Goya is with her son and her grandchildren building sandcastles. Gail, Lisa and their husbands are chatting with Sam and Tom about what they should do during their holiday (other than the two day visit to Sky High Happiness I'm treating the girls to) and Dad is deep in conversation with Old Joe.

Dad turns around to wink at me and smiles. A happy man - his daughter's settled down and he's visiting somewhere he's always wanted to. I see he and Joe have something in common - they turn to look at me as if they are both thinking 'our job here is done'.

I look around in complete and utter delight at how my life has changed in just a year, and wonder when Sam and I should tell everyone that my champagne glass is actually filled with fizzy water.

Printed in Great Britain
by Amazon